EXIT PAPERS
FROM
PARADISE

LIAM CARD

EXIT PAPERS FROM PARADISE

A NOVEL

DUNDURN
TORONTO

Editor: Allister Thompson
Design: Jennifer Scott
Printer: Webcom

Library and Archives Canada Cataloguing in Publication

Card, Liam, 1980-
    Exit papers from paradise / Liam Card.

Issued also in electronic formats.
ISBN 978-1-4597-0611-8

    I. Title.

PS8605.A688E95 2012   C813'.6   C2012-901544-X

1   2   3   4   5   16   15   14   13   12

 Conseil des Arts   Canada Council
du Canada   for the Arts
 Canada
 ONTARIO ARTS COUNCIL
CONSEIL DES ARTS DE L'ONTARIO

We acknowledge the support of the **Canada Council for the Arts** and the **Ontario Arts Council** for our publishing program. We also acknowledge the financial support of the **Government of Canada** through the **Canada Book Fund** and **Livres Canada Books**, and the **Government of Ontario** through the **Ontario Book Publishing Tax Credit** and the **Ontario Media Development Corporation**.

Care has been taken to trace the ownership of copyright material used in this book. The author and the publisher welcome any information enabling them to rectify any references or credits in subsequent editions.

J. Kirk Howard, President

Visit us at
Dundurn.com
Definingcanada.ca
@dundurnpress
Facebook.com/dundurnpress

Dundurn
3 Church Street, Suite 500
Toronto, Ontario, Canada
M5E 1M2

Gazelle Book Services Limited
White Cross Mills
High Town, Lancaster, England
LA1 4XS

Dundurn
2250 Military Road
Tonawanda, NY
U.S.A. 14150

For anyone who knows the depth of a rut

"It's never too late to be who you might have been."
— George Eliot

I

I'm as alive as my prey but feel nothing but resentment toward him. Does his brain refuse to shut off, like mine? Does he have trouble falling asleep, fearful of what he might dream? Is he constantly on trial with the voice in his head?

No.

He simply exists, and as an envious witness to this, I notice the pressure on my trigger finger increase as the final grains of sand in his egg timer of a life race to the other side.

Nature's scent has led him to this field, like a teenager to a high school dance. Fuelled by opportunity. You won't find what you're looking for, Mr. Buck. She's not here. She doesn't even exist. I tricked you. Life is what you smell, but there's nothing but death for you in this particular field.

After much voyeurism through the scope on my Winchester Model 70, it strikes me once again how strange a fetish voyeurism truly is. But I completely get it. I fully understand the desire to lay eyes on something beautiful, while remaining anonymous. No judgmental eyes staring back. No expectations. That, mixed with the excitement from getting away with it, which I'm sure for the "peeker" is more thrilling than the act of physical lovemaking itself. Voyeurism isn't right. It's a violation of privacy and I would never do it — but I felt obligated to investigate the fetish. I clicked on "voyeur-cam" Internet porn once (to try to get a sense of what it's like) and watched a supposed sorority collegian towel dry after a hot shower. Brushed her long brunette hair for awhile in the nude. Skin cream went on next. Deodorant was then applied under her arms, but I couldn't tell if it was anti-perspirant, which contains aluminum, and aluminum has been linked to Alzheimer's. Regardless, she then lay splayed while leafing through a magazine on the edge of a motel-looking bed — the kind you put quarters in. But that's not real voyeurism. I knew the camera had been set up and the fraud was likely a coked-out amateur porn star or failed actress. *Are you sure that she knew the camera was there? Because if she didn't, then it classifies as true voyeurism, and you violated her privacy, Isaac.* No, she knew it was there. Every stilted action was blatantly played to the camera. *Let's hope that was the case — or you're a huge pervert.* No I'm not, because it didn't get me off, and it was for research purposes. *Fair enough.*

My diagnosis, then, is that voyeurs are either addicted to the endorphin rush yielded from the act itself, or they suffer from severe lack of confidence — bordering on depression. Either could be dealt with professionally. No one is born a voyeur, and that is a fact.

I find myself increasingly concerned at the tense in which I talk to myself. I hear the word "you" get thrown around a lot in my head: "'You' should do this." "'You' can't say that." "'You' need help." "'You' shouldn't think that."

Who is that speaking to me in my head? Is it me? It can't be.

It sounds exactly like my regular inner voice — the one speaking right now. Which thoughts are my own, and which don't belong? Or do they all belong to me? Could it be that my inner voice has more than one personality? *Possible.* I'm not schizophrenic. I don't suffer from hallucinations or delusions or incoherent word salad. My inner voice must be schizophrenic.

How would a professional even begin to treat a schizophrenic inner voice? There can't be medication on the market for that — something to make the conversation in my head stop talking to itself. Or me. Even for a second. And what if it stopped? Would I cease to be me? *You'd be bored.* Maybe. That's scary, too. In no way is this a professional prognosis, but I may be fucked in the head. *Inconclusive. Perhaps this is all very normal. You have no idea what the inside of someone else's head sounds like.* That's a great point.

It is too hot for a late October day, and I am beginning to smell bacteria multiplying in my armpit as the scent escapes from the neck of my camo, waffle-knit thermal. I am going to define this natural fragrance as vinegar mixed with gym sock and a hint of Parmesan cheese. *You smell like a hobo.*

Slaves must have worked on hot days like this, and I have no idea how they managed that. *You would have made a shitty slave.* They would have lynched me for repeatedly boarding the Underground Railroad. *Some slaves didn't get caught.* I would have. I, Isaac Sullivan, would have been made an example of, but would be proud to go out that way — having defied an institution. Taking a stand. Changing the world. Doctors change the world. *Yes, but you are not a doctor.*

Not yet.

But I could be.

You are a plumber, Isaac.

A plumber in Paradise. *That is an oxymoron.* No, that is an oxymoron on steroids and, of those steroids, most likely Winstrol-V. That oxymoron is not passing a urine test. That oxymoron rebuilds damaged cells faster and can train harder than other oxymorons. That oxymoron suffers from rampant acne, increased aggression, and testicular atrophy. Still, no matter how often that oxymoron sticks a needle in its ass, it remains both a tragic and accurate description of my role and location on this planet.

But the dozens of online IQ tests I've completed tell me that I, in fact, am quite capable of handling a college-level, pre-med curriculum. My SAT score placed me in the ninetieth percentile. *What kind of loser takes the SATs in his thirties? Pathetic.* I am, apparently. I'm the loser who took them in his thirties. Proud, and ready to secure my notch on the SAT measuring stick, I sat with two hundred seventeen-year-olds battling oily skin who couldn't give a shit about their scores and who lacked the capacity to appreciate their opportunity. Unable to understand what it felt like to take the test at my age or what it felt like to be on the receiving end of their confused, dirty looks.

More resentment to add to my toxic pile.

Raised by a father who instilled in me the idea that my aspirations of being a doctor were ridiculous, I wonder if it's possible to grow any more resentful of him. "You're not college material," he would say. Obviously, my SAT score and online IQ results have proved him wrong. But the evidence of that would never matter. I could never present it to him, and it wouldn't change anything or his estimation of me, because I'm still here, in Paradise, living someone else's life.

Someone else's career. Not mine.

I could have been a college student at the University of Michigan. Ann Arbor. The Wolverines.

An undergraduate, first. Medical school after that. Then a real doctor. The thought, the image, the words — they make my stomach flip as though catching a glimpse of the object of one's affection.

I hope Mr. Buck didn't sense my intestinal acrobatics. Yes, he's that good, and the last thing I want is to scare him off. *Stay still.* He's chewing right now, and I will wait to end his life until he finishes his mouthful. His last supper. *How thoughtful.*

The hundreds of medical textbooks and journals that line my antique bookcase have all been read twice. I'm like the kid who begs his coach to get in the game and play, but whose talent is left on the bench undiscovered. I could have gone to college. I could be a surgeon by now, but there is no M.D. after my name. Instead, I followed orders, did what I had to do, and took over the family business: piping routes for water, shit, and piss to travel, and maintaining them.

For now, I lie flat on my stomach just inside the tree line, peering out into the soybean field where Mr. Buck's chewing is nearing an end. Barely even breathing, I lie hidden, looking through the scope into the animal's retina. This isn't hunting. From this distance, I couldn't hit him with a baseball or a small stone — not even with a slingshot. But through the scope, I can almost smell him.

The fly on my arm cleans his wings, in no danger. A snake could cross in front of my mud-streaked face. It could even touch me or coil itself around my arm. I wouldn't budge. *Lie. You hate snakes.* True. But maybe I just haven't met one I liked.

The woods behind me are alive with noise, random chirps, rustling, calls, mating, and digging, but my prey is intelligent and in tune with nature and is deaf to these sounds. The wonderment here lies in the fact that one wrong breath from me, one cough, one small clearing of the throat, one misplaced body shift, and the balance is off, and so is he. *No, the wonderment here lies in the fact that he hasn't smelled you, because your armpits are a Petri dish.* True. Lucky I'm downwind.

I look over to Gilby crouching silently beside me. He knows better than to pant, despite the fact that it is too hot for an October day. *You're a good soldier, Gilby. You're a Marine, pal. We are an army of two.* His dirty yellow coat seems to blend in nicely with our current vantage point. He looks back at me. I agree. It's time. I feel the calculated intake of air into my lungs. Fuelled by power and poise, I have to remind myself why I do this. It's not about the buck. Resentful as I am, this is not about the buck. *It might be about the buck.* Enough. It's time to get focused.

Crosshairs sit between his eye and lower ear, dancing a few inches in every direction because I can't hold perfectly still. If I popped a Diazepam, I would be more still. Snipers take Diazepam. *Two things: Diazepam can be tough on the system, and its side-effects include depression and impaired learning, both of which you can't afford.* True. I walk the line of depression daily, and I can't afford anything to impair my continual intake of medical knowledge. *Also, you're not a sniper. You're a plumber.* Shut up.

Focus.

Focus.

Focus.

The mounting pressure on the trigger is too much. I feel it give way. It's at this point that I close my eyes. The weight of the rifle kicks back into my shoulder, but I am too strong. The cracking sound of the bullet, ignited with new purpose, is succeeded by two of my favourite things: the smell of the powder, and the thud of the fallen kill.

Eyes re-open. Mr. Buck lies on the ground as his peers dash away. Don't worry, peers. No more bullets. I only brought one. And thank you, Mr. Buck. You have unwittingly volunteered your body to medicine and will be this week's surgical practicum.

Home schooling is hard and takes tenacity and creativity. There are no fetal pigs, and there are no rats or other small mammals soaking in formaldehyde to operate on, so I'm forced to provide for myself. As a result, I shot Mr. Buck, and the more hours behind the blade, the better.

Training.

Preparing.

You can't qualify cleaning Mr. Buck as surgery. Why not? *It's more of an autopsy, except you already know the cause of death.*

Fine. It's surgery and it's an autopsy. *An autopsy isn't surgery.* I agree — but a heart transplant is, and he has one coming.

One day it will not be a buck or a wolf or a mallard. It will be a human being. That human being will unconsciously rely on my confidence with a scalpel and, like an athlete in training, I am dedicated to perfection. Fact: It would be much more beneficial to practice on humans, but I won't be granted that divine right until medical school. Fact: There are a few characters in Paradise I would love to select for an educational dissection — Tyson Fleming being the highest on the list. Second highest on the list is Mrs. Bennett on West Portage Lane. Mrs. Bennett, whose hot water heater I installed three months ago and who hasn't paid me yet.

Dressed in a Mossy Oak, Realtree HD camouflage jacket and pants, lying at the edge of the tree line, I stare back out onto my fallen buck.

Gilby licks my face, pleading to go check the kill. I motion with the slightest nod, and he takes off like a malnourished greyhound chasing a plastic rabbit. Gilby. So loyal. If I installed a water heater in his dog shed, he would pay me on time. I release the bolt on the Winchester and slide it back. A smoking brass shell pops out.

I approach my fallen prey with my tools and a large blue cooler in tow. Precious time has elapsed since I downed Mr. Buck. I should have raced to slit his throat and let his heart pump out as much blood as possible before it got the memo. *Surgery will be messier now.* Understood.

Crouching down beside the noble creature, I lay both of my hands on his torso, carefully, as if not to wake him from an afternoon nap. Gilby has come over to sit next to me, panting heavily and biting at the flies circling his head. He knows what comes next. He is my operating room nurse.

"Thank you for your contribution to medicine, Mr. Buck."

Even in his death, I am more resentful than ever of this animal. And why you? Why you, out of all of your qualified peers? There must have been a reason. There must be karma, and if there is karma, then I am begging for it. While digging a ditch for a sewer connection, do I get to be unsuspectingly crushed by the shovel on the backhoe? Mercifully released from this nuclear meltdown of a life to start from scratch sometime in the future or in tandem or however that afterlife thing works — if it works at all.

Enough questions. The sun is burning hotter, and I have to clean Mr. Buck to salvage the meat.

"Gilby. Scalpel please," I order. He looks at me and sniffs the air. Typical.

From my tool bag, I grab the transportation tags and wrap one around the right ankle of Mr. Buck like a hospital bracelet. *Honestly, don't call him "Mr. Buck." I'm sick of it already, and it's weird and really messed up.* I will call him "Mr. Buck" if I like. He deserves a name. He is a patient, and one day they will be real people who have real names. I remove the plastic cover from the scalpel and catch my reflection in the blade.

Not sure what to think of what I see.

I bring the white surgical mask to the ready position, and it hugs tightly to my nose and mouth. Two rubber gloves are snapped on over my sweaty, dirty hands. Will someone catch me this time, out here with the mask and gloves and scalpel instead of a proper cleaning knife? *Why not add the white surgical cap for good measure, moron?* The cap would be too much. *They would still call you a freak. The lack of a surgical cap is not saving you from that.* True, but this freak is dedicated to saving lives, and no one can see me because this is my property and it is private.

My scalpel cuts away Mr. Buck's genitals. Not my fault. It has to be done: Step One in field dressing and the worst part. *Your hand is shaking a bit. Are you nervous?* Shut up. *Why are you cutting with your left hand?* Good point. I'm right-handed, but I also cut my food with my left hand. *That's odd.* In medical school, they will force me to cut with my right hand because I am right-hand dominant. *Be proactive and switch it up then.* Next time.

From around the genitals first, the scalpel travels backward, cutting a circle around the anus.

The hard part is over. I insert my scalpel under the hide and make one single incision up the belly all the way to the base of his neck. Skin spreads apart behind the blade, releasing it like a zipper.

With purpose, I walk into the O.R., dressed and scrubbed for surgery, my gloved hands arrogantly positioned in the air awaiting surgical tools.

"Status update," I demand from the eager team already in place.

"Penetrating ballistic chest trauma," says the Blonde Nurse. "Patient is in hypovolemic shock."

"More info," I command.

"B.P. is 70 systolic, and blood ox is 88 on 10," she fires back.

I love Blonde Nurse. She looks like Gwen Stefani mixed with Madonna, and Madonna attended the University of Michigan for a brief academic romp — which makes her significantly hotter. So I guess Blonde Nurse looks more like Madonna than Gwen Stefani for my purposes. Focus. There is a human on the table dying. Who is he?

"Name?" I yell.

"John Buckley. Fifty-five. Hunting accident," says Asian Nurse.

"Let's get an X-ray up here for a portable chest. I want a chest tube in there to get the air out of the pleural cavity," I order.

I understand that this is a high-pressure situation, but Asian Nurse had better watch herself. She has given me two looks now in the span of only a few seconds. Two flirty looks. My general rule of thumb is that the first two are free. The third will result in my asking her out for a post-op martini or ten — the preamble to waking up beside her the next morning with a hangover and several important questions that need answering.

"Let's get three bags of O-negative up here, stat," belts out Asian Nurse.

I look into John Buckley's chest and then over at Blonde Nurse's.

Both equally fascinating.

"Give me a 10 blade!" I yell. Instantly, a 10 blade is placed in my hand by an overweight Fat Male Nurse.

Larger issue: Asian Nurse just gave me the third look. She is mine.

Larger issue: John Buckley's chest — spread open on the table in front of me. I begin to hunt for the bullet with my scalpel but can't see shit from the bleeding.

"I can't see shit from the bleeding! More suction!"

My request is instantly granted. Blonde Nurse returns with blood bags. A new Brunette Nurse, who looks like the real-life version of Belle from the cartoon *Beauty and the Beast*, enters with the chest X-ray. *Cartoon Belle was hotter.* I really can't debate this right now.

Focus on the dying human.

Just as I thought, the bullet is lodged against the heart — the trickiest of removals. One wrong move and life is over for our calamity-stricken hunter. I wonder if Blonde Nurse would join me in a threesome with Asian Nurse. I'm getting self-conscious now. *That's weird.* Why did I just get self-conscious? *Is it because there are two of them? Maybe. Are you afraid that they will pleasure each other more than you possibly could?* That's impossible. I have hardware that they lack. *You do have hardware, but your refractory period isn't great.* True. Conclusion: In a threesome, I am quickly expendable.

"B.P.'s dropping," announces Fat Male Nurse with a sense of purpose. I'm working as fast as I can, for Christ's sake. *No, you're not.* Fat Male Nurse looks over to me, his eyes suggesting he could do a better job. Really? Do you think so, Fat Male Nurse? Fact: He should be fired and forced to jog five times a week for at least forty-five minutes, because only then will he utilize the most recently metabolized energy and force his body to tap its fat stores. *Good general advice, but bad idea. He should simply try walking quickly, first.* Fine. Do something, Fat Male Nurse. Do something to help yourself. Obviously, typing, playing video games, and passing me tools isn't burning enough calories. *It may not be his fault. This could be a thyroid issue in which a significant decrease in the release of thyroid hormones causes cellular activity to drop off, thereby allowing more energy to be stored as fat.* If Fat Male Nurse does, in fact, have a thyroid issue, then I am empathetic to his situation. Having said that, if he is truly a lazy slob, then I want to tie him to a stationary bike and force him to watch the movie *Seven*, on repeat, for a month.

Miraculously, I have located the bullet. "Tweezers!"

"They're called 'Adsons,' sir," says Fat Male Nurse, swapping the bloodied scalpel for my new tool. It's official. He thinks he can replace me. He thinks I'm a hack. I know they're called "Adsons," Fat Male Nurse. *Then why didn't you call them that?* I didn't feel like it. *Wrong. You forgot the proper term.* Fuck off.

Focus. Dying human on table.

Without complication, I remove the bullet from John Buckley's chest. All in attendance clap at my amazing retrieval. The crimson bullet glistens under the hot O.R. lights. One of my personal favourites: a Winchester Supreme .300 WSM bullet. Boat-tail design and polycarbonate Silvertip for bone-smashing fragmentation built on a lead core for optimal expansion, providing a devastating terminal effect and wound channel for easier extraction. The tooled contours in the nickel-plate jacket maximize range and reduce crosswind drift but now do nothing more than provide trenches for coagulated blood. I love this bullet and technology, and I love my job. *Well done, Isaac.* Thanks.

"Well done, sir," whispers the Asian Nurse in my ear. I smile back. She lets the tiniest of giggles escape as she walks away. Tonight could not come soon enough. I have championed this surgery, and I want my victory lap. *Will you wear a condom?* I hate condoms. *Yes, but as a medical professional, you have to lead by example.* True. I really don't want to, but I will. Beyond the medical and ethical implications, I simply don't want to run the risk of knocking her up. *That is racist.* No, it's not. *Yes, it is. What you're saying is that you don't want to run the risk of knocking her up and having a mixed child.* Could that be what I meant? No, I fully disagree. That is not what I meant. I'm just not ready for kids.

Blonde Nurse and Brunette Nurse have suctioned the last amounts of bleeding from the chest cavity and begin to sew up John Buckley.

Where is Fat Male Nurse? I trust him as far as I can throw him. My eyes scan the room and quickly confirm my suspicions. There he is in the corner chatting up Asian Nurse. Do you think you could do a better job than me in that regard as well, Fat Male Nurse? Not sure why I should feel threatened, but I am. I'm not possessive, and she's not mine, and no one should own anyone else, but she was into me, and now I have an urge to cut this guy's head off.

Escalation: He just told a joke and made her laugh. She's laughing. Loud. Showing all of her perfect teeth in a mouth that obviously housed braces at one point. *He thinks they are perfect teeth, too, I bet.*

Escalation: She just touched his arm. He liked that, and now he's asking what she's doing later tonight.

It's official. His fat head will be removed.

I grab the bloodied scalpel from the stainless steel tub and prepare for surgery of a different nature.

Enough.

I'm out.

I blink hard several times. Sweat drips from my brow into my eyes. Stings them. More sweat from the tip of my nose drips into the body cavity of my patient. *That's not professional. Put the mask back on.* Fair point. Gilby scratches the back of his mud-caked ear with his hind leg. Most of the work has been done, and Mr. Buck's four-chamber heart, the last of the organs to come out, awaits transplant surgery.

With my scalpel, I detach the heart where it marries the aorta.

Day in and day out, the daydreams continue to sneak in as they please, but I still remain in full control of my escape from them. Usually, I let them play out in their entirety, simply for entertainment value. I should have known to pull out halfway through that last one. They've been getting away on me lately. I didn't like myself in that one.

I wonder if I would have mixed kids? They were always the best-looking kids in school. And the smartest. And very athletic. It makes all the sense in the world: the hybridization that occurs from two genetically different parents masking recessive traits and leaving only the superior qualities of both parents to be expressed in the offspring. This process is called "hybrid vigour." *Nice one. Thanks.*

The second incision severs the heart from the pulmonary artery. Applying the slightest bit of pressure to the heart, while cutting, has forced the remaining blood in the chambers to spill out over my surgical gloves. I could use some suction here.

Hybrid vigor is essential to the advancement of plants and animals on this planet, and I am more than willing to jump on that bandwagon with regard to progressive human reproduction. I vote YES to the advancement of the human race. Genetic All-Stars. Isn't that what all nations should aspire to — an intelligent, talented, attractive, athletic population?

Carefully, I make the third incision — carving the heart away from the left atrium, leaving a circular portion of it containing the pulmonary veins.

Success.

Mr. Buck's heart is now hanging from its attachment to the superior vena cava. With my right hand, I cradle the heart and rest the scalpel on its final mark.

The world is changing, and I hope this change continues to bring variations of mixed people to the White House and to the head of Fortune 500 companies and brings stem cell technology into standard practice and begins an era of sustained socialized healthcare. *Bad idea. You would make less money as a surgeon in that scenario.* I don't care. It's the right thing to do, and I would be doing what I love and still making more than I do now as a plumber.

Mr. Buck's heart rests in my hand. Should I save it for future mock transplants? I hate to waste anything. *No.* And I'm not going to eat it. The heart is tossed on top of the "viscera pile" I seem to have created a few feet away. Successfully, I have vented the body cavity of the animal and begin to pack it with ice bags from the cooler to cool down the meat. From the bottom of the cooler, I remove the freezer bag containing the donor heart, which, thankfully, feels not to have frozen solid. But the sun is hot, and it will thaw quickly. I shot the donor a month ago, and he was delicious, grilled to medium rare on the barbecue and topped with a Scotch sour sauce.

"Mr. Buck, your donor heart is coming from a healthy, non-smoking candidate who suffered ballistic trauma to the brain on account of my exceptional marksmanship. I have determined that the blood type and tissues match because he was shot in a field only a mile south and, due to proximity, is likely your relative." I say this to the patient with heightened intonation, as if his hearing was impaired slightly. *That was weird.*

Gilby's head pops up from its resting on his front paws, and the reproachful look he pitches me suggests that I have broken code. *You have.*

"Too weird. Me talking to the patient, pal?"

His silence, like a master professor, forces me to answer my own question.

"Yeah, I agree. No more of that," I say. Gilby seems satisfied with this and returns to his resting position, enjoying his front-row, platinum-level seat.

Wetted thread makes its way through the eye of my large disinfected sewing needle in preparation for suturing the donor heart into place. Time is obviously not a factor, but I will work quickly. I have to learn how to create high stakes in situations like this. Perhaps, one day, there will be a ticking clock.

A life hanging in the balance.

A real sense of urgency.

Pop Quiz: List all of the endocrine glands and each of the hormones they secrete. *Go.* I list them. And then again for good measure.

The donor heart has now had enough time to reach its desired temperature, and I position it, like the missing piece in a jigsaw puzzle, up against Mr. Buck's anxious arteries.

Transportation tag spinning around his right ankle in the breeze, my deceased and disembowelled patient is soon to have a new heart and a second chance at life.

Thanks to me.
The almost doctor, Isaac Sullivan.

‖

After its recent service, the plumbing van runs very smoothly. Transmission almost seamless. I round the corner from Whitefish Road onto West Portage Lane, and the street looks good for being a lane. The leaves are falling, and raked calico piles mark each yard, only to be cannonballed by children of single-digit ages. Usually, Portage is filled with kids playing, but today it looks like an abandoned Hollywood set.

There it is. Fifty-seven West Portage Lane.

The home of Donna Bennett.

I pull into her driveway and leave the plumbing van in park. I apologize, Mr. Gore, but I'm leaving the van running this time. The purpose here is to collect. The visit will be quick, and if she wants to chat, I can rely on the fact that "the van is running." The remaining coffee from the to-go cup is downed like a shot of courage before I exit the get-away vehicle. *Get-away vehicle? Where did that come from? You're here to get what's owed, not stick her up.* You can't stick someone up in a small town like this.

You can't do anything in a small town without everyone knowing.

"Stay in the van, Gilby."

He sniffs at me.

My finger presses her doorbell button so hard that the tip of it becomes translucent. Instantly, she answers, as if the two of us had rehearsed this for weeks.

"Mr. Sullivan! Wow! So nice to see you," she says, with intonation suggesting old friendship.

I'm not your friend. Not even close. I think about you never, except when you owe me six hundred bucks. But your breasts look great for sixty. Should I be looking at her sixty-year-old breasts? Don't look. *Yes. Look at them.* It's not my fault that she wants to shop at Abercrombie, and it's not my fault that she fits their clothing so nicely. If she wants to advertise her wares, then I'm entitled a glance or two.

"Pleasure's all mine. Do you have a moment?" I ask.

"I most certainly do. Please, come in."

"I don't really have time, Mrs. Bennett. I'm here because you owe me six hundred dollars for the water heater installation three months ago."

"What?"

Oh, please. Don't play dumb. Don't play dumb, and don't subtly arch your back and use your tits to get out of this one. Yes, before they were breasts. Now they are tits and she made it that way. *Fair enough.*

"Oh, right! The water heater. Yes," she says. Here it comes. Forgetful Jones seems to have clued in.

"But I can't pay you this month. Bear with me on this one. I can get you the money by Christmas."

All I heard was "Christmas," and all I can focus on is not looking at her tits, wrapped up like a perfect Christmas gift. The kind of perfect gift Santa would deliver to me, if he existed. What a crushing letdown: the whole Santa thing.

Before Mom left, she always worked so hard at making Christmas special and Santa real. Every year, she would help me write the letter to Santa that we mailed together. Every Christmas

Eve, the milk and cookies were laid out. And magically, the cookies and milk were nothing more than crumbs and a dirty glass on Christmas morning.

Too bad Dad is such a jackass and stormed in on us writing the letter together one year. "Santa isn't real, for fucksakes. Stop acting like retards, the both of you," he said. Mom cried hard, like when you can barely breathe, and she tried her best, between the tears and quick gasps for air, to tell me he was kidding, but I knew he wasn't. He never kids. He never smiles, and I'm sure you have to smile to have the capacity to kid.

Mom loved Christmas all the way up until she abandoned us.

Who knows if she still loves Christmas.

Reality check: Mrs. Bennett just said that she couldn't get me the money until Christmas. I have gifts to buy for people I downright loathe. Don't get worked up. Stay focused on the task at hand. Try a new approach.

"Look, I apologize, and I would never normally do this, but I really need the money now, Mrs. Bennett."

"And I'm genuinely sorry, Isaac. But I can't do it."

Apparently genuine.

I'm calling bullshit, and I am starting to question if those tits are even genuine, they look so damn perky. Stay focused.

"I hate to be a stickler, Donna, but I need it today. It's been three months, and I feel I've been fair."

This is progress. This is masterful. This is coming out much better than expected. How could this be going so well? Why is she lighting a cigarette? Her demeanour has changed. The whole temperature of the room has changed.

She pulls on her menthol cigarette, and hundreds of wrinkles, unseen prior to this, appear around her mouth. Menthol. Who came up with that? Mint should be served with an order of spring lamb, not emphysema.

Mrs. Bennett, you are destroying the elasticity in the structures supporting your alveoli and the capillaries that feed them, with every gum-rotting puff. Sooner than later, your only hope will be a lung transplant, and in most cases, patients aren't strong enough that far into the disease and die on the table during surgery. If you are choosing not to pay me to buy cigarettes instead, then you are ultimately fucking yourself, and no one wins here.

"Why don't you stop staring at my tits and get off my property, Plumb," she says casually, flicking her cigarette toward me. End over end it goes until it strikes the faded fabric next to the Sullivan's Plumbing logo on the left breast of my T-shirt.

I love this T-shirt, and now there is a hole in it.

Rage.

It's amazing how women strike a certain position once they have drawn a line in the sand. Unfortunately, the only line that will be drawn around her will be in chalk.

As swiftly as a cat bats at a toy, a screwdriver from my tool pouch finds the temple of her skull. The look in her eyes tells me she could, indeed, have paid me and truly regrets her decision not to. I can tell by the ruby colour of the screwdriver's handle that it was a slot head, which explains the easy entry. Lucky grab. The Robertson or Double Hex could have been awkward and messy.

Bottom line: It was a horrible idea to introduce a screwdriver to her brain. One of the worst I've ever had. Red and white and blue lights begin to flicker in her eyes, as if the flag itself was waving at me, mocking the American dream. *Look more closely, Isaac.* My body pivots, and my head spins around to witness the horrifying image behind me: a sea of police cars surrounding my plumbing van, still running. Every single squad car within fifty miles sits in Mrs. Bennett's front yard with lights flashing. What is Dad doing out there? *You can fix this, Isaac.* She needs surgery, and I know penetrating head trauma removal procedures. *Even if*

EXIT PAPERS FROM PARADISE

you save her life, yours is over. The University of Michigan will never accept you after this gross indiscretion. That is undeniably true.

Panic.

Ringing.

I'm out.

That ringing sound is the alarm clock, and it rings, oblivious to how annoying it is. No human should ever be forced to wake up like this. Cruel. Unusual. And we would be a far healthier species without the alarm clock. There would be less cancer and anxiety. *You have no medical proof of that, and potential doctors don't go around spouting ridiculous shit without facts.* I'll do better.

I hit the snooze button much harder than I hit it ten minutes ago. Did I hit the snooze button so hard because I thought the alarm clock could feel it? *The alarm clock is made of plastic.* Am I pissed off at the clock, or Donna Bennett, or am I pissed at myself for having to wake up and be a plumber? *Good question.* Easy answer.

You killed Mrs. Bennett with a slot screwdriver in a fit of rage after salivating over her breasts-turned-tits. That's disturbing. *You say that, but you're really not disturbed by it at all.* True. So that must mean something — my non-disturbance. *Sociopaths are never disturbed by their actions toward others.* Right, but these are dreams and not actions, so I'm fine. *Thoughts manifest actions.* True. Every action starts as a thought, which is likely why the Bible says anyone who looks at a woman with lust in his eye has already committed adultery in his heart, and I can't stand the Bible or anyone who thumps it.

Including my father.

Gilby gets off his mat beside the bed and performs one of those wild and violent total body shakes that start at his head and end at his tail. Like clockwork, front paws come to rest on the edge of the bed, and he props his body vertically, allowing an unobstructed view of me.

Tongue hanging from his jaws. Tail wagging. Hot, stale breath pluming into my face.

How can you be so happy, pal? I reach out and scratch his ear. He leans into it, and the panting ceases.

This will buy me a few minutes of distraction.

Other than my bowl of generic corn flakes, my breakfast experience this morning has been far from mundane. Listening to medical experts on this morning's webcast wrap-up, I sit in wonder at their recent discovery: significant amounts of adrenocorticotropic hormone found in human tears. If this polypeptide, parasympathetic hormone, often released into the body due to biological stress, has found its way into human tears, then there is a reason for it. Nothing in the human body is accidentally found in large amounts. Nothing in the human body is an accident, which is the sole reason I can't rule out a higher being of some form or title.

The human body is a perfect design that fits into a larger perfect design called Nature, and both are so perfect that they remain a mystery to us in many regards. And if the human body is, in fact, a design, then I am forced to agree with Mr. William Paley. There has to be a designer. If a watch has a design, and a watch exists, then it must have a designer. My coffeemaker exists because it has a designer, and so does my car and my shirt. My underwear even has the designer's name on the waistband.

"Argument by Design."

I get that.

I buy that.

That makes sense to me, and I have no idea what the name of the Earth Designer is, or the Nature Designer, or the Designer of

Species or how many designers were allocated to the Milky Way Creative Team, but I have to agree that (from a logical perspective) something designed all of this in order for it to exist.

Regardless, given this morning's reporting, mankind has unlocked yet another secret.

Therefore, if researchers have found large amounts of adrenocorticotropic hormone in tears, then the act of crying is not only beneficial emotionally, but required physiologically. I will have to do more research on this tonight. Fact: The presence of adrenocorticotropic hormone (ACTH) increases the production of cortisol, so the million-dollar question is: What are the effects of prolonged cortisol production? If my hypothesis is true and the absence of crying is actually harmful, then Oprah will catch wind of it, and the world will see the emergence of high-end crying clinics and crying retreats, and people will cut onions at close-range, but that won't work because those kinds of tears are composed differently than emotional tears, and that is also a fact.

I haven't cried in a while. Not since Mom left. If my pending research supports my hypothesis, my failure to do so may be killing me. But not fast enough. I will still have work today. And tomorrow. And even next week and next month.

Not killing me fast enough.

Gilby hoovers his kibble from the stainless steel bowl on the floor beside me. I could never eat that fast, pal. I would get heartburn, and gastric acid would pound against my cardiac sphincter until the flesh levee broke and my esophagus was exposed to the burning hydrochloric juices. But I don't get heartburn anymore because I chew properly and go to bed no sooner than three hours after I've eaten or consumed alcohol. Listen to me, Gilby, chew your food more thoroughly. You don't want heartburn, because heartburn is gastroesophageal reflux disease and that is the precursor to esophageal cancer, and once you have that — you are cooked.

The bird's-eye maple floors in this century-old farmhouse creak under the legs of my chair with the slight transfer of weight. Deep in thought, I slowly lean from side to side on my chair, like a lazy metronome.

What about another podcast or another webcast? Podcast. They're usually shorter in length. There's time.

No, there is no more time.

My calendar wears the battle scars of pencil marks on top of erased pencil marks, which is ridiculous given that I have a BlackBerry. This is different. This is backup, in case the BlackBerry fails.

First up: Mrs. Dunfield, on Tahqua Trail — toilet issue. If I were to pray to a named higher entity and my faith was blind, this would be the time where I would pray for said "toilet issue" to be nothing more than a flow rate adjustment or a broken lift rod. I would pray for that.

After locking the door, I turn around to face the world. Gilby sits patiently at the passenger door to the plumbing van, tail wagging. The property looks fairly good, although one of the huge maples lining my quarter-mile driveway needs taking down. Raking needs doing. Why would I do it? *Hire the kid across the street to rake.* He's likely too busy trying to convince his girlfriend to show him what second base looks like. I could always ask him to rake and pay him enough so he can't refuse. *You have nothing better to do, so do the raking yourself.*

I make my way to the passenger door of the van and unlock it. Gilby is alive with anticipation. I admire you, pal. Your daily enthusiasm. As soon as I swing the door open, he is up and in the front seat facing forward.

My navigator. My first mate.

As I make my way behind the van to the driver's side, the unsightly amount of rust on my Michigan licence plate catches my eye. The words "Great Lakes" are barely visible, and my back-left tire is balding. *So are you.* I'm thinning. *Is that denial?* Not really, it depends on the lighting. Overhead lighting exaggerates the thinning. *To make it look more like what, Isaac? Balding?* True. Why do hair plugs look more unnatural than a reforestation project? Our species can take MRIs and land objects on neighbouring planets, but we fail to combat male-pattern baldness. That is ridiculous, and I need new tires and a new licence plate.

The driver's side door bears battle scars of small dents and scratches in the paint, and I need to deal with that, too. *The entire van needs replacing.* No, I will be gone to school soon, so replacing the van is a waste of time. *Says who? When did you apply? Who accepted you?* Stop. That's why I said "soon." It's relative. *It's delusional.*

I flip through the similar-looking keys to unlock the door and question the amount of keys on one ring. How in Christ can I have this many keys, and why do they all look the same? I look like a janitor. *You can't call them janitors anymore. They are sanitary engineers.* Yet, somehow, everyone's still allowed to call me a plumber. How is that fair? That's bullshit. *What would you rather be called?* Good question. I have no idea.

Like clockwork, pulling myself up into the driver's seat inspires cursing the early morning aches and pains. How can my body be this sore at thirty-six? *Because you lift, dig, carry, and crawl for a living.* What if I got a helper? If I had a helper, I could stand back and drink coffee while he did all the work. *You don't make enough money for that.* What a piss-off. More importantly, where would Gilby sit? He would refuse to sit in the back with the tools. No, he would do it if I asked him nicely. He would do it because he loves me. If I had a helper, then I would have to participate in small talk with the helper, and I hate small talk. *Hire a chick.* Nope. Nothing would get done, and I would eventually get charged with sexual harassment. *Fine, hire a lesbian.* Gilby would still have to sit in the back in that scenario, for sure. I couldn't ask a lesbian to sit in the back with the tools. I don't think that's P.C.

How would I begin to find a lesbian in Paradise?

There should be more of them, by definition.

Gilby and I make our way to the coffee shop like we do every morning, but which route to take today? *Drive past the high school.* Always a good choice. I'm sure Gilby agrees, though his preference is to drive past the park. Many more of the canine persuasion hang out there, providing him his needed eye candy. I think it's only fair that I get mine, too, pal. *Hold on, why is driving past the high school providing you eye candy?* Relax, some seniors are eighteen. I will only look at the seniors as we roll by. *How can you tell the difference?* Fair point. What if I get all excited over one that I think is eighteen but is really seventeen? Or sixteen. Or fifteen. *That would be against the law.* Wrong. It's not against the law to look. *Still, you will look really creepy driving past the high school gawking.* I wasn't going to gawk. It would have been more like brief glances. *Equally as pervy.*

I pull a mean U-turn and steer clear of the sociological and legal quagmire that driving past the high school was causing to surface. *It had already surfaced.* True. I am choosing to avoid it.

There are more parking spaces than usual at CoffeeBuddy. Gilby's now alive with interest. No dogs in sight. "Relax, pal." *Telling him to relax is futile.* True. As soon as I leave the van, the barking will commence.

Through the dirty window, I can see that Linda is working. Ron Green dated Linda. He said she had the most interesting cum faces. He said that once she got on top and slid back and forth a few times, her pretty face would contort into something that resembled pain, fear, and electrocution. I would pay a thousand dollars to see what Linda's cum face looks like. A picture of it. Even a grainy one. I've tried to imagine it in my mind for months, but reality is stranger than fiction, so I understand that anything I've come up with in my mind pales in comparison.

I lower myself down from the van and feel all hundred and eighty-five pounds of myself. My knees feel as old as my weight. I need to start taking those glucosamine or devil's claw tablets again. Oddly, they worked. *Ibuprofen is better.* True. The herbs don't work as well as ibuprofen, but they still work.

In public, I do my best to walk without emoting pain. Who would hire me if I allowed myself to walk the way I felt? *People would still hire you, Isaac. There are only two plumbers to choose from in the area, and one's likely busy.*

I open the door to CoffeeBuddy, and the annoying bells jingle.

"Mornin', Plumb," says Linda, without looking up from her pouring. What a pro.

"How are you now?" I say, well aware that in Paradise, this question breeds the same answer every single time.

"Been better."

And there it is. I believe her, fully.

But Linda braves a smile and manages a happy face every morning of every weekday. Despite the fact that she's "been better." No clue how she pulls that off.

Question: Does she force the smile, or worse, does she mean it? Is she actually happy here — a lifer in Paradise pouring coffee for the tradesmen and welfare recipients? I can picture her getting ready in the morning, selecting a pair of high-rise jeans that make her ass look like the Midwest. Selecting one of three CoffeeBuddy jersey-shirts that hang in her closet. Overdoing her hair and makeup the same way she's overdone it since high school. And finally, starting the engine to her rusted Chrysler to chariot her to work. If it is, in fact, bravery that allows her to force the happy face, then I want to applaud in admiration and award her an Oscar. Alternatively, if she is genuinely happy, then I believe she is mentally ill.

"How 'bout you?"

"Not bad for a Wednesday, Linda," I reply, much more audibly. *Why the louder voice there?* Not sure. *Don't be weird.*

"Here you are, Plumb. Two creams. Two sugars. Just how you like it."

"Thanks," I say, noticing the button of her Levis hanging on for dear life. Stretched to capacity. Get over it, Linda, the jeans don't fit anymore. You are a size bigger now. Does she even realize the gravity of the pending social nightmare? I can see it now — the button releasing like a cork from a shaken bottle of champagne in the middle of our coffee transaction. There is only one thing that will get Linda into a larger size. One antidote to counteract her denial. And that is the drama and trauma of a "button launch." The button will launch, and the taut zipper will splay halfway down its track, and Linda will be left standing, mid-conversation, wishing she hadn't actively chosen to give these jeans one more wear. It will take that scale of nightmarish reality to break through her tough exoskeleton of pride.

"Beautiful weather this past weekend," she says, working hard to get me talking. *Stop being a caveman and be more interesting.* All I can think of is the button.

"I hope it stays."

Oh shit, was I talking about the weather or the button?

EXIT PAPERS FROM PARADISE

She hands me my coffee in exchange for the one-dollar bill I have pulled out of my worn wallet. This wallet looks like shit. *Make a new one out of Mr. Buck.* That's not a bad idea.

"Look, I know this ain't none of my business," she offers in a hushed tone, as if to brief me on a redneck secret mission. "And I don't even know if you're lookin' ... but my girlfriend's younger sister, Mandy Klein ... you know her?" she asks.

Jesus Christ. I know exactly what's coming.

"No," I say, lying through my teeth. "Never heard of her."

"Thought you knew almost everyone, Plumb?"

"Well, I'm sure I'd recognize her face ... is what I meant."

"Here's her picture right here," she says, proudly unfolding today's paper. "Look right here. She won an award at the softball banquet last Friday night. She's one hell of a pitcher. Lemme tell ya."

Gosh, Linda. I was hoping she was more of a catcher.

I look hard at the picture, pretending to strain for recognition. "Oh, yeah! 'Course I know her. She lives on Albert Street in the ..."

"That's right! That little white bungalow with that thing in the garden."

"The gargoyle."

"Yeah, the gargoyle. You know, I keep telling her to get rid of that weird thing. I tell her it's a little devil chasing away all the good men from her doorstep."

This conversation is now painful and requires a potent opiate analgesic. Most likely morphine.

"I have a hard time believing she's without a man," I say. I actually admitted that. I must believe it. *Interesting.*

"Look, Plumb ... again, none my business, but I just happen to think the two of you would make a great couple. What d'you say you let me hook the two of you good lookin' singles up on a date?"

35

What do I say? Dammit, Linda. You've backed me into a one hell of a corner here. My heart is beating fast and my fight or flight response has kicked in. I have to say yes. *Why? Are you experiencing peer pressure?* I believe so. *Pathetic.* You have caught me with my pants down, Linda, despite the fact I saw it coming. If I say no, she's going to think I'm a homo. *Why would she think you were a homo for saying no?* Guys are supposed to jump at everything, right? Is it even possible for guys to turn down an opportunity to get action and not look like a pussy? *That is a tough one.* The answer must be yes, but only if based on an attempt to upgrade the proposed option. *Too much time has passed. Answer.*

"I think that would be a great idea," I spurt out awkwardly.

"Really? Yay!" Linda makes tiny clapping movements with her beautiful hands. No ring on Linda's hand. How can Linda not be married, either? To be single in Paradise at her age must mean something bad. Perhaps her terrifying cum face scares away all the good men — like Mandy Klein's gargoyle.

"I'm gonna set the whole thing up. All you have to do is show up and be the handsome devil you are," she says. I feel more devil than handsome these days, Linda.

"And just the other day, over a beer, she was just talkin' about how chivalry was dead. No more gentlemen out there, she said. So, be extra charming, Plumb. Just a little tip."

I pull my body carefully back into the van, so as not to spill the coffee. Gilby stops barking immediately and looks back out the window on alert. I scratch the top of his head.

"I love you, buddy," I say. His eyes close as he enjoys every second of the scratch. I'm not even sure he has an itch there. In fact, I'm sure he has a terrible itch somewhere else, but he leans into my hand as if scratching him in that exact spot was doing him the greatest of favours. How could I not love something that grateful? I want to be more grateful. I am envious of you, Gilby. You are a Zen master. You are a Buddha, and I am a knot of anxiety, resentment, and fear. Fearing most that I will never make it to medical school and instead be sentenced to stay here in Paradise, caged, arguing with myself in my head.

As for Mandy Klein, I didn't need Linda's help to get that date. I mentioned to Rob Parker last year that I thought Mandy Klein was hot, and I bet Rob Parker ran his mouth to Linda. Small town. Now I don't want to have anything to do with it. That was my hunt, Linda. A lion doesn't want to have an antelope steak tossed into his cage. He wants to chase that hard-to-get antelope and enjoy that succulent meat once he's earned it. *You haven't even introduced yourself to Mandy Klein.* That, sadly, is the undeniable truth. I have made zero moves in her direction.

The coffee is extra hot this morning, and I've burned my tongue.

"She said chivalry is dead. What do you think about that, pal?" I ask Gilby.

Gilby sniffs in my direction, having recognized the question posed. No comment from Gilby. Typical.

Men will not and cannot take the blame for the murder of chivalry. Chivalry is dead because women killed it. I shouldn't say that. The Others killed it. The Others killed chivalry. Have women not thought about why chivalry existed in the first place? It existed because men had to fight to earn the infrequent gift of winning a woman's heart, and then, ultimately, her body. Chivalry is time-consuming, expensive, and inefficient, and that is a fact. When The Others decided they would embrace a new sexual playbook and sleep with men on the first or second or third or fourth or fifth date, they pushed the dagger deep into chivalry's aorta. Why would men be chivalrous when they know they can get laid without it? And quickly, I might add. We refuse. We are efficient, if anything, and refuse to be chivalrous if not required. But here's the catch:

We want to.

Know that, beautiful women. Understand that. We want to be chivalrous. We want to court.

To chase.

To care that much.

Others, you have soured proper courtship, and you have debased the title "woman." It takes more than a vagina and the ability to menstruate to be a woman, the same way it takes more than getting a boner and drinking beer to be a man. Women command respect and chivalry, they don't have to ask for it. Women, you should line up The Others who continue to ruin it for you and kick them between the uprights. Witch-hunt the celebrities who expose themselves when getting out of limos, who make grainy sex videos, who dress like hookers and who influence the younger generation to carry the Olympic torch of unbridled promiscuity.

Hunt those ones down especially. Kick them harder.

Until the revolution takes place, may chivalry rest in peace.

Gilby licks my arm, relieving me of my imaginary address to the League of Females.

Linda, I promise I will be a chivalrous gentleman, so long as Mandy Klein adheres to the Dogma of Classy Women. However, should she give me the slightest inclination that my penis has been conscripted for duty after the first or second or third or fourth or fifth date, I will not be held accountable for my actions.

"Let's go, pal," I say, changing the subject. "Off to see what's up with Mrs. Dunfield's shitter."

I press Mrs. Dunfield's doorbell so hard, the tip of my finger becomes translucent. *Déjà vu.* Weird. The large oak door creaks open before being caught abruptly by the safety chain. The small sliver of space allows me to see a section of curly grey hair and old hands.

"Oh, dear. One moment, Isaac. Just one moment, dear," she says apologetically. Honestly, I'm in no rush to be enlightened as to the state of your porcelain throne.

"No worries, Mrs. Dunfield. Safety first, right?"

"This damn thing was installed last week, and Heaven help me if it hasn't been a pain in the …"

She fusses away for a few more seconds before I hear the brass chain lock release. Does she go through this with every guest? *How many guests a week could she possibly have?* Does Meals on Wheels count? *It shouldn't.*

"There," she says, opening the door fully. "Come in."

I walk through the door, careful not to scratch the oak frame with my tool pouch. Mrs. Dunfield still looks the same — like a weathered old man, but with larger, saggier breasts. Still, she was blessed with the kindest green eyes. From her eyes alone, I'm sure she was beautiful two hundred years ago when she effortlessly roamed Paradise.

This is not my first visit to this house. I remember installing her toilet several years ago but had forgotten what a museum this place truly was.

Hats. Hundreds of them.

Hundreds, maybe thousands of hats. Hung from every imaginable place. Hats of all different shapes, sizes, colours, and all women's hats. This is scarier than I remember. The layer of dust on some of these hats has to be older than me by thirty years. My eyes scan the room, quickly, hunting, and determined to find a picture of her from seventy years ago.

"I just can't imagine what could be wrong with this toilet of mine."

I can imagine. You are likely constipated and take shits the size of Coho salmon. "It's likely an easy fix, Mrs. Dunfield. No problem at all."

"Not when you get to my age. Everything is major. Nothing is easy. You know what I mean?"

Who am I to argue with that?

"Take this lump on my throat," she indicates by touching. "It's getting harder and harder to swallow."

"When did you first feel it there, Mrs. Dunfield?"

"About three weeks ago, when I woke up one morning."

"Have you had it looked at?" I ask. This question prompts tears in her eyes

"I'm sorry," she struggles. "Cancer runs in my family, and ..."

Instantly, as if programmed, I set my tool belt down and find myself with an arm around her performing some kind of pathetic half-hug.

"Hey, it's okay," I assure her. "Come here, sit down and let me take a look at it." She nods and I escort her to the red corduroy loveseat, backed against the westerly wall of hats.

"Let me just touch it. Do you mind if I touch it?" I ask politely. *That sounded very professional.* I agree.

"Dear, I didn't know that you ..."

"Yes, I went to medical school, believe it or not. Before the plumbing career."

"Well, how about that. The things you learn about people," she whispers.

With both hands, I gently touch around her neck until I locate the Titleist lodged below her hyoid bone. I don't need a scalpel. I need a fucking sand wedge to get at this thing.

"Difficulty swallowing, you said?"

"Yes. Especially when I eat."

"What about breathing? Any trouble there?"

"Not so much."

Difficulty eating was an understatement. She's downplaying her symptoms. My bedside manner must need work. *So don't make your questions sound so textbook.* Fair point. The questions were a bit cold. I can work on this.

"What do you think, Isaac?"

"I think you'll be fine."

Her tears fight to hang onto the bottom lid.

"You have a thyroglossal duct cyst, Mrs. Dunfield," I correctly diagnose.

"A what?" she asks, obviously in need of a hearing aid as well. *Then speak up.* True.

"It's a thyroglossal duct cyst," I articulate, four tones louder.

"Is it … umm?"

"No, they are rarely malignant."

"So, I will be okay?"

"Yes, but you need to have it removed before it becomes more of a problem."

"Surgery?"

"It's an outpatient surgery. No big deal. You are going to be fine."

"Thank God!" she cries as she throws her arms around my neck. "I'm going to buy many new cashmere sweaters to hide the scar."

The scar is not the superficial item *du jour*, Mrs. Dunfield. It's the whiskers that make you look like a catfish, and I have pliers in the truck that will work for those.

As if new life had been injected into the basilic vein in her arm, made it past the giant cyst and reached her brain, Mrs. Dunfield dances around the living room. *That is barely dancing. It's more like a choreographed seizure.* Be nice. I sit back on the ugly red corduroy loveseat in disbelief at the joy I have created.

"I am going to shout it to the world: 'Isaac Sullivan is not a plumber! He is a doctor!'"

Your stellar marketing initiative is welcomed, Mrs. Dunfield, but dancing was a bad idea. With that, she trips over the coffee table and free falls to a guaranteed compound fracture.

Enough.

I'm out.

"Isaac? Do you know what I mean?" she repeats.

"Yeah, I do."

No clue what the question was. You clever little daydream. You sneaky bastard. Seamless entry. I didn't even see you coming. Entertaining, as usual.

"Well, let's take a look at this toilet," I say.

"Yes, dear. I'm sure you have many other places to get to today. It's the upstairs toilet next to my bedroom."

I make my way up the hardwood stairs, fearful of what I could find. Pictures line the stair wall and upstairs hallway. Still, no shots of her as a younger woman. *Why so curious?* Nothing really, I simply want to see if she was beautiful. *Understood, but for what reason? Is it to prove that even the most beautiful still fall victim to time and gravity?* Possibly. *What if she wasn't hot as a young woman? What then? Would you feel better or worse about her current state?* My instinct is to feel better. *Interesting. So, if she was ugly as a young woman as well, then, that explains her current exterior?* I must be afraid that good looks can turn that tragically sour with time and gravity. *Why so focused on the exterior? She's ninety. She doesn't have to walk a fucking runway, draped in Armani.* Good point. *Your concern with her former looks is a projection of your own fear of aging.* Fuck off, please.

I arrive at the toilet in question and set down my tool pouch on the black and white tile floor. The lid is down. Bad sign. The sink is a mess and is lined with dozens of balms and creams and ointments, and I have never seen so many different kinds in my life. What could each one possibly treat? I never want to use that many creams.

I want to prescribe them.

With my right hand, I lift the toilet seat and delay looking with my eyes. What am I so afraid of? *Is it the possibility of a shit-clogged toilet?* I've dealt with that before. Dozens of times. Hundreds. True, but not from such a haggard old woman. *What if, instead, the toilet in front of you belonged to a young, attractive woman? Would you be so afraid to look?* The answer is no. *Weird.* In fact, if she were attractive enough, I might even reach down there and set the captured turd free with my bare hand. *You are fucked in the head.* No, I just seem to have more ease with the fecal matter of attractive women. *What if this was Harrison Ford's shit-clogged toilet?* I find myself less grossed out than if it were Mrs. Dunfield's. *Why?* Because he's famous. *You said famous, but you meant handsome.* Stop. Seriously.

Today, I have learned that the shit-clogged toilets of very attractive women and stars gross me out less. This insightful revelation cannot distract me much longer, and I must look at what is in store for me.

"Don't try to flush it! The water is already near the brim!" her old voice belts from downstairs.

Impossible to be surprised at this point, I look into the toilet bowl. There we have it: a shit-clogged toilet from someone who looks like a cross between Yoda and a transvestite version of Bob Barker.

"Thanks, Mrs. Dunfield!" I yell back.

She has powdered the water with toilet bowl cleaner to dampen the smell, which is kind, but I am fully aware *What Lies Beneath.*

—»—

The rear doors of the plumbing van swing open and reveal my organized masterpiece of tools and supplies. I marvel at this every time: stainless steel shelving, plastic bins, dividing bars, and the sectioned-off lengths of copper and PVC pipe that run down the centre. My van looks more organized than a passionate teacher's lesson plan. I could have been a teacher. *No, you couldn't. You don't have enough patience — at least not for teens. Or pre-teens.* I'm going to be a doctor. Doctors can still teach, so it's not out of the question. It's settled, then. In my retirement, I will teach medical students.

Gilby looks back at me from the front seat, as if begging to help. It's the Vietnam of clogged shitters in there, Gilby. I'm going in alone. I reach for the snake that will travel down the porcelain Ho Chi Minh trail in search of the MIA turd.

I remove my weapon from the van, and it uncoils. The stainless steel toilet snake. My least favourite tool in the van.

I take a breath for strength and sanity and make my way back into the DMZ.

I wind the toilet snake down and down and down. Mrs. Dunfield's toilet bowl now looks like a wave pool thanks to my hungry snake looking for its meal. And just like that, my snake finds its shit mouse and bites into it hard. I wind the snake back, and then forward, and then back, and then forward, forcing the shit mouse to its final resting place, like a spirit guide releasing a confused apparition from an old farmhouse. A final turn of the orange handle and the snake, and I have broken through the Berlin Wall of excrement. Well done, my stainless pet. Well done. Hopefully I'll put you back in the van and see you never.

The moment of truth has come.

The flush.

Game time.

I press down the silver handle on the side of the cistern, and like a pitcher releasing a split-finger fastball in the bottom of the ninth, I just hope and watch. Everything looks and sounds good so far.

Please flush.

Flush.

Flush.

Flush.

Spin around and disappear forever.

If my assumptions are wrong, my work boots are soon to be swimming in Mrs. Dunfield's brown trout, and should that happen, I will snap like the button on Linda's Levis — which, I am certain, has happened by now. There would be a mini flood, and the water would seep between the cracks of the hardwood floor, and there would be water damage, and I would be blamed, and the hundreds of hats below would be covered in shit water, and I would be sued.

The water cyclone meanders down the bowl and disappears as clean water begins to fill the bowl in preparation for the next transportation of waste.

The toilet is back in working order. Well done, Doctor. *You're not a doctor. Doctors don't deal with this type of shit.* What about proctologists? They deal with this type of shit all the time. I could never be a proctologist. I would rather be a gynecologist. *No, you wouldn't.* Why not? *That lineup is not populated with beautiful and healthy vaginas.* Right, but once in a while a patient would come in and have nothing wrong with her — just a routine pap. *That's unlikely, and let's go back to the fact that most of the vaginas would be sick or covered in STDs.* That could seriously disturb me for life. Fine, I would rather be a proctologist than a gynecologist. *No one is forcing that decision. Relax.*

"Is it all better now?" I look behind me and Mrs. Dunfield is standing in the doorway. Mrs. Dunfield, please add a regular laxative to your diet to decrease the instances of backed-up, heavily compressed, clog-prone shits.

"It's working fine," I say.

"Fantastic. What do I owe you?"

Truth: If I had a flux capacitor installed in the plumbing van, I would hook it up to the nearest clock tower and travel back seventy years to determine, with my own eyes, if she was beautiful or not.

She reaches into her purse and finds her chequebook. Mrs. Dunfield, your purse looks more like modern day carry-on luggage. No wonder she has spine-curling kyphosis. She looks more like the letter "r" than a human.

"I'll send you an invoice."

"That would be kind of you, but I would rather pay this way. I lose those darn invoices."

That pisses me off. I want it done my way. I have a method. Now I want to insist that she send me the money via email money transfer. That would really make her smell burnt toast.

"Okay, a cheque is fine."

"Good. How much?"

"Let's call it fifty even."

"Fine. That is fair. Fifty even. And how much for you to scoop Alfred's poop from my yard?" she asks.

What? Who is Alfred? Where is he? He must have dementia if he is shitting on her lawn.

"Who's Alfred?"

"He's my husky. He's rarely around."

Mrs. Dunfield, I don't clean up dog shit. Unless you want me to outfit his kennel with a urinal, bidet, sink, or carbon-fibre shower with overhead rain-drop head, then *no*, there is nothing I can do to service your husky.

Albert may still have dementia.

"I don't typically do that sort of thing," I say. *Did you just say "typically?" What a pussy you are, Isaac. Stop, please.*

"I would really appreciate it. Guests are coming over tomorrow for tea and a walk around the property. It would be so embarrassing for one of them to step in Albert's mess."

But not too embarrassing to ask me to clean it up, obviously. "Why don't you call a landscaper?" I suggest. *Great save. Beautiful idea.*

"No, they are so busy, and they never come on time."

"I would help you out, but I have no time today."

Actually, I do have time. It's easy to resort to the lie. The lie seems to get me out of so many situations. What would I do without the lie? What would humans do without it? We would be plagued by the truth. Marriages, certainly, could not last. Friendships would be ticking time bombs. I don't believe that society could function without the lie. There could be no government, because the politician would fail to exist. The workplace, the infrastructure of our economy, would be torn apart in a matter of hours. I want to publish this. No. It's too controversial, and it would tarnish my application for the University of Michigan. *You haven't applied. You've never applied.* I need to apply this year. This is the year. *You say that every year.*

"Isaac, I will pay you whatever you like. Name your price," she says, calling me out on my lie. She refused to accept it, and now she is bribing me. Does she think I'm poor? *You could use the money.* I don't need it that bad. If I take it, am I furthering some sort of tradesman stereotype? Let's say I do the job. If she tells people I did it, I will never get laid again. Ever. I will be the plumber that moonlights as a dog-shit-cleaning yard janitor.

"It's not about the money. I just don't have time."

No response. Her bottom lip is quivering as if she is about to cry or tell me to piss off. She simply gazes at me. Inside me. This is a Mexican standoff. This is the Cuban missile crisis. The nuclear clock is at 11:59. Who will break first? How much money will be too much money for her? On the other hand, how much money will be enough for me to do it?

"I'm desperate to have it cleaned up, Isaac, and I'm too old and tired to do it myself," she pleads. Her lip is quivering, almost uncontrollably. Her eyes are welling up. This is hell. I would have rather she told me to piss off.

"Please put yourself in my shoes. This is not easy for me to ask, as I used to be able enough to do it myself," she says.

I stand and watch as she plays the "old woman" card. It lands with such a commanding blow, and I immediately feel like an asshole for having said no the first time around. Fine, I will shovel Albert the Missing Husky's shit, but I am asking for a thousand dollars, and I want it in cash, and I will spend it all on beer and lap dances. That means that the total for today will be one thousand and fifty dollars, Mrs. Dunfield.

Cash.

"I said it wasn't about the money, Mrs. Dunfield. So I'll do it on the house. No charge."

Isaac, you are now cleaning up yard shit for free.

"Wonderful, but will you be late for your next job?"

"It's Mr. Kendall on the tenth line. He's not going anywhere. Don't worry about it."

"Well, this cannot go unpaid. I refuse. Here is a check for the fifty dollars for the toilet, and another fifteen, in cash, for the yard work. But don't go telling Mr. IRS on me," she says with a wink.

Fifteen.

Fifteen dollars. A ten-dollar bill and a five-dollar bill. Fifteen one-dollar bills.

My hands and feet go numb.

I walk back up the flagstone path to her porch with a white bucket filled with Albert's treasures in one hand, and the shit-tipped collapsible spade in the other.

Gilby looks at me from the front seat of the van with his big lazy eyes. Look away, pal. Look away.

The white bucket is heavy. That's because the only thing that takes bigger shits than Albert is Mrs. Dunfield. I refuse to believe Albert is a husky. He's her pet grizzly.

Mrs. Dunfield comes out onto the porch to greet me, as if I was returning from a great expedition. Ice cubes tinkle the sides of the crystal glass she holds in her right hand. Is it Scotch? Is it iced tea? Is it apple juice? Regardless, I am going to lose it. The decrepit old hag has been sipping a nondescript, tasty, chilled beverage while I was collecting Albert's lawn sausages.

I drop the white bucket in my left hand and switch my grip on the shovel to javelin-style. I stride three graceful steps and begin the motion that will hurl the shit-tipped shovel in her direction. This throwing motion is not natural. Micro-tearing is taking place in my ulnar collateral ligament. I know it is. However, adrenaline is the greatest human gift of all, and I feel nothing. When the doctors perform the Tommy John surgery to reconstruct my elbow, I hope they are fully aware that this was not an incident of Olympic nature, but instead, a plumber hurling a shovel at an old woman.

The spade is launched from my hand like a surface-to-air missile and heads, impartially, toward Mrs. Dunfield.

Instantly, I regret this decision. This was a poor judgment call. Possibly, she will duck or move. I give myself too much credit. The odds of hitting her are slim. I am no Greek hero. I am no decathlete.

Gambling is based on odds, and odds are only probable. Fact: My aim was impeccable. Mrs. Dunfield, the airborne spade is going to hit you if you don't move, and it will cause significant damage to your brittle frame. Even if it's a glancing blow and barely breaks her skin, the amount of bacteria on the tip would send her to her cemetery plot, which, I'm sure she has picked out by now.

Enough.

I'm out.

"Where do you want this, Mrs. Dunfield?"

"Just empty it in the compost beside the shed. Everything turns back to soil sooner or later," she says.

I agree with you, Mrs. Dunfield. You're closer than you think.

III

"You Are Leaving Paradise," the sign reads. I break a half smile every time I pass it. What a superior ring it has in comparison to the sign facing the other direction. That sign might as well read, "Welcome to Hell," but Hell, Michigan, already exists, ironically. *I'm not sure that's irony.* It's something, though.

Gilby is not the kind of dog who hangs his head out the open window. He quietly sits shotgun and gives that thousand-mile stare down the county road. Comically, his body language is very similar to my own. He really loves me.

"We have to get ready for a date, Gilby," I say. Gilby says nothing. Typical. But if he could talk he would say, "Really, Isaac? Is it going to happen? Linda hasn't called you with the date and time." That's what he would say, and Gilby doesn't have to get ready for the date at all. He's a dog. Dogs don't have to get ready for anything. *That's not true, they have to sniff the area.*

Imagine if humans had nothing more to do than give a few sniffs before deciding to date or mate. No dinner. No manners. No baggage. No social barriers. No trying to make plumbing sound interesting over coffee.

Simply, a sniff. That's all.

Perhaps introducing yourself as a doctor is the canine equivalent to successful sniffing.

Sniff: "Hi, I'm Isaac Sullivan. I'm a doctor."

Sniff: "Really?"

Sniff: "Yes."

Sniff: "That's amazing. You should enter me."

Makes perfect sense. Instantly the woman knows I'm a financially, mentally, and genetically ideal candidate for procreation.

I have a pending date with Mandy Klein and need to decide how much effort I am going to put into it. I can't court or date Mandy Klein, because I will be leaving for college at some point. *Speculation aside, why not date her long distance?* I refuse. I can't have any ties to Paradise. None. *But you like Mandy Klein. There is potential here, and you need to get over the fact that you didn't set this up yourself.* Fact: She is cute and always in the paper for doing volunteer work. I bet a large percentage of people who do volunteer work do it for something to talk about. *You have no proof of that.* I agree, and collecting the data would be painful and useless.

I reach the laneway to my next destination. "Dawson" is barely legible on the rusty mailbox that has seen too many winters and too much salt. Maybe Linda from CoffeeBuddy should hook this mailbox up with my license plate. They have tons in common. They are perfect for each other.

Vultures circle in the neighbouring field. Something is dead, or something is about to die. Always the case around Paradise.

I complete the turn into Bill Dawson's driveway and proceed slowly. A driveway that looks more like the surface of the moon.

I steer to miss the largest of the craters, but the remainder tax the shit out of my suspension. Items are falling out of bins and tools, displaced from their homes. What a shit show this is. Now I'm really pissed at Bill Dawson. And more pissed than before when he married Jenn Slate. Jenn Slate who dumped me six years ago because she said I was going nowhere.

And she's wrong.

I am going somewhere. I am a surgeon in training. Not just some loser townie.

But she said I was just a loser townie going nowhere and she wanted someone who was going to make it big. Someone who was leaving Paradise. So she dumped me and married Bill Dawson because he bragged about starting up a construction company in Lansing. That was before his business went tits-up, and now both of their silly asses live on this back-country plot of land collecting pogie. Who's the townie now, Jenn? *You really liked her, and this is how you're dealing with the hurt.* Fuck off, please.

The driveway from hell turns into a very well-groomed roundabout in front of his log house. That's a genius idea, Bill — have the area where people park be well-groomed, but make it Beirut to get there. Asshole. No cars or truck in sight. The only sign that anyone is home is light grey smoke that billows out of the stone chimney. Drilled into the side of the house, a tattered American flag gently dances on its pole.

A golden retriever bursts through the screen door and dodges the van as I come to a stop. What was that retriever's name? It was a planet, I think. Gilby is poised for action and mumbles a low growl.

"Easy, pal," I say, reaching over the glove box and popping it open. Old road maps, random keys, and dog treats are its only contents, and the dog treats are running low. I grab the first two free-floating dog biscuits my fingers find and toss one up in the air. Gilby snatches it like a seal snatches a fish. For a few minutes, the treat will take his attention away from the gorgeous retriever, who (I'm positive) is named after a planet.

"Plumb! How're ya now?"

Bill Dawson bursts through the screen door, pulling on a tan winter coat as he exits his log house. It's the kind of winter coat that has the fake fur sewn into the hood.

I can't stand those coats. I can't stand Bill Dawson.

"Been better, Bill."

"I hear that, Plumb. Jesus Christ, I hear that."

I want to tell him how many times I ravaged his wife — her passionate screaming and the way she would bite down hard on my trapezius muscle to muzzle herself while she churned out multiple orgasms.

I expose an open left palm to the retriever, who calms instantly and begins sniffing it. You smell Gilby, don't you, lady?

"Thanks for gettin' over here today. The wife said she left you a voicemail last night but you didn't call back, so I didn't think I'd be seein' you today," he says. I smile, wondering if she still knows my number by heart.

"What are we looking at today, Bill?"

I find it very useful to use people's first names as often as possible. Especially early in the conversation. It has occurred to me that a person's favourite word in the English language is their own name, and the best thing I can do is to use it whenever possible. I'm also sure that this has occurred to someone before me.

From hidden around my back, I swing my right hand forward to present the dog biscuit. Tail wagging has increased by fifty percent. Why isn't the dog eating the treat? Too much sniffing is taking place. Sweetheart, I assure you it's not laced with Rohypnol. This is not a date-rape bone or a ploy to get Gilby laid. Eat the treat. Take it. Eat it. *This is getting awkward.*

There. Good girl.

My hand is wet now and smells weird, likely due to tartar buildup and some gingivitis.

"Ganny loves that! Don't you, Ganny?" says Bill, rubbing the head of his excited retriever.

Ganny! That's right. Ganymede. I was wrong. She is not named after a planet, at all. It's one of the moons of Jupiter. *Stop.*

No one around here knows the moons of Jupiter, especially this backcountry goof. I'm positive that Mr. Flint, my science teacher, didn't know the moons of Jupiter. I won't let this rest. It cannot be Ganymede. It just can't.

"Bill, that is a great name for a dog."

"Yeah, she likes it."

She's a dog, Bill, and she can't tell whether she likes her name or not. All she hears are sounds and syllables in varying pitches.

"The first wife picked that one out," he says.

All I want to know is if the second one is home. *What if she came out to say hi?* Horrible. I hope she's laid up in bed with the shits, and "the shits" is really called "diarrhea" and is caused by viral infections, parasites, or bacterial toxins and is the second leading cause of infant deaths worldwide. *Nice one.* Thanks. Jenn Slate, if the shits are prohibiting you from experiencing an awkward exchange with me, then please stay hydrated and be sure to replenish your electrolytes.

"Really?" I say. "What inspired the name?"

"Short for Gananoque. Pretty little town in Ontario. Met the first Mrs. up there on a fishing trip. She was Canadian."

I knew it was too good to be true. Ganny could never have been short for Ganymede. However, Ganny the Retriever was named after an equally obscure small town in Ontario — one of the moons of America.

"Here it is, Isaac," he says. The two of us stand beside an old concrete well. Weathered plywood rests on top of it, bearing the scars of several consecutive seasons. "The pump is about eight feet down resting on soil, but bolted to a plywood square."

"Okay."

"From there, the submersible dives down a hundred and twenty-five metres to the water table."

"So what's the issue?"

"The damn water pump just stopped pumping. Just like that," he says, snapping his worked, cracked fingers for punctuation's sake.

"Weird."

"Cocksucker's only five years old, too."

I don't remember installing it, so it must have been Dale. Why would he hire Dale? Dale is a slob with a chronic hairy plumber's crack. You do a disservice to all plumbers, Dale. Wear a belt and tighten it if you have chosen this profession.

"Well, don't write it off yet. Let me take a look," I say. "What's the board for?"

"Keeps the wildlife out. And I fixed a ladder in there to climb down to the pump."

I remove the plywood lid from the well, and sunlight hits the cold, damp air inside it.

Snakes. Hundreds of them.

Sitting in shock after having their roof torn off. Many of them wound around the rungs of the wooden ladder. The same wooden ladder that is to take me down to the inactive water pump. Several of the others rest, coiled among the tree roots that have broken through the walls of the old concrete well, in search of water themselves.

My hands and feet go numb. This sensation has happened before, but it was rage that caused it. So, am I feeling rage or fear? Is it possible that anger and fear are the same base ingredient to a very similar physical reaction? More possible: Could fear and anger be the same?

Bill throws a rock into the well. It hits the ladder.

Snakes dart in every direction. A manic sea of varying shades of green and brown disappear into the walls and depths of the old well.

Gone.

Not a trace. Not one snake remains.

Your shitty plywood board did NOT keep the wildlife out, Bill. *Don't look frozen — he'll think you're afraid of them.* I *am* afraid of them!

I seem to have an issue showing fear or pain in front of others. *That had to be instilled by Dad.* I blame him for a lot. Almost everything. *Who cares if Bill Dawson thinks you are afraid of snakes?* I do, obviously. I'm going to tell him there is no way I am going down there.

"I'm just going to wait until they get comfy," I say. Bill laughs. I take a step back from the well. Bill laughs at this, harder.

"Yeah, there's lots of those buggers down there, but they're harmless enough."

Is that true, Bill? Are they harmless? If you are so sure, why don't you get down there in the snake pit and get your broken fucking pump? *Focus.*

I make my way down the wooden ladder, equipped with my hacksaw and flashlight. Odds are, I will have to cut this pump out in order to fix it above ground, in better light. Fifteen minutes is enough time for all of the snakes to have hidden, and I don't believe snakes hold a grudge. Although they should, being forced to live on land with no legs. *Snails don't have legs either.* True. I'm sure both taste good with enough garlic and butter.

Jenn Slate said I would never be married because I was the loser townie plumber and that's all I'd ever be. *We know.* I wanted to slap her in her ignorant, filthy mouth for uttering such bullshit. But you can't hit women. It's wrong and I would never do it. But patience is a virtue and retribution is king, so the heavyweight-style uppercut I will deliver her will come in the form of someday hanging my framed diploma from medical school on her front door. Hammering it there with twenty nails so it takes her longer to remove. Maybe that, plus ten or twenty voicemails to her all starting with, "Hi Jenn, it's Dr. Isaac Sullivan calling ..." But that might just be too mean. *The bigger man would take the high road and do nothing at all. The bigger man would let her find out through someone else in town.* True. This debate can continue when the time comes. *It won't.*

My last moments of aboveground vision hurry themselves, and I am now completely engulfed by the walls of the old concrete well. Up close, the inside of the well is quite beautiful. An uncountable amount of small bugs, several with feelers, travel back and forth while performing their chores. A millipede enters the well from one of the larger cracks to the right of me and meanders south into the bottom. What's at the bottom for him? Can he actually know where he's going? Do any of these poor bastards know where they're going? The millipede, for all intent and purpose, is sprinting. Can bugs understand the concept of hurrying? Would there be a situation where he would travel at a slower pace, or even a brisk walk? No. Reason: When you can be eaten by something else, you don't walk.

Humans should take note of this. We would behave quite differently if we were not at the top of the food chain. For starters, we wouldn't take the future for granted. Statements like, 'This time next year ..." or "By the time I'm forty ..." or "I will call my parents next Christmas ..." simply wouldn't exist. It would be a gift and strategic struggle just to see another day. There would be no depression. No Prozac. No Tony Robbins. There would be no body dysmorphia and no plastic surgery. There would be no fat people because they would be the easy-to-nab, succulent, low-hanging fruit for predators. No mortgages and no I.O.U.s. There would be no dating and no hand jobs, and more sex would be had. There would be no calendars because there would be no plans — because the only plan would be to eat and breed and survive one more day.

If there are aliens out there, please come and land now. Immediately. Land and be scary and huge and have teeth and eat us. To establish your M.O., and to make it interesting, eat all of the genetically unfit first. If you are exceptionally hungry, I suggest you land in Paradise. In Paradise, you will find a buffet of unattractive idiots who should never pass on their DNA.

Surprisingly, even in the midday sun, the bottom of the well is a shade darker than dusk. I click on the flashlight, terrified of what could be illuminated once it points downward. The light beams across to brighten the left side of the well on its journey south and lands on the out-of-service pump.

Panic.

Entire body is numb.

There is a snake on the pump.

Not true. There is a snake in *the pump!* How is that possible? *Is he stuck in the pump? What kind of snak*e? I moved the light, so I can't tell. *Move it back!*

My flashlight finds the pump again in time to spot the snake striking. I should have moved when I spotted him. Now, I'm frozen. All I can do is watch him sink his fangs into my gastrocnemius. And this is no regular snake. This is an Eastern Massasauga Rattler, the only poisonous snake in Michigan. The strike hits unexpectedly hard, like the force of ten sledgehammers, and my left knee buckles, but I clench the rungs of the ladder instinctively to support myself. Shortly, the loss of muscle coordination, nausea, and blurred vision will cause me to fall to the bottom of the pit, where I will be slowly consumed by my fellow diggers, builders, lifters, and crawlers. The vocal cords in my throat beg to scream out in pain, but I make no sound. My left leg continues to burn, numb. I look down with the flashlight once more to see the mighty Massasauga extended with his open face pressed up against my jeans and his hypodermic fangs buried in me. Is he caught on my jeans or in my leg or is he just happy to be killing me? *Shake him off!* My leg is paralyzed. *How in Christ didn't you hear him?* His rattle must be in the belly of the pump. With every second, more and more toxic droplets drip into my bloodstream. I will use the hacksaw to cut him in half, the bastard. *You're already dead, Isaac. Too much venom is in your system for a shot to counteract it.* Why did he strike me? I was here to help him. This is uncommon for a snake to strike, unprovoked, but he is trapped and confused — so I forgive him. I will not saw him in half. We are both already dead. Perhaps he just wanted a companion for the journey to the other side. I will go with you, Mighty Rattler.

As it turns out, I would have liked that date with Mandy Klein, regardless of Linda's game of matchmaker. I should have spent more time dating and less time looking at Internet porn. I bet a lot of guys my age think this before they die.

Bill has returned to the well and quickly figures out what is going on. Take that look off your face, Bill. I'm the only one allowed to be in shock right now. His hands grab me by the collar of my work shirt and I feel his attempt to lift me. I thought you were stronger than this, Bill. Seriously, I did. Fact: There's a rattlesnake buried in my leg, and I am about five minutes away from dinner and a movie with the Reaper.

You learn something about people every day. I, now, have learned two things about Bill Dawson: His first marriage was to a Canadian from Gananoque, and he has a large vein that pops out of the centre of his forehead when his blood pressure increases. Twenty bucks says that vein surfaces as an element of his cum face, as well. Thanks for the help, Bill, but I am going to stay and die in the snake pit and become more intimate with the millipedes. My left arm brings the hacksaw up to his right bicep and I expel the last energy I have sawing into Bill Dawson's humerus.

Enough.

— » —

I'm out.

A large ant is running across my hand. I wipe him off against my jeans. Sweat is beading down my face. I'm still inside a well on a shitty old ladder. How long did I gap out for? That would have looked funny to see from a third-party perspective — me, staring into the side of a well for several minutes. What blows my mind is how a daydream can be so clear and vivid, despite the fact that my eyes are wide open. It's like an IMAX screen exists behind my eyes and turns on whenever it feels the urge.

This is a problem.

This is not entertainment.

I should talk to someone about these daydreams. They are becoming too violent. I don't like myself in them.

The light from my flashlight hits the pump at the bottom of the well once more. Low and behold, an Eastern Hognose is stuck in the gears of the pump. Still alive. Waving his head around in search of answers. Poor little guy. I know how you feel to be stuck, good buddy. I will get you out.

I climb down the last few rungs and stand with the flashlight fixed on my harmless poikilothermic patient.

The pump, still fastened to the square piece of plywood, sits in the middle of the lawn in direct sunlight. The Hognose repeatedly lowers his head toward the grass in an attempt to silently slip away but can't understand what's holding him back. My heart is breaking. How does that sun feel on your body, good buddy? Does that feel better? I hope it takes some of the pain away. Try to relax.

"Well, that's gotta be the damndest thing I've ever seen," says Bill, poking the belly of the snake with a long stick. Poke him with the stick again, Bill. Do it. I dare you. Poke him again and I will make a fucking kebob of you.

I hear the front door slam.

It's Jenn.

Hands and feet go numb.

"Jenny! Get over here, you gotta see this," he yells, grinning, as if this was the circus. This is not the circus. This is a tragedy.

I hear her walk up, but my focus is the snake. My patient.

"Morning, Isaac."

I nod. That's it. No eye contact. Just nodded. Me, the "loser townie fuck-up go nowhere plumber who will never find a wife to love him" just nodded back and that's it. *Pathetic.*

"Business been good?" she asks. What kind of question is that? How could the plumbing business ever be good? *You're missing the point.* Which is? *You're still* in *the business.* That was mean of her. *Really mean.*

Rage.

Rage inspires a glance over at her.

She stands there, Jenn Slate. Glowing. Beautiful. And well into her second trimester, rubbing her pregnant belly alongside Bill, father of the giant redneck creature growing inside her.

"Business is fine, thanks."

"I can't believe that old van of yours is still running."

I want to puke.

Saliva floods my mouth, and I want to spit it, but saliva is chock-full of bicarbonate, so I will swallow it and pre-emptively combat the acid reflux that this situation is sure to instigate. Her fetus is somewhere around twenty-four weeks, marking the emergence of eye lashes, eyebrows, neurons connecting the brain to the musculature, air sacs lined with capillaries ready to someday be lungs, and eyelids getting ready to open — and when those eyelids open, post-partum,

62

that child will see Jenn Slate's nipples, and so have I, and they are lovely.

Her breasts are visibly swollen and she just caught me looking at them.

Awkward.

Focus on the patient.

"I think I'm going to disassemble the pump and try to save the little guy," I say.

"You gotta be kidding me!" says Bill, howling with laughter. He thinks this is a hilarious joke. I want to take his stick and blind him with it.

"I think that once he's out of there, the pump will be fine, and he can go on his way."

"He doesn't look fine," says Jenn.

Hands and feet numb again. This is really becoming an issue.

She's right. Mr. Hognose is not fine. He found a way into those warm gears when the pump wasn't running, but once a tap was turned on, the pump fired up and crushed his body before he could escape, thus seizing the gears.

"I'm not paying you your going rate to disassemble and then re-build the pump. I'm just not. The snake is fucked. The pump is fucked. Now kill the little bastard before the dog gets at him."

Kill the little bastard. I will be forced to, but I want to be as humane as possible. The quickest way is likely with the long-handled shovel or with the axe. Yes, the shovel is the quickest way. Guillotine-style. Coming down on him from above, as if he were a snake of the French aristocracy. *The shovel is the quickest, but it's not the most humane, and if you miss, you could just maim him more than he already is.* True. What he needs is 50cc of morphine to get him comfortable, followed by a second injection of potassium chloride to arrest his little snake heart. Better idea: There is a cardboard box in the back of the van large enough to hold the snake and the pump. I can rig a hose from the tailpipe and send him out gently with a little help from carbon monoxide. Tell Bill Dawson that is your plan.

"What are you waitin' for, Plumb?" he asks. Don't rush me, Bill Dawson, or you'll be coaching your legs on how to walk again.

"Just kill him, Isaac," chirps Jenn.

No.

"Jesus, son. Give me your hacksaw," he orders, palm open.

I notice my hand extend. *Don't give him the fucking hacksaw. Stop. He'll be a butcher!*

I just gave him the hacksaw. Now, I can only stand and watch as Bill steps on the head of the Hognose with his boot. Mr. Hognose struggles more.

I want to puke.

"This is how you do it, dammit," he tutors.

This is cruel. This is wrong. There is a better way, Bill. I strongly advise against this. *So tell him that!* Bill places my hacksaw on the taut body of the Hognose, close to the pump where he emerges. With one forceful down-stroke, the Hognose is in half and a burning lump hits my throat.

Don't cry.

Do not fucking cry.

Don't. Not in front of Jenn. Not like this.

Don't cry and don't look away. My jaw clenches hard, and I go twelve rounds with the ACTH-laden tears desperate to escape from my body. I win by decision.

Bill picks up the severed section of Mr. Hognose and pitches him to the bottom of the well.

"Jesus, Bill! I'm already nauseous enough!" Jenn says.

So am I, Jenn. The nausea I feel for the life you've made with this toolbox of a human is only trumped by the nausea I feel for my own. Her comments toward me five years ago should have been fuel enough to get me to the University of Michigan.

To get me out of Paradise.

To prove me right.

To prove her wrong.

But me standing here, still a plumber, and still on the verge of tears (exactly how she left me five years ago) has only proven those heartless comments to be true, and now two hearts beat inside her. *You hate that.* Yeah, I hate that.

Revelation: I don't even want the child in her belly to be mine. I just don't want it to be anyone else's.

Hognose blood drips off my hacksaw and disappears into Bill Dawson's unkempt lawn.

"If you can't take it, then get back inside, Jenny. Christ. We're out here doing work. Fixin' things," he says to her. She blankly turns on her heel and heads back toward the house.

Not even a look to me.

Nothing.

Her gait has changed. Hint of a slight limp. *Likely due to the pregnancy.* Jenn, try sleeping on your left side to ensure that your sciatic nerve isn't pinched and also to provide good blood flow and nutrients to your uterus. *Nicely done.* Thanks.

Whether her departure was out of embarrassment or whether she was gloating over her accurate summation of me five years ago, it didn't matter. Both of us are equally sad.

The truth is, she should be happy and I should be a doctor.

Before she abandoned us, Mom used to tell me that everything happens for a reason.

I need to get out of Paradise.

I need to apply to the University of Michigan.

Tomorrow.

IV

The Internet is a fascinating and culture-changing phenomenon that has put knowledge, news, blogs, art, sports, politics, and an unlimited amount of porn at our fingertips. My outdated computer may not have multiple processors or an LCD display, but it can receive and send emails, surf the web, and stream video, which is all I need it for.

Eighteen years ago, I never could've logged on to the University of Michigan's website for all my prospective student needs. *www.umich.edu.*

Look at this site. Gorgeous. *Don't get melodramatic. You've been to this site once a month since 1996.* Yeah, but it was only to check football scores and broadcast schedules. Looking at this website with different purpose has made it the most beautiful thing I have ever seen. This is my future. *You hope.*

My hands and feet go numb.

The University of Michigan?

Home of the Maize and Blue.

Home of the Wolverines.

Home to three Heisman trophy winners.

Home of fifty-two National Championships.

Home to President Ford and James Earl Jones and Arthur Miller and Lucy Liu and Michael Phelps and the home of my forthcoming undergraduate degree.

Michael Phelps is incredible and superhuman, and I would love to have sex with Lucy Liu. In fact, I would love to watch Michael Phelps have sex with Lucy Liu, and that, sadly, is something you can't find on the Internet.

Mom bought me my first U of M cap and T-shirt when I was four. Before that, I had several Michigan Wolverines terrycloth baby jumpers that I puked on and shit in, but I don't remember receiving or wearing those, so they don't count. I will never forget the cap and T-shirt combo, wrapped under the Christmas tree at four years old. The card said that it was from Mom and Dad, but that was impossible because it was wrapped. Mom was the only one who wrapped gifts. Dad refused. His Christmas gift-giving included pulling unwrapped items out of a black garbage bag and tossing them in the general direction of the intended recipient. This went on until the bag was empty, and then everyone would just sit and stare in silence as he would get up and leave to go chop wood for the rest of the day. But the U of M cap and T-shirt gift has to be my earliest memory and my best one. Second to that would be the Wolverines football game Dad took me to for my eighth-grade graduation, which was the most thoughtful thing he has ever done.

Ever. For anyone.

The only reason it happened was because he was going for himself and dragged you along for company. That, sadly, could very well be true.

Regardless, the anticipation and excitement that pumped through my pubescent veins during the van ride from Paradise to Ann Arbor is something I feared I would never feel again.

Until now.

Until viewing this website and clicking the only tab previously undiscovered by me: "Prospective Students." *Click it.* Done. Heart rate elevating.

"Undergraduate Admissions." *Click that tab.* Done. *Good.* BP rising.

"Applying to Michigan." *Click that.* Difficulty breathing and numbness. *Breathe.* Good. *Take your time, Isaac. Soak in all the pages, alive with interesting graphics and happy faces.* No. Too excited.

"Apply Online." Stop. Let's think this over. As progressive as I claim to be, I am not comfortable applying online. I want something tangible to fill out and hold on to. I want something to put in the mail when I'm finished. *Agreed.*

"The freshman application is also available here." *Click the word "here." It's a hyperlink.*

Like Alcoholics Anonymous, this seems like the first step to recovery: Download the application, fill it out, send it in, get accepted, pick my courses, pay tuition, find someone to rent my place in Paradise and get the hell out of Dodge. *Notice how "tell Dad" wasn't in there, and where are you going to live?* I can't live in the dorms. At my age, that's creepy. *Is there residence for mature students?* Likely, but who in Christ wants to live there? *Exactly.*

What about Dad? I would have to either tell him or not tell him and just disappear, but that isn't heroic. I'd essentially be running away from home. No, I'd be branching out. *What if he gets weaker and gets worse? What if he needs you on a daily basis instead of a weekly basis?*

I'm doing it again. Looking for a reason not to go. For my clever mind, a reason to stay put is easier than finding a resident in Paradise without a GED.

Not this time. This time, my balls have finally dropped.

The hyperlink has been double-clicked, and a box pops up on my desktop.

"You have chosen to open Application.pdf which is a: Portable Document Format from: http://www.admissions.umich.edu.

What would you like to do with this file? Open with PREVIEW or Save File."

Save the file. Click "Save File." Done.

Yes, I have Adobe Acrobat 7.0, thank you for asking.

Waiting.

Waiting.

Also, I seem to be hard. Is the erection due to the thought of Mike Phelps banging Lucy Liu, or is it the pseudo-orgasmic buildup that downloading this application has kindled? Someone famous once said you should never waste a boner, but I can't remember who it was. It may have been a line from a movie. Maybe I should surf some porn while the file downloads? *Good idea.* Internet porn is extraordinary, and I'm fascinated by it half the time. Disgusted, the rest. What amazes me is how many young women and middle-aged women and grannies put their bodies on display. Nude grannies, desperate for retirement income, getting plowed by well-hung young men is wrong, and I have no idea how that can turn someone on. Some things are sacred, and grannies are one of them. Tied for second place in the category of "How in the Hell Does That Turn Anyone On" would be hermaphrodite porn or anything involving an amputee.

To each their own.

I suppose.

But there are thousands and thousands of girls on there. All from somewhere with an address and a postal code. All from a mother who birthed and cared for them. *Or sometimes not.* And all with a story and dreams and aspirations. Yet somehow their image is streamed into my little computer in Paradise within seconds, and I see them in all their glory. To me, that is fascinating. Sometimes I try to attach a name and a story to each face I see, which usually results in a complete loss of erection. Then

I feel attached. It's like farmers eating a lamb they have raised since birth. It just feels wrong.

But with Internet porn, the user gets exactly what they ask for. Whenever they want. A myriad of fetishes involving different races in different positions. Never any risk of bad breath, body odour, or bad conversation, and the girls never pressure for a relationship. But that's not what fuels the worldwide addiction when it comes to Internet porn. Choice does. Unlimited selection. Tired of one? Move on to the next — minus the awkward conversation or lame excuse. It's the same reason that with seven hundred channels on cable, nothing seems to be on. We are obsessed with surfing, flipping, and trading up. It's dizzying. A generation of commitment-phobes obsessed with what's next.

Basketball great Wilt Chamberlain is supposed to have slept with ten thousand women. Excellent. Brilliant effort, Wilt, and I applaud you. Online, anyone could see that many naked women over a long weekend if they put their mind to it — and without the risk of pregnancy or venereal disease.

Having said all that, what should I search for today? Black girls? Interracial? Amateurs? College girls? Asians? Asian lesbians? No, I always end up there. Something different this time. *How about petite?* Getting warmer.

The U of M file continues to trickle in.

Fact: If you accidentally pull up a minor and they trace it back to this computer, you are ruined for life. Michigan would never let you in, and the residents of Paradise would be notified that you are a sexual predator.

That's not good.

Understatement.

That would ruin my life.

The sites say they are all eighteen, but a few have been questionable. True. What a dirty industry. What a disgusting bunch of low-lifes who make this material. I'm as embarrassed to consume it as I am a slave to it. Like an addict. I get the slightest bit horny, and it's a knee-jerk reaction to turn on my computer. Long gone are the days of strategically stashing the lingerie sections of the Sears catalogue because you didn't want traces of actual porn in the house. Or worse, you didn't want to have to go to a store to buy it. No way. That would be totally embarrassing. But via the web, even the world's academic elite and political leaders can't resist the urge to do a little anonymous surfing. *Isaac, are you addicted? It really sounds like you are.* I don't believe I am, but I can't be addicted to anything when I get accepted to Michigan. Not even almost addicted. Doctors can't be addicts.

This has to stop. Cold turkey.

My erection seems to have donated most of its blood back to my vasculature. More importantly, the file is already ninety percent downloaded. The little blue indicator bar struggles to reach the finish line, as if my download request were a marathon for my old computer. I'm inclined to start cheering for it at this point. The mental image of that makes me laugh. I must be in a good mood. I never laugh at myself.

91%

. . .

92%

93%

. . .

. . .

95%

. . .

97%

98%

99%

...

...

Download Complete.

Among the stars of the Crab Nebula, which I have selected as my background desktop picture, there sits the file. It reads, "Application.pdf." Even the tiny document graphic of the thirty-foot Greek-style pillars that adorn the entrance to Angell Hall is powerful, welcoming, commanding, and inspiring.

If I get accepted, I will definitely get a new printer. After a ten-minute self-cleaning and awkward-sounding warmup, my old ink-jet printer coughs and sputters out the twenty-five-page application like a cat does a hairball. A new computer would be good, too. The best of laptops. I need to be trendy. Likely a Mac. I like their ads. Being a mature student at Michigan, I need to show people I mean business. *Having an expensive computer doesn't do that. Having the best marks and the best work ethic, and being the best student, shows you mean business.* True. Still, I don't have a laptop, and I need one. With five pages to go, I feel the obligation to scrub up and operate on my old printer in order to retrieve the final pages, via Caesarian. In this case, I may save the life of the pages, but lose the printer in surgery.

Fact: Jenn Slate is a beautiful pregnant woman.

This colourful visual trumps even the U of M application, now fully printed and sitting in the plastic printer tray, safely delivered.

You really need to get over her.

Jenn Slate is blonde with the facial and physical features of an almost model.

Search engine: "blonde model xxx."

20,960,000 results.

The application can wait five minutes. No. This is happening. Today.

—»—

Under the light of the hanging stained-glass lampshade, the University of Michigan application glows on the kitchen table.

My exit papers from Paradise.

Stapled in the top left corner. *Turn to the second page, Isaac.*

"APPLICATION COMPLETION CHECKLIST" it reads.

"STEP 1: make sure you are a freshman!"

Yes. I am. Check. Old, but a freshman.

"STEP 2: decide which school or college you would like to attend, and read carefully the instructions for applying."

Easy. College of Literature, Science and the Arts. Done.

"STEP 3: fill out the application completely."

Yes, I will do that. I promise.

"STEP 4: write your two short answers and one essay."

That will suck. What am I going to write about? Maybe they give me some options? How about: "The Influence of Pornography on Retail Cosmetic Surgery." Fantastic idea. *Too provocative. Horrible idea for this situation.* Agreed.

"STEP 5: complete your application and sign your name."

Isn't that basically STEP 3 all over again but worded differently? Obviously, a significant number of people submit the application without filling it out.

"STEP 6: pay your application fee."

I may be the only applicant who is genuinely happy to pay. If Michigan asked me to pay more, I would, and if Michigan raises tuition, I will not join the picket line.

I promise.

"STEP 7: obtain your counselor recommendation."

My counselor died three years ago. *Relax. There will be a work-around.*

"STEP 8: obtain your core academic teacher recommendation."

I have now gone from the pan into the fire. Will I have to track down one of the old crotchety teachers from almost two decades ago? Maybe U of M drops this requirement for mature students. *Maybe, but they are not called "Mature Students" anymore — they are called "Non-Traditional Students." That is a* much easier pill to swallow. I need to find out, exactly, what a non-traditional student is required to submit. *Call the university.* No. I will visit Whitefish High on Monday and ask the secretary to forward my transcript. Maybe she will know what's required or, better yet, a current counselor. *Good call.* I must know one of them. Or done plumbing for them.

Many of the remaining pages of the application don't apply to me at all.

Not interested in the arts, thank you.

Or engineering.

Or design.

No, I won't need an audition for dance or performing arts, although, if I get accepted I will dance like a maniac and sing out loud — so, I will end up two-thirds a musical theatre major by proxy.

Fill out the application, Isaac.

Full legal name: Sullivan, Isaac Harding

Country of citizenship: United States of America

Birth date: 03/30/1972

Birthplace: St. Ignace, Michigan, USA

Gender: Male

High school graduation date: June/1990

Permanent email: isaac.h.sullivan@gmail.com

Cell phone number: (906) 306-3333

Permanent street address:

    31 West Tepee Lane

    Paradise, MI

    49768

Valid since: June/1994

You are a: freshman

When do you want to start?: next fall

Have you applied to U-M before?: no

University housing preference: none

U-M school or college: College of Literature, Science and the Arts.

Area(s) of interest/ program of study: pre-med/ sciences

Parent/Guardian: Sullivan, Norman Harding

Relationship to you: Father

High school graduate: No

Any college?: No

Highest degree: middle school

Employer: Sullivan Plumbing

Occupation: plumber (retired)

Michigan resident?: yes.

Siblings?: no

Immediate family member who attended the University of Michigan: none

Please estimate your family's gross income for 2008: $25,000–$49,000

Did any of your grandparents attend college?: no

If applicable, please tell us about anything you do to provide significant support for your family, either by working, by providing care for family members, or through other work that you do at home: I am a non-traditional student with no dependents.

Which best describes you: Caucasian/White

What is your native language?: English

Are you a U.S. Veteran?: No

I authorize the release of my academic, demographic, and financial information on file with the University to alumni clubs and other organizations that may consider me for scholarships: No

Why not apply for scholarships? I don't want people in my business. I just don't. I don't need the money, and that scholarship should go to someone who really needs it. *Right, but if you are deserving of a scholarship, then you should accept it and be proud of it. LeBron James doesn't NEED the money anymore, but he takes it because it is deserved.* Good point, but there are obligations and pressure associated with scholarships, and I don't want those thoughts creeping in. Ever. I am at Michigan for me, and I can afford every penny, so I will not be accepting scholarship money. *But it would sound pretty cool to tell a girl that you're on scholarship.* True. There's value there.

Is everything we do as men directly or indirectly for the sole purpose of impressing women? *I think it is.* That can't be true. *Really? Think about it.* I can tell this is going to be a long and depressing debate, and I have work to do.

I would rather not be on any kind of scholarship and still

be at the top of the class. America loves underdogs and, in this situation, I will be looked upon like a three-legged Pomeranian up against a rabid pit bull. I wonder what odds Michael Vick would give me?

I can fill out the rest of this boring stuff later. Where are the essay questions? *Near the back.* Here. Good.

PART 1: ALL APPLICANTS must answer the following question: "Share an experience through which you have gained respect for intellectual, social, or cultural differences. Comment on how your personal experiences and achievements would contribute to the diversity of the University of Michigan."

Well ...

I could talk about the Native Americans in the area and my experience with them not paying me. Does it count as pro bono work if you invoice someone who doesn't pay you? *It should.* What about the time I did all the plumbing for the new community centre on the Reservation in Brimley, "pro bono," and what I learned about the rich Ojibwe culture? That sounds good. *There is a ring of racism in there, Isaac. Be careful.* True. But I do love the people and culture of the Ojibwe, and I have to make sure the actions of a few don't cloud my perception of the rest. *That sounded very mature.* Perhaps the essay topic could be the right-sizing of my perception of a culture through a direct, working interaction with them. It's edgy, but it's honest and would definitely garner attention. Not only that, it shows that I'm not stuck in my beliefs and am open to change and open to learning. Isn't that what college is all about? *Yes. Perfect. Be sure to leave out the part where the chief's daughter invited you over for lunch and guided your sexual vision quest.*

True.

The things we did to each other over the course of that hour should have been written on birch bark scroll and passed down to future generations. But there was no way the chief would let her date me. He smelled heavily of Aqua Velva, and the rumour was he drank it, but I paid no attention to that. *It does contain alcohol.* I don't care. He chose it as his aftershave. Besides, he was the chief and the father of my beautiful Native American Princess.

I loved when her hair smelled like campfire.

When we interlocked our fingers, it looked odd, but beautiful.

Search engine: "native american nude xxx."

53,900 hits.

Then the essay portion can wait five minutes or so.

V

"Here's what you do, Isaac," he says. My father wipes his mouth with the sleeve of his plaid shirt after uttering the preamble to some sage advice. Tiny pieces of food are still caught in his salt-and-pepper beard, post-wipe. *Tell him.* No, let him finish his thought. Dad pauses then takes a long pull from his can of Miller High Life. Obviously, the advice hadn't completely hatched, and he is now in the process of editing it as he chugs. One of his oldest tricks.

He enjoys Saturday brunch with me. I think he does. I love it, which is crazy. I shouldn't. And the man has to be sick of eating the same thing every weekend. *Prepare something different for him then. Try an omelette, for Christ sake.* No. It's tough to screw up bacon, scrambled eggs, sausage, and toast, and the punishment of his complaints are not worth the culinary risk of preparing something new. *At least change up the dessert.* Why? *Because apple boats are boring as all hell and should not constitute dessert.*

The chugging has ceased.

Here comes the advice, which historically has been the parental equivalent of an oil spill. *Give him the benefit of the doubt.*

I'm all ears.

Small droplets of beer have decided to hang out with the crumbs in his beard. It's all I can focus on. *Reach across with your napkin and clean them off.* No, he will tell me that I am acting like a woman. *Focus, advice is coming. Look interested.* There they hang, like tiny beads of water on a spider's web after a light rain.

"You need to find yourself a woman, Isaac … who doesn't piss you off too much," he says. Wow. I wasn't sure you could pull it off, but you have raised the bar with that gem, old man. "Besides, you can die from pussy these days."

"You mean AIDS?"

He nods, gazing out my kitchen window. "Hardly an aid if you ask me. Fucking thing kills you."

Tell him it's an acronym. Why? To make him feel stupid? *No.* Yes. I won't do it. "It's an acronym, Dad."

"What!"

"Acquired. Immune. Deficiency. Syndrome. That's what AIDS stands for."

It can also stand for immunodeficiency syndrome. *Don't confuse him.* His gaze remains fixed on the wilderness of my backyard.

"What a world we live in, champ … where you can die from pussy."

"They pretty much insist on the rubbers these days."

"Before your mother, back when I was sowing my oats in and around Paradise, the most you could get was a few critters runnin' around in your pubes. And what the fuck is condom sex? I don't even count that bullshit. Never did. Neither should you."

I do.

I count it.

"Sex is when you enter a woman without a rubber on. That's the only time it's sex," he says.

I disagree. Penis in vagina is sex, and I don't care if you have a condom, garbage bag, or a neoprene sleeve wrapped around the bastard, it's still sex. Plus, you overshot the birds-and-the-bees conversation by twenty years, Pop. Please, do us both a favour and do not start now.

It was a bad idea to tell him I had beer when he asked. Five crushed cans on the table in front of me await the remaining member of their family. He is coming soon, cans. And the advice is flowing just as smoothly as the beer. I should have said I was all out. "Sorry, Dad. Fresh out. No beer today." Another example of how a lie would have improved my quality of life.

Dad tears into the last sausage with the old wood-handled steak knife. A knife from the set he bought me in 1999. *Why do you put the steak knives out for him to cut eggs and sausages?* Not sure. They look better. Tougher. Maybe it's just to prove to him that his gift gets used.

I pick up my matching steak knife and cut into one of my remaining sausages as well. Thank God for manners — you can't eat when you talk, so as long as we're both eating, I don't have to attribute the silence to awkwardness.

"You a fucking southpaw now, son?"

"What? No."

"You're cutting with your left hand. What's that all about?"

"Not sure."

"Your mother teach you that?"

"No, Dad. She would have left before carving manners was a real issue," I say. *Too heavy for breakfast conversation. Get back on track. Lighten it up. Fast.* Agreed.

"In a few of the old pictures, she fed me a bottle with her right hand, so she was likely right-handed. Wasn't she?"

"She was a fucking drunk, and she fed herself the bottle."

"Right," I say. "Of course."

"So why are you cutting lefty, or is that how queers eat these days?" he zings at me. His best attempt at a joke. *Pathetic.* With the tip of his steak knife, he swats the back of my cutting hand.

Interesting.

He swatted my cutting hand without having to cross his body or the opposite side of my plate to get to it.

Like a mirror. A mirror image.

We have eaten across from each other since Mom bailed on us, and our silverware has been facing each other ever since. That explains it, Dad. *Explain it to him.* No, I like it better that just I know. Could it have hurt him to come to my side of the table thirty years ago and teach me properly?

Typical. He's never been interested in my perspective.

"Not a queer, Dad."

You shouldn't have acknowledged the question at all. True.

"You been single for too long. Small town like this, people are gonna start to think things."

I would love for people to start to think in this town.

"So, I should go out and find someone … anyone … so the people in Paradise don't think I'm gay? Is that the advice?"

"Aren't you lonely?" he asks genuinely. I think he almost cared there. That's something.

How can I be lonely? Books and journals and the Internet are my best friends. Knowledge is my best friend. Does he realize how busy a pre-med undergrad will be? No. *That was a mean and unfair question. And he didn't mean friends, idiot. He meant women. He's asking if you're lonely for a woman.*

I would assume it's much easier on the ego to be single in a small town than in a large one. One has the excuse that "it's a small town, and there's no one here worth dating who isn't already taken." On the other hand, I imagine it's more difficult to be single in a college town or large city, which are overrun with attractive and intelligent people in the same way Paradise is overrun with deer.

My diagnosis, then, is that it is far more taxing on one's confidence to be chronically single in a city or college town.

"There's really no one here worth dating who isn't already taken," I reply. *Pathetic.*

"Forget the other thing," he says. "All I'm sayin' is this … Find someone before you get the AIDS, because no piece of tail is worth dying over."

Dad stands at the sink with his back to me, having insisted on doing the dishes by hand. I have a new stainless steel dishwasher that he wants no part of. The cluttered kitchen island separates us, but it might as well be an ocean or galaxy. Have I run out of things to talk to him about? *Find something to say. Start a conversation.* I hate small talk and refuse to subject anyone else to it. *Tell him that you printed out the Michigan application.* No way. Not yet. *You said you would today.* Drop it, please. *You're terrified of his reaction. That he'll make fun of you.* Fuck off.

Fact: All I want to discuss with Dad is his current medical condition. *Ask him about the prostate.* I'm not supposed to know about the prostate, and ignorance was bliss until Nurse Fincher let the secret slip halfway into installing her new sink. She figured he would have told me. Incorrect, Nurse Fincher. He doesn't tell me fuck all.

Truth: His medical coverage won't remove his grossly enlarged prostate because the biopsy came back benign, thereby forcing him to stick a lubricated tube up his cock hole three times a day to piss.

He is sandbagged with a coverage provider that won't preemptively spend money on a laparoscopic prostatectomy to remove the prostate before it becomes malignant. He couldn't even get them to pay for a nurse to come and do the catheterizations for him in the meantime. A trusted plumber for thirty-five years, he is now forced to pipe lines for waste removal up his own manhood. That is sick and unfair. There will be a time when he can't do it any longer himself. Could the proud bastard ever muster up the courage to ask me to do it? Would I do it? This visual is too disturbing for my highly creative mind. Possibly, I would do it just to see him swallow his pride for the first time — ever.

It could always be worse. It could be Alzheimer's.

The thought causes my forearms to come alive with tiny bumps. What an evil bastard ... Alzheimer's. Of this affliction I am by far most terrified. People get a kick out of zombie movies, but the harsh reality here is that zombies do exist. They do. They exist in every hospital in every town and every city in America, and they are called Alzheimer's patients.

Leaving its prey nothing more than a shell with a heartbeat, Alzheimer's eats away at our coveted grey matter and consumes us with confusion and sadness. What are we, as humans, without the ability to recognize the faces and relationships we've built, or the memories and moments that define us?

What do you call someone who is alive, but dead?

You call them a zombie, and the only way to kill them is to blow their head off with a shotgun, slice the head clean from the neck, or completely crush the skull, thus mashing the infected brain.

Dad's swollen prostate seems much more manageable now, considering the alternative. Would I kill him if he had Alzheimer's? Yes. *You can't kill your own father.* No, but you can kill zombies. In the movies, you are required to kill them. I'm reminded how our society fails to view euthanasia as a humane exit strategy. Instead, we all get to sit, wait, and watch our familial zombies suffer. Perhaps the most terrifying zombie movie ever made is the one where you can't put a zombie out of its misery. A starring role thousands in this world are forced to play.

Have I just lessened my father's condition? No. He is still suffering and needs to be reached out to.

Words bubble up with intention, but continue to get trapped in the invisible lump in my throat. Dad, I know what you are going through, and I am here for you. If you have any questions, I have the wherewithal to answer them. *That sounded great. Say it.* Can't.

Pussy. You'll wish you had. Why not say it? Because I will cry, and then he'll tell me that I'm emotional like my mother, and that's where I get it from. Fact: I do have the wherewithal to answer any question on the subject of the prostate gland — its function, secretions, structure, regulation, and development. Since Nurse Fincher spilled the beans, I have become an expert on the topic, including the pros and cons to each of the three methods of removal.

He washes the paring knife that I used to cut the apple for him earlier. It's time I grew some alligator skin, and if I did, it would sound like this:

"Dad," I'd say.

"What?"

"What if I told you that I could take the paring knife, the one you are holding in your hand, and with my medical knowledge and skill, I could cut out your angry prostate? Would you hand the paring knife over to me? Would you let me do it? Would you let me excise that angry prostate that will eventually kill you?" I'd say.

Nothing more frustrating than knowing what to do and having your hands and feet tied.

Tied tight with no feeling.

That's me. A doctor without a licence.

"You've done a hell of a good thing with the family business. Marv Pearlman was sayin' good things about you the other day. I had to agree."

"Thanks," I reply. Thanks for forcing me into it, you selfish prick.

Before I know it, he is back around to the sink and working on the dishes with the check-pattern drying towel slung over his shoulder, as it's always been. The same belt from fifteen Christmases ago is looped into the jeans from three years before that. It makes me feel good that I bought him both of those items, and it makes me sad that I haven't replaced them yet.

Empathy is a strange emotion to feel toward another human who warrants such resentment. However, the only soothing thought — which allows me to continue to invite him over for Saturday brunch and to love him unconditionally — is the fact that the simple bastard likely did the best he could.

"Next week as usual?" he mumbles on his way out the door.

"Yeah, Dad. Of course."

He manoeuvres his rickety old frame painfully down the first wooden step from my porch. Other men his age are in shape and quite active. There are golfers and cyclists and marathoners his age. But my old man, at age seventy, looks ready for admittance to the nursing home and is one of Death's top twenty prospects for the new year ahead. I hate the nursing home. It wouldn't matter if he begged me, I would never visit him there if that's where he lived. First of all, I hate the institutional smell of lingering death, and secondly, such places are infested with zombies.

My polished black steel-toe boots kick in the main entrance to the Paradise Acres Retirement Home. The door flies open a hundred and fifty degrees before connecting with a large potted yucca plant sitting in the main reception. SMASH! The glass from the door shatters into a million tiny cubes, and those cubes dance like dice on the tile reception floor. Shatterproof glass is genius. *Why didn't you just open the door? Now some retirement home janitor has to clean up your mess. Why? For the sake of a great entrance?* Yes. The reception is as disturbing as one could imagine. Stark. Cold. Even the coffee table at the end of the worn leather couch is made of stainless steel.

The weight of the Remington eight-gauge shotgun in my right hand is almost cumbersome. But this is not battle. Nor do I have to move quickly. The leather ammunition pouch that hangs from my belt almost counteracts the weight imbalance.

Not for long.

The ammunition pouch will only get lighter.

"Thank God you're here, Isaac! They're that way!" points Receptionist.

Take note, Receptionist, I think you are really sexy. The collar of her pinstripe dress-shirt emerging from her v-neck, cable-knit sweater is only outmatched by her brown hair, wrung into a perfect bun. Gorgeous. This kind of dedication to professional appearance makes me think that, when she lets her hair down and loses the Gap look, baler twine and ball gags are definitely in play.

"How many of them?" I ask.

"Two!"

"Room?"

"178."

My steel-toe boots make a rhythmic tapping on the terrazzo floor as I march past residents and visiting family members down the hallway toward my targets. Eye contact would be nice, people. Except that, like the grim reaper, I may be coming for you, or the one you love, in the not too distant future. So I get the point and understand your fear of me. Wrong. You should all bow down and thank me for taking on this role of superhero.

The door numbers fly by:

167.

168.
170.
172.
174.
176.

Here it is. Room 178. I clear my throat and tap gently on the door with the barrel of the Remington. No answer. They know I'm here. They always do.

"I already made a mess in the reception! I really don't want to destroy this door!" I yell hoarsely.

Count to three. Not out loud, though. That is stupid and cliché. My first stepmother used to give me to the count of three before she would whoop me with her size nine-and-half shoe. I'm glad she died when I was thirteen. There is nothing worse than getting whooped by someone with no genetic relation to you. It feels wrong. Unfair. Who was she to reprimand me? She came from a family of hillbillies. My genetic code was like the Matrix compared to her simple plan.

"I'm gonna count to three!" I yell. *Pathetic.* Fuck off.

"One!"

"Two!"

The door opens just enough to allow a controlled and graceful panoramic of the horror inside. The unforgiving overhead lights pound down on the infected and infirm. Four bodies lie on gurneys, well tucked-in by coarse, white hospital sheets. The room is a sea of white and aluminum.

Stark.

Cold.

Receptionist said there were two infected. Which ones are they? Where are their families? Best they aren't here to see this. Best the retirement home contacts me the minute they suspect one of their residents has turned. *Who opened the door?*

Automatic door release from the front desk, perhaps. *Who cares?* True.

Start the questioning on the far right, Isaac. Fine.

His medical bracelet reads: "Almont, Fred." On the stainless steel tray beside his gurney rests a silver-framed picture of his family. They looked happy.

I tap the old man on the forehead with the tip of the shotgun barrel. His dead brown eyes open slightly. Like rings in a tree stump, the lines on this man's face tell an epic story. I can almost read the twists and turns. But can he remember them?

"Who the hell are you?" he says.

"Who are you, sir?" I reply. Save yourself, old man. Tell me your name.

"Fuck off," he mumbles under his tired breath.

"I need your name please, sir."

He hears none of my question. His eyes dart around the room in search of answers.

"Where am I?" he strains. Use the picture. The chubby girl with the perm and bad Christmas sweater has to be his daughter.

"Tell me your daughter's name, sir."

"Do I have one?"

He's fucked. He's a zombie. *Wait. Maybe she is a friend of the family. Move on to the wife in the picture.*

"Your wife's name, sir?"

"Never wanted one in the first place," he says.

"Is she dead?"

"No, I never had one!"

Is that his mother, then? No way, too young. Are they his sister and his niece?

"What's your sister's name, sir?" I ask.

"Do I have a sister? I don't have a sister."

The questioning period has now ended, Mr. Almont. His

answers are good enough for my due diligence report. The Remington fires a shell that pastes his diseased contents against the back wall.

One down.

The old woman on the gurney to the left of the recently deceased zombie will now be questioned. I tap her on the forehead with the tip of my index finger. Her Carolina blue eyes open up, filling the room with new colour and hope. She can't be one of them. She can't have turned. This woman is delightful, and I know nothing about her but her current expression.

"Who are you, Mr. Handsome?" she asks. *She is flirting*. No, she can't be.

"What's more important is who you are."

Her bracelet reads: "Price, Mabel." Her beautiful wise eyes instantly become submerged.

"Bill?" she asks innocently. This is not a good sign, Mabel. I am not Bill.

"Bill? It is you. You came home!"

Her nasolacrimal ducts are now pumping tears without pause.

"Oh, Bill, I got the note they sent in the mail after the raid on that island … but I didn't believe it! I knew you would come back! We won, Bill! We won the war!"

In no way could I have been prepared for this, and in no way do I know how to react. I am a superhero, sent to put zombies to rest, and I have been drawn into a comforting hug with this sobbing widow. *Isaac, are you crying? No. Yes you are. Good. Cry it out. Cry out the ACTH. Get it out of your system.* I hate this.

Perhaps she has dementia and not the disease. *Stop. Isn't Alzheimer's a form of dementia?* I should know this and don't have time to research the definitive answer. *It's bullshit that you came out into the field unprepared like that.* Relax. Being a superhero isn't easy. Dig deeper.

"What's your name, ma'am?"

Say "Mabel." Say it! Say it, and I will blow the head off the person lying next to you and leave. I promise.

"Bill, it's me."

"I know, but what is your name?"

"It's … well … certainly you can remember, dear."

"Just please tell me your name. I need to hear you say it."

Her wrinkled face gives her situation away. She has no clue.

How can such a beautiful, kind old woman be staring down the barrel of my Remington eight-gauge? *Pull the trigger.* I can't. *She's infected.* Right, but there was a flash of memory. She definitely knows who Bill is. *No, dear little Mabel Price is long gone. She is a zombie now. Do it.* Can't. It's like she can't even see the gun or my shaking hands cradling it in the firing position.

"Why are you crying, Bill? Were you injured in the battle?"

"Ma'am, tell me who Mabel Price is," I say. Come on, that was a gift. A lay-up. A fastball down the middle.

"Mabel Price?"

"Yes, Mabel Price. Who is she?"

"I'm sorry, Bill. I have no idea. Is she someone you met during the war? Oh, my. Did you meet someone special in the war?" she asks, now weeping.

You have ruined my day, Mabel. You are infected. You carry the zombie disease, and it is visible to me, and it is eating away at your mind like a bat eating mosquitoes.

Barely able to see, I line up Mabel Price's adorable little wrinkled face in the sight of the Remington.

Enough.

I'm out.

Dad has one step to go, down the porch stairs as I return from my daydream, broken out in a full sweat. I should really install a railing for him. He braces his knee with his right hand to support the final reach down to the gravel path with his left leg. This is horrifying to watch. *Take a look, Isaac. That is what your body will look like. That is what your body will feel like, and you'll end up like your old man — laying the burden on your first-born son to carry on the torch of mediocrity.* Cycles are inherently that way. They can't help but repeat themselves.

These steps are killing him, and he is making strange noises, as if trying to pass a kidney stone. *Help him down the steps!* Too late, he's reached the bottom. *What kind of a son stands and watches his father struggle like that?* One day he won't make it down on his own and he will break his hip, and it will be my fault. I will help him next time. I feel horrible. *Tell him you love him, then.* No.

The tips of my hands and feet go numb as I watch him hobble down the gravel driveway to his rusted red pickup truck. The same red pickup I lost my virginity in to Sarah Cliffton. What a beautiful girl. What could Sarah Cliffton be up to these days? *Likely married with kids.* She had the most beautiful body I have ever seen — the first one I saw naked, anyway, which may distort my ranking. Before laying eyes on Sarah, I had no clue what a vagina looked like. I hadn't even seen a picture of one. Russ Davidson's dad used to press two heavily buttered pancakes together and hold them upright, forcing us to touch the edges where the pancakes met. Or stick our finger between them. He would yell, "That's what you put your pecker in, lads," and would laugh and laugh and laugh. But I was just a kid, so I took that redneck example as gospel from that point forward. Several years later, in that rusted truck, I was thrilled to find out he was full of shit. In fact, I've never seen a vagina that looks or feels like two buttered pancakes pressed together and held upright.

And for that I am thankful.

I loved Sarah Cliffton. However, like my old man and his red truck and my licence plate and Bill Dawson's mailbox, we all seem to rust with time. I'm sure that Sarah Cliffton is fat and ugly now and stuck in a dead-end job. At least we have one thing in common, and the other is subjective.

Dad wrestles his way into the old red truck, and I almost have to look away. This is too much. I can hear him cursing with the same words that I use — except my cursing is done in my head. Is there a point at which the pain is too much and it becomes mandatory for the cursing to be vocalized? I refuse to find out. If I am to walk this earth at seventy years old, then I want to golf and cycle and run and drive a really expensive and rust-free red truck.

If the encounter with Jenn Slate started the ball rolling, then this one solidified my decision.

So calm, now.

I can feel the seismic shift rattle in my brain as the layers of bullshit and fear flake off my once-prominent life plan.

This is really happening. Tomorrow, I will cut my umbilical cord to mediocrity and go to Whitefish High, in search of answers.

Tell someone my plan — out loud.

Make it real.

And get what I need to apply to the U of M.

VI

Whitefish Township High School — home of the Rockets. I have no clue how they came up with that particular team name, because it doesn't apply at all. In no way has there ever been a rocket in this neck of the woods. There have been many guns, crossbows, cannons, and small aircraft, but no rockets and nothing armed with a rocket engine. That's not entirely true. My good friend Jeff Grant and I used to shoot bottle rockets at tourists from the woods.

Actually, the Whitefish Bottle Rockets is a pretty good name.

The late eighties was a weird time to be in high school. The girls had fluorescent clothing, crimped or spiked hair, and all listened to Paula Abdul and Tiffany, and they laminated images of Kirk Cameron cut from teen magazines. As for the guys, our acid-wash jeans were way too tight, and that generation of Ford Mustangs was, by far, the worst design to date. All said, the best thing to come out of the eighties were Thundercats and Guns n' Roses and my personal sweet child o' mine, Sarah Cliffton. I should try to find her. *Why? What would you do if you found her?* Not sure.

I throw the plumbing van in neutral and stare at my old stomping grounds from the high school parking lot — the same lot where fights took place after school dances or gym classes. I never got in a fight in high school, but that was because I never gave anyone trouble or looked at anyone the wrong way. The closest I came to getting in a fight was when Brittany Hamill told her boyfriend that she wanted to date me because she thought I was hotter than he was. An impartial jury would have ruled me more attractive, and I was a boatload smarter, to boot. I can't remember his name. Regardless, when he and his crew of Cro-Magnons eventually found me — I was making out with Brittany Hamill's best friend behind the electrical transformer — I was exonerated due to a combination of insufficient evidence and my threat to press charges. *What kind of pussy threatens to press charges in a high school fight?* The kind who was trying to graduate at the top of his class and go to medical school — that's who. Fact: Had I known I was destined to be a plumber for the next two decades, I would have thrown hands that day. In tandem with the jealous Cro-Magnon, I would've had nothing to lose, and that's when humans become most dangerous and do horrible things to each other. Poetically, I did end up doing horrible things to Brittany Hamill three months later, after the winter semi-formal in the back of her dad's '76 Chevelle.

Students in the smoking section watch me like hawks as I enter their nest. I must be old, but these little bastards don't look a day past ten. Are all of your parents idiots, kids? They must know you are all smoking, and this is not 1985. Now there are health warnings and images of diseased organs and gums on the packaging. Truth: The parents *do* know the little bastards are smoking, and, in most cases, it's the parents who buy the cigarettes for them. Likely a parent who tossed them their first dart from an already opened pack of their own.

Once again, the cycle continues — because that's all it's good at.

One of the pimple-faced smokers ashes his cigarette on the redbrick exterior of the school, now covered in graffiti. For being considered "destruction of public property," I have to admit some of the misplaced art is quite beautiful.

My tape measure, clipped to my right side pocket, bounces on the upper thigh of my worn work jeans as I notice my pace increase through the smoking section. Racing to the heavy side doors of the east entrance to disappear out of sight. I wish they wouldn't stare at me like that. What are they staring at? *You are a grown man (not a teacher) walking into a high school, wearing a quilted plaid jacket from the mid-nineties and a tape measure on your pocket. You are a lesson to others to stay in school.* That was uncalled for.

A young, black-haired Goth cuddles into her tall, lanky boyfriend as they hold hands under the overhang of the east doors. Her dark eye makeup, deep purple lipstick, and lip ring, are all strategically designed to force attention her direction, and her bait has been successful. Perfectly lined, her bangs run horizontally across the tips of her eyelashes, and two longer bands of hair frame her adorable little face. *You're staring at her like a creep.* I realize that, but like a train wreck, or a Wolverines football game — I can't look away. You are so beautiful, little Goth Princess, and you can do much better than Lurch Adams. I bet he holds your hand wherever you go, providing him superficial insurance that you won't leave. Yes, you could do much better, Goth Princess. *Like who, Isaac? You?* Maybe.

Lurch Adams could care less about me, and he refuses to acknowledge my presence. But the blue eyes of the teenage Goth meet mine and electricity is shared. *Sexual?* No, not sexual. More of a mutual transfer of sadness and disappointment.

"You got a light, sir?" she asks.

My left hand is already grasping the staple-shaped stainless steel door handle. I could easily pretend I didn't hear her. I do have a lighter. I always have a lighter on me, but it's not for cigarettes. It's for lighting my portable propane torch that melts solder into copper piping joints. *I wouldn't tell her that.* Agreed. I hate smoking and smokers, and I don't want to be listed on the scorecard with an assist in her death. Keep going. Walk away. *Did she just call you "sir?"*

That seals it — I am a "sir."

I am a relic.

I am archaic.

I am the Old Testament.

"Yeah, I have a light," I reply, cramming my hand into the pocket of my jeans. Styles have changed. My jeans are obviously too tight compared to the other guys around me. No one out here works this hard to get at a lighter.

"Just a sec. It's in here somewhere."

That was the wrong thing to say. Now there is a penis joke on the tip of both their tongues. True.

Goth Princess smiles at me, revealing some of the deep purple lipstick that has migrated onto her straight, pearl-white teeth. No one has teeth that naturally straight. She's likely the daughter of a wealthy dentist who pays her no attention. That would make her Dr. Spencer's daughter. *You are speculating, Isaac.* I don't care that there is lipstick on your teeth, Goth Princess. You are gorgeous.

"Ready when you are," she says, pulling a single white dart out of her pocket and holding it to her mouth between glossy black fingernails.

Lurch Adams is still looking away. Lurch, you stupid bastard, looking away will only ensure that you don't see it when she's snatched from you. *By whom? You?* I didn't say that. *You meant it, though.*

I hold the yellow Bic lighter up to the end of the cigarette and snap back the serrated wheel. Goth Princess and I use our free hands to create an air pocket, protected from the wind. The flame flickers and dodges the cigarette while our house of phalanges protects it long enough to ember its tip. Her darkened eyes close as she draws the smoke through the paper chamber and far into her ballooning alveoli, making the lobes and bronchioles of her lungs a shade darker.

Lurch finally looks over at her and takes the cigarette for his own tar consumption. Goth Princess looks up to me, searching for something to say.

"You're the plumber, right?"

The punishment of that title becomes increasingly cruel each day. *Is she flirting with you?* No.

"Yeah, that's me."

"Cool."

"Shadow me for a day and you'll think differently."

Was that an invitation?! No. *It sounded like an invitation.* Relax. I was making a point.

"You here to fix something?" says Lurch, handing the cigarette back to Goth Princess.

Obviously, he thought it was an invitation. His exhale of smoke is controlled, smooth, and amply rehearsed. Well played, Lurch. What a subtle way to tell me to fuck off.

"I am, yeah."

My life is what I'm here to fix.

"Thanks again for the light," she says, pulling her hoodie up over her head, as if to remove Lurch Adams from her peripheral vision and out of her life completely.

"No worries. But you should think about quitting."

Who are you to give her advice? Don't be a creep. You are really perving out here. Am I flirting? What if she mistakes advice for flirting? Doctors give advice. This is the first medical advice I've given a stranger.

98

Ever.

A breakthrough.

"I'll try," she replies, cocking an adorable half smile.

Is that all it is, Goth Princess? Are you looking for someone to genuinely care about your well-being and someone to prove that you are the centre of their universe? Someone to prove that they'll do anything to keep you happy and healthy? I bet your father hasn't mentioned your smoking. I bet Lurch hasn't mentioned it. Are you having sex with Lurch, Goth Princess? I hope not. *What do you care who she's having sex with?* Is she a junior or a senior? I want to ask her, but it's too obvious what the inspiration for the question is. *Don't ask.*

"Good. Cold turkey is best. I hear the patch sucks," I say.

She smiles and looks down at the butt-littered asphalt. *Isaac, that was outstanding work. Well done.* Thanks.

The long corridor down to the main office remains as dull and brown as it was when I attended the school. Looks like they took out the Coke and snack machines. Not a bad idea, given what we know about nutrition these days. Sarah Cliffton and I would pool our money together each lunch period to split a can of Cherry Coke.

Right there.

We would sit right there in that nook, and my heart would pound against my ribcage with nervous energy. I'm obviously not over her either.

Plaques of graduating classes line the wall encompassing the library. *Don't stop to read.* I'm on there somewhere. *Who cares? Move on.*

Photos of Whitefish High's top athletes and their achievements hang encased in glass, preserved forever. *You're not featured in there, Isaac — keep walking.*

The reception area isn't as alive as I remember. Three un-showered teens sit on the floor with their greasy hair glistening under the pot lights. What an awkward time — high school. I sympathize, greasy teens, but get your shit together and get it together quickly, because before you know it, you'll have knocked up your girlfriends and will be forced to take on employment without a college degree — limiting your options to farmhand, butcher, or plumber.

I want to puke.

The coast is now clear, and I walk toward the reception counter.

"Isaac! Thank God you are here!" shouts Susan Grant, the school's secretary.

I have a bad feeling about her enthusiasm. No one should ever be that excited to see a plumber unless they need some-thing fixed.

"Something has sprung a leak in the boys' change-room. We tried to call Dale, but he hasn't come yet."

Even as I try to better myself, even as I try to improve my life situation, I cannot escape who I currently am. My hands and feet are tingling again. Not quite numb, but tingling.

"I'm not here for the leak, Susan."

"No?"

"No, not this time."

"Oh. Okay. Could you do it anyway, since you're here?"

Tell her no. *You're here on business of a different nature.* Don't get bullied into the job that drunk Dale has obviously skipped class on.

"Sure, I can help."

"Yes?"

"Yeah, no problem. I'm happy to do it."

"You're the best. Thanks."

"Don't mention it."

"And come back when you are done and I'll help you with ... whatever it was you needed helpin' on."

Exactly, Susan. You had no clue why I could possibly be here, if not to fix a leak, and now I have been relegated to the showers like a struggling pitcher in the seventh inning. *Isaac, you're the one who agreed to fix the showers.* True. The same showers where Tyson Fleming beat the shit out of your best buddy Russell, and the same showers where Tyson Fleming pissed on the retarded kid. Truth: I was present for both of those horrible situations and did nothing to stop either of them. That's not fair. In the first case, I had nothing to do with the issue between Russell and Tyson. *True, but he was your buddy, and you should've stuck up for him.* I was naked! Who fights in the shower, naked? The situation caught me off guard, and before I knew it, Russell had been punched and was suffering from nasal septal hematoma, and that is the proper term for a bloody nose. *Nicely done.* Thanks.

As for urinating on the retarded kid, there was nothing I could do for the poor bastard. The jocks had encircled him, and he was left, caged by muscular bodies, to get pissed on as he sat and cried under the cold shower — turned cold, to guarantee he could distinguish it from the ninety-eight degree yellow water being blasted at him. Sitting on the wooden bench in the change room, I could barely hear his sobbing from the showers, as it was drowned out by the laughter of the Neanderthal jocks. There was nothing I could've done, unless I was the Hulk — because if I was the Hulk, I would have turned green and twice my size and fucked everybody up.

After that day, I dreamt of catching Tyson off-guard in the halls and unhinging his mandible from its attachment behind the zygomatic bone with my fist. Is that enough punishment? I can't even begin to imagine what punishment would fit that crime. I wish that Tyson was sentenced to trade places with the retarded kid, even for a week, and that he be bound to struggle down the school hallways with bent limbs and a crooked neck — drooling uncontrollably all over himself. One week, stripped of his ability to communicate coherently. One week, ignored by the fickle popular crowd he called "friends." One week, invisible to good-looking girls. One week, the brunt of insults and strange looks. One week, where his aspirations became governed by his situation.

Bound to that torturous situation for a week, my wish for Tyson would be to experience empathy, but mostly, to learn compassion.

Instead, Tyson's disciplinary lumps were nothing more than a three-day suspension and a forced apology. Apparently, he was too valuable to our school teams to be expelled indefinitely, and marking wins on the Whitefish scorecard was more important than deserved punishment. It also helped that his mother sat on the town council. Since when does a mother stick up for her son and plead for a slap on the wrist when he's held a retarded kid captive and pissed on him? This world is incapable of justice. I leave it to the universe, if not in this life, then in another. Tyson, you'll pay dearly for that colossal act of inhumanity.

I'm not going back to the boys' change-room. The place of stinging towel flicks and social posturing and fights and alpha males nicknaming each other's cocks and the oddly shaped cocks of others. Someone once nicknamed someone else's penis "the crooked hammer." I forget that person's name, but I remember seeing the hammer in question, and it was, in fact, quite crooked.

I refuse to go back.

"Forget the leaking showers, Susan. Get me my transcripts and have that disgusting skin tag on your eyelid removed."

Enough.

—»—

I'm out.

"Isaac Sullivan! So great to see you!" yells Susan from behind the counter.

She removes her dated reading glasses and sets them beside an equally ancient computer. Keeping up with technology has never been a priority at Whitefish, the same way switching from asbestos to a non-toxic insulation has, obviously, been overlooked as well. Does the school board supervisor not come to this shithole, ever? Do parents not complain? Do *you* not complain, Susan?

She should complain about her skin tag. Skin tags are small, benign, tumours that form in areas where the skin forms creases. In your case, Susan, the skin tag is too close to your eye for excision or ligation, so I would opt for electrolysis or cryosurgery. From what I've read, the corrosive creams can cause bad skin reactions and, again, it's too close to your eye to take that risk. As for the less noticeable skin tag on your neck, peeking out from your blouse — you can tie a string around that ugly little bastard, and it will fall off in a few days.

"Susan! How's your boy?"

"Daniel. Yes. He's growing like a bad weed. In ninth grade this year, he is."

"Girlfriend?"

"Naw. Not yet. Too into his sports and his guitar."

"Well, both lead to girlfriends, so you've got your work cut out for you."

Good for you, Daniel. I love it. Be a sports star, wail on that guitar and wear fox skin and ride around on panthers. Do this, Daniel, and you'll have more naked, sex-craved women chasing you into the woods than Dionysus.

"I don't want to think about it." She blushes, filing papers to let me know she wants a subject change. Fair enough, Susan. You shouldn't have to think about the fact he's likely behind the portables, rounding second with some beautiful brunette, as we speak.

"I'll tell you what I need, Susan."

"Yes. Of course."

"How easy is it for you to find my high school transcript?"

"Very easy. I'm good at my job."

How nice to see someone proud of their position and excellence in their field. *She's a high school secretary, Isaac.* So what? I don't care if she cleans the shit out of hog trucks. She is proud of her job and good at it.

I want that.

"I need you, or whoever does it, to forward the transcript to the University of Michigan in Ann Arbor, please."

Susan covers her mouth with her hand in an attempt to bottle her excitement. The massive diamond in her wedding ring catches one of the pot lamps and performs laser eye surgery on me. Jesus, Susan — where did your husband find that glacier? I wonder what he does for a living? *It might be fake, and fake diamonds are made from cubic zirconium or moissanite, which is a synthetic diamond, and synthetic diamonds are created using a high-pressure, high-temperature process of compressing carbon.* Regardless of its quality and authenticity, he must really love her. Do they still make love? I've had a hard time with this concept: How do married couples continue to have sex with one another long past the point where they've let themselves go physically? Perhaps the visual of a once-beautiful bride is just a light switch away? Is the deed done out of pity or mercy? Or because you simply have to, and the current version of the woman you married is your only outlet? *Yet another reason to be addicted to Internet porn.* True. I'd much rather lock myself in a room clicking images of attractive and toned bodies and wait until my wife got her de-conditioned self back on the treadmill. Then, and only then, would proper intercourse recommence. *That is unfair and mean*. Really? I think it's mean to allow yourself to look like shit for your lifelong mate.

"You're going back to college, Isaac!" she bursts.

"Well, I never went … in the first place."

"Oh, right. I knew that. Forget that. But you are going to college!"

"I'm going to apply, anyway."

"At your age? Wow. You're so brave. I'm so proud of you!"

"I have some questions about applying, if there's someone here I can talk to."

"'Course there is, hun. 'Course there is. Yes. Mr. Swanton is the guidance counselor, but I believe he's on lunch right now."

Shit, I know Robert Swanton. Did work for him recently. *He's late a payment, too, I believe.* Leave that for now. *Leave the whole thing. He's on lunch.*

"Oh, I can come back later," I say.

"No. No way. Let me buzz him. I think he's still in his office."

The phone she picks up was easily made in the same year that the neighbouring computer on her desk was top-of-the-line, and the same year asbestos and brown and yellow colour swatches were a good choice.

"Mr. Swanton? Yes. Isaac Sullivan here to see you. Yes, the plumber. No, he's not here with an invoice, sir. It's important. Okay, I'll send him in. Thank you, sir," she says, wearing a proud grin, as if having pulled a string for me.

"You can go right ahead, Isaac. First door on your left is his office. Just knock before you go in."

—»—

There are those who insist on knocks before entering a room and there are those who have an open-door policy. I have always believed that someone who insists on knocking has something to hide, something to clean up quickly, or pants to be zipped up. After sitting behind a desk all day coaching hot teenage girls how to apply for college, this dude likely has a few skeletons in the closet. *That would make him a pedophile, and guidance counselors do more than just coach on college applications.* True, but that's what I'm here for, and that's all I need him to be an expert in. As much as I want to catch him in the act of … something … I will knock, because getting the advice I need is more important than humiliating him.

Knock.

"Come on in!" he yells.

That yell was approximately three seconds after the knock. What are you hiding, Mr. Robert Swanton? I turn the knob and push forward.

"Plumb! How are ya?" he asks as he goes back to another bite of his sandwich.

That is a serious sandwich. Look at all the ingredients on that son-of-a-bitch. Is that avocado? His wife loves him. Adores him, if she's carving up avocados to put on his sandwich. An avocado is way beyond the call of duty. *Yeah, because he's in great shape and she loves that.* Well done, Robert. I tip my hat to you.

"Fine, sir. Thank you."

"Look, I know I'm a little late on my payment for that hot-tub install, but it's on my list," he promises. That's good that it's on your list, Robert. I will have tuition to pay for soon.

"Not a problem, Mr. Swanton."

"You can call me Rob, Isaac."

Why? Because I'm too old to be in your office? *Chill out, he's just trying to make you comfortable.*

"Rob it is."

"Good. Now, what can I do for you?"

Well, you could start by putting down your sandwich and giving me your full attention. Confirmed, avocado is definitely present in there, and slices of brie and sprouts have now made themselves visible as well. Robert, you must service your wife better than a NASCAR pit crew.

"I … umm … Well, I …" *You sound like an idiot. Get the words out.*

"Isaac, sit down. Make yourself comfortable."

I sit down in the same chair I sat in eighteen years ago when I told Mr. Fredrick that I wouldn't be going to college because of Dad's injury.

Oddly, Mr. Fredrick was the one crying over the news, not me. Only now do I understand his tears over the situation. As fate would have it, I'm back in the same red leather chair voicing my intentions on college. My heart rate is increasing. There go the hands and feet again.

"I'm applying to Michigan."

"That's a good one. Nice. Seriously, what do you need?"

Two more laughs are snorted before tearing back into his avocado, brie, prosciutto, and tomato sandwich. The starting pistol has officially gone off.

I have encountered the first slam.

The first zing.

The first poor reaction of many to come. How unfortunate for it to come from a man in a guidance position. Is this how they treat non-traditional students? Am I ready for this, and is my skin thick enough?

Robert Swanton continues to laugh as he chews his oversize bite. I seem to have really amused him with my news. Robert, you shouldn't laugh and chew. I'm serious. It's not safe.

The whites of Robert Swanton's eyes reveal their full circumference to me as his laughing and snorting ceases instantly. Robert, remain calm. The laughing has ceased because your airway is blocked and you can no longer breathe. Your Cadillac sandwich has now turned on you and become a high-end means of asphyxiation.

The sandwich is dropped, and its contents spill out onto his desk.

A shame. I would have finished it for you.

I may still.

Instinctively, Robert taps his throat and fails in every attempt to vocalize that he is choking. I know you're choking, Robert. Try to relax.

"Try to relax, Robert. You are choking and your trachealis muscles are trying to figure out what to do with the foreign object in your throat," I say calmly. Like a pro. Robert points to the phone on his desk.

"I see the phone there, Robert. Do you want me to call someone?"

His pointing at the phone is offensive. He doesn't believe I'm capable of saving his life. Lowly plumber that I am. You've made a poor assumption, Robbie. However, I will respect your wishes and call someone else to save you. What would you like me to tell them? *Perhaps he wants to call his wife and not 911. That's a hell of a good point.*

"Here's the deal. I'll call when you tell me who to call ... and what you want me to say. Fair?"

The look in his eyes has shifted. Confusion. Frustration.

Wait, he wants *my* help now. Interesting. Robert, you are starting to get the point that your time is running out.

"Do you want me to help you?" I ask.

Robert nods. He's really beginning to panic now. The tapping at his throat has now turned to frenzied scratching. You want so badly to reach in there and retrieve that rebel piece of sandwich, don't you, Mr. Swanton. This is fascinating to watch. *Stop letting him suffer, Isaac. You are a medical professional.*

With one swipe, I remove all of the contents from his desk and onto the floor.

"Robert, listen to me. Lie on the desk, on your back," I demand.

He rolls himself onto the desk and faces the ceiling, his body starting to shake as he can sense Death licking his chops. Relax, Death. Go back to Mrs. Dunfield's house or my father's. Your odds are much better there.

I pin Robert's head down on his desk and grab the No. 2 pencil from my pocket — the same pencil I use to make measured cut marks on copper pipe. Yes, Mr. Heimlich's manoeuvre could have worked, but this way is far more interesting, and I haven't tried it yet on a human.

"Close your eyes, Robert."

With one strong jab, I puncture through the trachea with the pencil, below the vocal chords and thyroid cartilage. My fingers spin the pencil in the hole like a wooden dowel in an old-fashioned Christmas toy.

I've thrown the perfect strike, right between tracheal cartilages seven and eight. *Find a pen, fast.* From the floor, I find a plastic Bic pen and remove the blue ink tube and connecting ballpoint from inside the clear plastic casing. Robert's mind, I'm sure, has resigned itself to the fact that he will die on his own desk, at work, and not in the loving arms of his wife, but instead, with the local plumber stabbing him in the throat with a pencil while he chokes on the finest of ingredients.

Carefully, I remove the pencil from his trachea and, quickly, replace it with the hollow plastic pen tube. Very little bleeding so far. Good sign. *Wet your finger, Isaac.* Done. Gently, I push down on Robert's chest and force the last ccs of air out of his lungs and through the plastic tube. My wet finger senses the cool air on its tip, and I have successfully performed my first tracheotomy. *Congrats.* Thanks.

"Breathe, Robert. Breathe in."

He does. The sight of his chest expanding is one of the most rewarding to date. The look of gratitude softens his expression as he grabs my left arm with his hand. I saved your life, Robert Swanton.

"You're welcome," I say.

Rob Swanton's office door flies open to reveal Sarah Cliffton, circa 1990, standing in the frame, crying her eyes out. Crying, because I just broke up with her. The worst mistake I ever made.

Enough.

I'm out.

"No answer, huh. Wow. You weren't kidding," he says, swallowing the masticated bite of sandwich safely.

"I wasn't. No. I'm applying to Michigan."

"Okay. Great. That's fantastic. I assume you had Susan forward your transcript?"

"Yes, she said she would do that for me."

"And she will. She's great at her job. We're lucky to have her."

He meant that. I've found the one thing that trumps Susan's self-proclamation of excellence in her field — the same proclamation of her excellence from a peer.

"I just have a few questions on non-traditional students and what their application requirements are."

"Like?"

"Mainly the counselor and the core academic teacher recommendations."

"Right."

"Also, there was some stuff on the application that didn't seem to apply to me."

"Yeah, 'course there was. Was that frustrating for you?" he asks. I'm not here to talk about my feelings, asshole.

"I just need to know what's required, please," I say.

"And I really want to take a second to commend you on your bravery here. I think it is so special that you are taking this risk."

Don't need the pep rally. Just need the answers. You feel bad after having laughed at me, and I get that, but I'm past it. Much more disturbing is the one ingredient that I hadn't previously noticed in his sandwich: the raw red onion. This evil little ingredient is making his breath smell worse than old body odour. And here I sit. Captive. Tasting his apologetic tone. What is it with people who eat raw onions? Where is their social decency? I don't care how good it makes your food taste. I don't. The trail of social destruction over the course of one day just isn't worth it. I have more respect for people than to subject them to the unrelenting stink of onion. How does your wife put up with it? *Maybe she puts it in the sandwich? Maybe she is so well satisfied that she puts it in there to ward off the threat and possibility of her man going elsewhere?* You are a genius, Mrs. Swanton, and there is one good use for the raw onion after all: the anti-pheromone.

"Yes, thanks. I appreciate your support," I say. "So what's required?"

"Well, you don't need either of those recommendations you mentioned."

Thrilled.

I believe in the argument by design, so now is the time I should say, "Thank Designer" over the good news. *That sounds weird and will never catch on with the masses.* I like it a hell of a lot better than "Thank God." *I could give a shit if you like it, and you need to put the brakes on this religious bullshit if you are going to be a doctor.* Why? *Because no patient wants someone religious operating on them. Patients want doctors who study textbooks — not bibles, and who explore science — not their spirituality.* Stop. You're blowing this out of proportion.

"Yeah, and you're right … most of the application doesn't apply to you, but fill out what you can."

"I did that. Yes."

"You will need one reference letter, however."

Who the hell am I going to get to write that? *Ask Robert.* No, I'm sure there is a conflict of interest there. True. *You should ask Mrs. Dunfield, if only to get more out of cleaning up Albert's shit than an extra fifteen bucks.* Not a bad idea, but I don't trust her to do a good enough job, and I don't want it written in Olde English. This could be tough. *Isaac, everyone in town thinks you're a saint.* This will not be tough.

"Okay. I'll get that done. Thanks."

"And you don't need an SAT score, so you don't have to rush out and suffer through that."

"I took the SATs."

"When?"

"Two years ago."

"Why?" he asks.

I agree, Robert. Why would a plumber take the SATs unless he thought he would murder it? I'm sure the thought running through your head, Good Counselor, is that I flunked it miserably. That I seriously pooped the sheets.

"To see how I'd do," I say. "That's why I took it."

"How'd you do?"

"Ninetieth percentile."

"Je-s-us Mother and Mary," he trickles out.

I disagree, Robert. Jesus had nothing to do with it. I feel like the Jews got that one right. Jesus may have just been an enlightened messenger and not the son of the Designer. But if the Jews and I are wrong about Jesus, then I have no idea what the punishment for that is. The fact that I've been programmed to think that there is a punishment for thinking something is also wrong.

Robert rubs his face with his hands, trying to process the open-hand slap of information dealt. "That score of yours is good for three years, you know."

"Yeah, that's what they told me."

I know everything about the SAT. I even know which questions have been removed in the past years because of cultural bias or racial connotation. I know the national average, and I know how long the average person takes to complete the test, and I know that I'm in the ninetieth percentile.

"I'll tell you what, Plumb." He leans in.

"What's that?"

"I think you've got yourself a hell of a shot here."

After my visit to the high school, piping a new shower line, and installing two garburators, I arrive back on my doorstep fussing to find the right key. Gilby sits and waits patiently, staring into the seam where the door meets the frame. Anticipating the opening. I wish I had your patience, Gilby. If I were you, I would say, "Isaac, mark the proper key with a sticker or put it on its own fucking ring! We go through this idiotic scenario every day!" But I am not you, Gilby, and you would never say that to me or talk to me like that.

My hope is to learn patience.

No, your hope is that you don't turn into your father.

True.

The house smells like a Thanksgiving roast because of the frozen turkey stew I put in the crockpot this morning. This is wonderful. I love this smell of prepared food upon entry. Is this what married men come home to every day? This could force me to reconsider my cynical view of matrimony.

The flashing red light on my answering machine next to my home phone indicates a voicemail. No one ever calls me on that phone. They only call my cell. I'm not even sure why I have an answering machine hooked up to that touch-tone relic.

Press the button for messages.

Done.

"Hey, Plumb! Linda here. Well, I've done it! You have a date next Thursday night with the beautiful Miss Mandy Klein at seven p.m. sharp. I'm so excited! I'm just … well … I'm just pretty goddamn excited about all this, as you can tell. Oh, boy — I'm rambling. Ummm … the reservation is at the Precocious Sturgeon. Don't be mad at me. I know that place is fancy pants, but I know you can afford it, and Mandy mentioned at the last softball meeting that she'd never eaten there. Okay, well — that's a long message, so I'm gonna go now. I'll see you tomorrow, as usual. Bye, Plumb!"

This is real.

VII

November is flying by, like a car through a town without a stoplight, and the tail end of the month brings the first noticeably chilly air of the season. The lazy Indian summer must have enjoyed itself too much in Paradise and had been setting record temperatures late into fall. However, Paradise is partial to winter, and it was only a matter of time before the eviction notice was posted on the door of the tepid Fahrenheits. That sounds like the name of a rock band — the Tepid Fahrenheits. I should start a band. *You can't sing, Isaac, and you have more pressing issues at hand.* Fine, but when I'm a practising doctor, I will round up other practising doctors, and we will be a Guns n' Roses cover band called the Tepid Fahrenheits.

The first item on the "Pressing Issues" list has to be the writing of my required letter of reference. For being everybody's chum, everybody's pal in Paradise, I can't bring myself to ask anyone who lives here to write the letter. *Why?* Because if someone from Paradise writes the letter, the entire town will know in a matter of days that "Plumb" is applying to Michigan to become a doctor. Wouldn't *that* be the talk of the town.

The elimination process is a beautiful thing: If I don't want to ask anyone from Paradise to write the letter, then who do I know from outside Paradise? Graham McNamara would be a fine candidate. Graham McNamara is a lawyer who cottages in Paradise and, in my estimation, prefers the company of men. While trying to keep the van on the road, I leaf through my to-do list. Yes. There it is. Graham McNamara wants me to come and look at a leak in the crawl space of his cottage before he shuts down the place for the winter. Next week is too far away. I have to get my application in the mail next week. *What if you swung by his house right now? It's a Friday and he may have escaped the city for a long weekend.* Good call. The rest of the tasks for today are bullshit jobs that can wait. Besides, this is my future.

"Gilby, we are going to get ourselves a letter of reference."

Gilby doesn't seem to care. What am I going to do with Gilby if I get accepted? *Take him with you.* To Ann Arbor? *Why not?* Agreed. I have to, but he is a country dog who loves the open spaces and would hate the city. *Ann Arbor is not a city, it is a quaint college town of 114,000 residents, of which 36,000 are college students.* A town does not have over a hundred thousand people — that is a city. Paradise is a town. No, Paradise is a hamlet, a village, a whistle-stop, and my own personal hell.

It is decided. For Gilby's sake, I will rent a farmhouse outside of Ann Arbor and deal with a short commute. This solves the creepy dorm situation and also provides me a romantic getaway for dates, when the ladies want to escape the hustle of campus life and the concrete scenery. Thank you, Gilby. I think you just unknowingly scored me more tail. I scratch his head, and he turns and sniffs at me. I love you, pal.

Isaac, pay attention to the road and love the dog another time. You are too close to happiness to die. True.

Every year, tourists come from all parts of America to witness the natural beauty and purity of Paradise and Tahquamenon Falls State Park. I refer to the tourists as "terrorists" and can't wait until the last week in August when they pack up — only to return, like locusts, eight or nine months later. To be fair, some of them genuinely fall in love with the area, purchase a cottage and add to the diminutive population tally.

Graham McNamara bought his cottage five years ago, and it was five years ago when he first called me to replace his toilet and hot water heater. There's no way around it — Graham is stranger than a bull with tits. The part in his hair is against the grain, and his thick, dated, horn-rim glasses sit far too high on his proboscis of a nose. He's the only man I've ever seen to wear a dress shirt in the summer, buttoned all the way up to the top button — with no tie. He's never been married, and there hasn't been any mention of family. Ever. In fact, the only soul mate I've ever seen grace his side is his Alaskan husky, Tim. *And who names their dog "Tim?"* Agreed. The name is far too familiar. It's frequently used as a North American first name. It is the first name of my English teacher in ninth grade and the guy who owns the gas station, the local barber and Dad's second cousin, who thinks he gathers energy from semi-precious stones. The only people who name their pets with familiar first names are people who are lonely as all Christ. They need to come home every day and call out a normal-sounding name once they walk in the door, because entering and yelling, "I'm home, Fluffy!" mentally chips away at them, irreparably. As for pet names, obscure and uncommon first names are fine. Gilby is an example of that. Ganny is another fine example. But don't name your dog Sarah, Brian, Tom, Rob, Dave, Tom, Frank, Mary, Steve, Kate, Susan, Paul, Jenn, or Tim.

Graham definitely operates several lanes outside the normal social track. But he's harmless, and although we have nothing in common, I admire his talent and what he's sacrificed to make partner at one of the largest law firms in Detroit. *You always thought he was an uptight prick.* He is a bit of an uptight prick, but obviously, a talented one. *Who cares? Get him to write the letter of reference because he's an out-of-town lawyer who is sure to write eloquently.*

Here is the side road to his cottage.

Turn left.

Before I can shut the van off, Tim is dancing outside Gilby's window, and the two of them square off in an incoherent match of noisemaking. Obviously, Graham is here — likely in the bathroom combing his hair the wrong way.

"Gilby! Quiet!" I command. His barks instantly shift to Girl Scout-worthy bouts of whining, as Tim continues to twist and shout. Ringo would have been a better name for this noisy bastard.

"Good boy, buddy. I'll be back in a minute. Promise," I say, opening the glove box and fishing out a dog treat to reward his behaviour.

The cheese-flavoured treat is tossed gently in the air for Gilby, who snatches it like Tigers centrefielder Chet Lemon. Lemon, who unarguably made the difference in the Tigers winning the World Series in 1984 but who also, unfairly, lost the title of series MVP to teammate Alan Trammell. In that year, there was not a baseball game, there was not a practice or a game of catch where I didn't make it very clear that I was Chet Lemon and I was playing centre. If my childhood dream was to play catch with all-star Chet Lemon, my adult dream is to have been present in the operating room at the University of Michigan, December 1990, performing the surgery that removed his enlarged and diseased spleen due to polycythemia. *No, your adult dream cannot be something that has already taken place. You can't dream backward, that's counterproductive and living in the past.* Fair point. Fine. In the future, I dream to have the opportunity to save the life of a famous Detroit Tiger. *Much better.* I hope Gary Sheffield drops with appendicitis twelve years from now so I can cut into him and remove his sick and irrelevant organ. You won't even know it's gone, Mr. Sheffield. You are safer without it, given the appendix's ability to cause death via infection, and I promise no immunological or gastrointestinal handicap, post-removal.

Upon exiting the van, Tim is all over me. Standing on his hind legs with his paws on my chest, the animal stands almost as tall as I do. How in the hell do you house this beast in your downtown Detroit condo, Graham? That's like lodging a pet Beluga in a red wine glass. *No, that's not a great example, but the sentiment was there.* Whatever. Tim needs to chill out because he is displaying bad manners for a canine. Gilby would never misbehave like this.

"Isaac! You're a few days early!" shouts Graham, exiting the screen door.

"I know. I was in the area," I say, lying through my teeth.

"Sorry about Tim. He's just happy to see you."

"It's fine. Gilby does the same thing when he gets excited."

That's not true. Another lie. You just sold out and betrayed your best friend like Judas, Isaac. No letter of reference is worth that. *Be yourself. You don't need to kiss this guy's ass to get what you need. Have some self-respect.*

Graham snaps his fingers twice, and Tim drops from me, immediately, and sits. Nicely done, Graham.

"I hope it's not a bad time?"

"Nope. The Tim-ster and I were just putting the storm windows up for the winter. Isn't that right, Timmy?"

Really, Graham? Was Tim helping you with the windows? Did you hold the nail while Tim hammered? Or did Tim hold the nail? Or did you put up the storm windows while Tim sniffed your ass, tracking the scent of another man? *That last comment was uncalled for.* True. This is not the time to debate Graham's sexuality, despite some of the circumstantial evidence I've collected over the years. Like his taste in music and movies. The amount of ingredients in his cupboards. The monogrammed gloves he wears to garden. The fact that he's been single as long as I've known him. The obvious eyebrow waxing, fingernail buffing, and androgynous scent.

None of it counts. None of it matters.

The only thing that would make Graham gay is if he prefers guys. That's it. He could stand limp-wristed, dressed head to toe in carnation pink, belting out show tunes, but if he loves women, then that just makes him unique, not gay. I should check his browser history. That would solve it. That makes it simple. The tell-all for sexual preference: Does he google for nude women or nude men? *Who really cares?* Agreed.

"That's great," I say. "The two of you must've had those windows up in no time."

"Oh, yeah. We're a good team."

I bet you are. *Go to the dog treat now, Isaac.*

"Hey, Tim ... you want a treat, Buddy?" I ask, presenting the cheesy dog treat open-palmed.

Tim comes over and devours the tiny treat like it was a single-calorie breath mint. My hand is wet now.

"Oh, he loves that! Yes, you do, Tim! Thank you, Isaac. Say, 'Thank you' to Isaac, Tim."

I hate when dog owners ask their dog to speak English. Yeah, I get it — it's cute when they're instructed to say something and then they bark and everyone is impressed and laughs. Worse is when they don't speak, and then the dog and owner look ridiculous. In this case, both are looking very ridiculous.

"Well ... I guess he hasn't learned those particular words yet," Graham belts out with laughter.

Laugh with him, Isaac. Pretend it is funny. I can't. He's already annoying me.

I force a thin chuckle.

—»—

We both stand cross-armed beside the rust-coloured board and batten siding of the cottage. Cottages on Lake Superior are like cottages around any of the Great Lakes. They are predominantly built on sand and have no basements. Instead, they sit on top of the sand, raised by concrete blocks, stacked two or three high. There is always enough space to crawl underneath and do the plumbing — but never enough space to do it comfortably. This particular shack is only stacked two concrete bricks high, so it will be a tight squeeze and a pain in the ass if I have to crawl in deep and drag the torch and tools with me.

"So, here's the issue, Isaac … in August, I noticed that the water pressure wasn't all that great to the kitchen sink."

"Okay."

"And I looked under the crawl space two weekends ago when I called you, because I noticed a dripping."

"Okay."

"Dripping from one of the pipes, and I wasn't sure if it was condensation or if one of these old pipes was leaking."

"Is it right under here?"

"Yes. Right under there about two feet or so. Not far at all."

"And you only notice the pressure change in the kitchen taps? Nowhere else?"

"Right. Nowhere else. Correct."

"Okay."

"It's not the biggest deal. I just want it taken care of before I board the place up for the winter. You know?"

"Yeah, I get that. Completely."

"Or before it turns in to something bigger."

"True. Okay. Let me get my flashlight from the van, and I'm going to take a look under there and see what's going on."

"Here's a flashlight right here," he offers.

I like mine better. Yours is generic, Graham. *Don't be a tool snob. Take his flashlight and allow him to feel like he is contributing.*

"That looks perfect. Thanks, Graham."

This "thing" should not fall in to the flashlight category. It should be mounted on a lighthouse and spun to signal commercial fishing vessels. I want to smash it. I want to smash it on the ground and get my own light.

The all-too-familiar position of being on all fours in a crawl space hurts more and more each time. The sound of tiny pops, cracks, and bone-on-bone rubbing echoes through my body as I assume the position once again. A sharp pebble digs into my patellar tendon, which hurts like shit, and the sparse grass lining the edge of the cottage smells like dog piss. Tim must lift his leg around this area. He likely pissed here this morning.

I hate my job.

I am halfway in and halfway out of the crawl space, and I hope that my belt is tight enough or else Graham is getting a box-seat view of my crack, and that would make me uncomfortable.

I turn on the beacon of a flashlight and angle it upward, illuminating the hung plumbing system, piped efficiently underneath the cottage floor.

"Is it the pressure on the hot water or cold?" I yell.

If he says both, I'll know he's full of shit. Maybe not. Maybe the faucet is the issue and the screen needs cleaning. That would be too good to be true.

"Just the cold, actually!" he yells back.

Good. That rules out a hot water line issue, which would have meant draining the twenty-gallon hot water heater, situated smack dab in the centre of the crawl space, and I don't feel like dragging tools today.

"Graham, can you go inside and turn on the cold water tap in the kitchen?" I yell.

"Yup! Just a sec!"

"Thanks!" I yell.

The screen door opens, and Graham enters the cottage, exhaustively wiping his shoes on the mat. I'm under your cottage on all fours, Graham. Take your time and make sure your shoes are immaculate while I rot under here. Tim sniffs around my boots. You smell Gilby, Tim — that's who you smell — now piss off.

The sound of the kitchen tap running influences the water pump to kick in. That's a good sign. The same sharp stone is still digging into my patellar tendon, causing micro-damage. That area will ache for the rest of the day, I bet. The position I'm in is awkward, and the edge of the cottage is catching me sharply on one of my thoracic vertebrae.

Leak?

There it is.

I spot the steady dripping with the lighthouse beacon, but where's the water coming from? It looks like the elbow joint in the pipe leading up to the kitchen, but that wouldn't cause a noticeable change in water pressure. So, what is it?

This is Mystery, Alaska.

This is Area 51.

This is the Florida vote count.

This is the Kennedy assassination, and this is going to be disastrous if I can't figure out what's going on and then have to ask him for a letter of reference. My body floods with a flash of heated blood, inspiring a heart rate increase. I'm sweating. Calm down. *Focus.*

The drip is not coming from the joint. It seems to be coming out of the hole where the hot and cold water pipes run up into the floor of the cottage near the elbow joint. Once the pipes pass through the floor they emerge behind a wall and run vertically until they reach another ninety-degree elbow joint, sending the water through the drywall to the final destination: the taps.

The rubbing edge of the cottage has lifted my jacket and sweatshirt and I can feel Tim's cold nose sniffing at the exposed skin, mid-rib cage. Tim, I will filet you and ship your butchered meat to Vietnam, where they will throw you in a hot pan, add veggies and stir-fry the shit out of you — if you don't disappear immediately.

The leak is hidden inside the wall, at the elbow joint, which means tearing into the drywall to fix it. Graham won't like that. *It is too late in the season to be doing jobs like that.* Good point. *Suggest that he bleed the water lines, shut down the cottage for winter and save that task for the spring when a carpenter can come in and fix the wall the same day.* Agreed.

Have him turn the water on and off again, just to make sure.

"Graham!"

"Yes!"

"Turn the cold tap off for a second please!" I yell.

He obliges. The fast-paced trickle responds by slowing back to its chronic drip. Good. That was the predictable reaction given my diagnosis. Have him turn the tap back on now.

A significant and foreign weight has just been placed on my back. My core muscles tense to support it. Something is scratching at my stomach.

I lower my head and flip the light around to spot two giant paws crossed over each other, digging, violently, into my stomach.

This is not right.

Now, and only now, has the pounding sensation kicked in from behind.

Jesus Christ. I'm getting fucked by Tim.

Get up.

The recruitment of every fast-twitch muscle fibre in my body propels my torso forward, and the full genetic potential of my action introduces the back of my head to the old cast iron sewage pipe a foot above me. The matte thud of the impact sends my face in the opposite direction, like a baseball launching from a bat.

The kind of ball Chet Lemon would hit.

Lost vision.

Face hits the dirt.

Losing consciousness.

"Isaac! Hey! What's going on? Are you down there?"

The words grow faintly in volume, like increasing the digital numbers with the TV remote.

"Should I turn it back on for you?" yells the voice.

My eyes open but my vision is still fuzzy.

My face is in the dirt, open-mouthed and drooling.

I close my mouth and try to calculate what's going on. There is dirt in my mouth now, and it is grinding between my teeth.

I shift my head to look behind me using the one eye that isn't still in the soil. The image I see is first received by the lens, which condenses the information for the retina, who relays the image to the optic nerve, which translates and channels the most horrifying image my brain has ever processed.

My ass is in the air and my face is in the dirt and Tim is, in fact, pounding me without remorse. Given my current position, he can now reach me with his snout and hot dog breath billows up against the back of my neck. All my open eye can see is Tim's narrow dog hips mechanically grinding his pink thing into my denim.

I wish this was a daydream I could pull out of. *Really? Do you want to be daydreaming this?* I would be completely certifiable if I were daydreaming this. Much better that this is not a daydream but still horrific that it is happening.

How long have I been unconscious? How long has this violation been left unsupervised? *Isaac, you need to stand up. You need to get the husky off you.*

With my right hand, I reach down to the crossed paws and pry one of them from my stomach.

Success.

With my right leg, I bring it forward and kick back hard against Tim's hind leg. Tim squeals intensely and I feel his weight lift from my back.

Success.

I'm glad you squealed, you rapist — you sick, guiltless bastard! What kind of animal dry-humps people who are unconscious? I would've kicked you harder, Tim, had I been able to find more leverage. I hope that kick triggers hip dysplasia and you die from lethal injection.

Pushing back with my hands, I wiggle my way out from under the edge of the crawl space and stand on my own two feet again. Visibly shaken.

"I don't know what gets into him," says Graham, standing with his arms crossed and shaking his head, just a few feet from the scene of the crime. Graham? How long have you been standing there?

"He just gets out in this fresh country air and becomes another person."

Forget my hands and feet — my entire body is numb. My jaw clenches so hard, the masseter muscles are almost at failure. How long was he standing there — accomplice to the perpetrator? Where was the two-snap obedience routine I saw earlier? Where was that trick, Graham, when the molestation was taking place?!

"You okay, Isaac?" he asks.

Graham, I am not okay! I am fucking pissed. *Bottle it, Isaac. You need this dog-porn trainer of a lawyer to write your reference letter. Keep a level head.* How can I do that? How can I keep a level head? It's ringing and I may have a low-grade concussion.

"I'm fine. Yeah. I really hit my head, though."

"Do you need some ice?" he asks. No, I need therapy to combat the post-traumatic stress disorder.

"No, I'm fine. Really."

"Good. So, what's the issue with the leak?"

Graham, give me a minute here. *No, you give him the diagnosis now. He asked for it, and you have to keep your eye on the prize. Think — customer service.* Right, but customer service should never include servicing his husky.

"Yeah. Ummm. The leak is in the elbow joint behind the taps in the wall."

"Oh, no."

"Yeah, it's a big job."

"It sure is. Can you fix it today?"

"I can. But, it means tearing the wall out to get at it."

"Oh."

"Look. Here's my two cents. I say bleed the pipes and shut the place down for winter, like normal, and we take care of this first thing next spring."

"Really?"

"That way we can get a carpenter in here to fix the wall the same day I solder a new elbow in there and it's a done deal. There's no reason to go to all that trouble right now — in my opinion."

"Well, I guess that makes sense. Yes. We'll get at that first thing in May."

"Sounds like a plan."

"Thank you for coming over. It means a lot."

Now is my chance. Ask. The time is right. *He is happy with your work and primed. If you don't ask now, you won't get the application in on schedule and will have been dry-humped for nothing.*

"Graham, I've got a favour I need to ask."

"Sure. What's up?" he says.

He has no idea what's coming. Should I ease into it? Just get it out. Rip the band-aid off.

"Could you write a letter of reference for me, please?"

"Ummm. Sure, I'd be happy to. For what?"

"My application to the University of Michigan."

There. It's out. *You sounded nervous.* My hands are shaking. I am nervous, and still in shock. *Put your hands in your pockets, so he can't see them shake.* Good idea. Now, I wait.

"Seriously?" he chuckles.

"Yeah, seriously."

"Wow. That's amazing. Yes, of course. I'd be happy to."

Touchdown.

This is huge. This is the turning point.

How can Michigan not accept me with a letter of reference from a partner of a law firm? Another step up the ladder to my dream. Another integral piece of the M.D. puzzle.

"That would be wonderful. Thank you," I say. My voice just trembled. *Do not cry! Stop it! Don't cry! Focus.*

"When do you need it by?" he asks. Right now, please. Seriously, I'll wait in the van. I'll wait all day.

"By Sunday would be best. Sorry for the late notice."

"I can do Sunday. It'll be in the mailbox."

"Thanks again."

"And good luck. I'm proud of you," he says and swats the side of my arm. That awkward swat is the most masculine thing I've ever seen him do. "What are you going to study?"

"Pre-med."

"Amazing. But not surprising, given how gifted you are with plumbing."

"I'm sorry?"

"The plumbing of a house must be like the veins and digestive tract, right? The pillars and boards are like the skeleton and the siding and roof is like the skin."

"Yeah, that's true. Never thought of it like that."

"As long as I've known you, you've had the gift to be able to take all of those systems into account and solve the problem. I think medicine will be quite simple for you, actually."

I open the door to the plumbing van and get in, releasing a huge sigh of relief. Gilby looks at me, as if to ask, "Did he agree to it?"

At that moment came laughter. Real laughter. It feels good to laugh. This is the most ridiculous story, and I have no one close enough to tell it to. What good is a story about getting dry-humped from behind by an Alaskan husky named Tim while lying unconscious with my face in the dirt if I have no one to tell it to?

That is sad.

Someday, I will tell someone this story. Someday, someone will laugh with me. Someday, this story will cause someone to cry with laugher and rid them of stored ACTH, which will make them healthier, I think.

VIII

The funny thing about getting ready for a date is that, despite how badly I want Mandy Klein to be a respectable lady, I'm still standing in front of a mirror, naked, trimming myself in preparation. I usually keep the one-eighth guard on to ensure safety and an even buzz, but today the plastic guard is off, and I'm doing the detailed work around the base of the shaft.

This is important.

Yeah, because it makes you look bigger. Am I creating an optical illusion? Is this nothing but smoke and mirrors? If cavemen could see us now, they would laugh at how diligently we groom for the opposite sex. Maybe their way was better: smelly, raw, wild, and without conversation. *That's still available, you just have to pay for it now.* True.

I wonder if Mandy waxes? I should trim my chest and stomach hair, too. *Why?* Again, I'm trimming up just in case. *Isaac, you always have the opportunity to say no to sex if she proposes it.* No, I can't. *Yes you can. What might happen if you were to make HER wait, huh?* She would think I was gay. Women are too deep-rooted into being in control when it comes to dictating sex. So deep-rooted, the only way to process a refusal is to instantly slot the man into the "latent" category. *I disagree.* Many, upon shoot-down, would feel self-conscious and wonder what was wrong with them. "What did he see that turned him off?" they would ask. "What did I say to make him not want me?" "Am I not pretty enough for him?" "Am I too fat?"

The questioning would be endless.

Let's try making Mandy wait, regardless of her advances. What? No. Yes. Think. *That could shift the power so far to your side that YOU would then be in control of sex, and all aspects of it. Now YOU could dictate when and where it happened and in which position.* True. That could work, but the power scale should never be that lopsided. Relationships can't operate like that. That's like trying to play seesaw with the fat kid at recess. It just don't work.

I would be a sex-Führer.

A sexual despot. A sex-pot.

There has to be a happy medium. This is all bullshit, because I don't really want a relationship because I am going away to school soon, probably. *Fine. But let it be groundwork for the future.*

The current conversation has distracted me. I have not been paying close enough attention, and the sawing teeth of the hair clippers chew deep into the soft skin of my ball sack. So deep that that skin of my scrotum stalls the motor and the clippers come to an abrupt halt. *You're going to need stitches!* I'm aware. *Why didn't you just leave the guard on? How do you explain this to the doctor on call?* I'm not going to the hospital. I can stitch. I stitched up Mr. Buck's new heart. I can do this. This is no big deal. *This is a big deal!*

Blood runs freely all over my hand and clippers. The teeth of the clippers are so deeply embedded that trying to pull them out only yanks and extends the damaged sac skin. It looks like I'm trying to pull bubblegum off the bottom of a shoe — except it's mixed with blood. *You could get a serious infection here, and the infection could easily spread to the testes, and then there would be no chance of kids.* Have I done it? Have I performed a home-vasectomy? Have I clipped the vas deferens? No, the wound is too superficial, but it feels like some serious damage has been done. *Isaac, go to the hospital immediately.* I can't. It would be the talk of the town. It would make the paper. "Plumber cuts his balls off with hair trimmer," it would read. *Doctors take an oath — they can't tell anyone.* Right, but the nurses would. They gossip like old grandmothers in a knitting circle. How could I be so careless? *You have to cancel the date with Mandy.* There is no other option.

Enough.

I'm out.

That was unpleasantly realistic and would have been a disaster. I turn the clippers off, without delay, and proceed to clean out the hair collected in the stainless steel teeth with a toothbrush. A toothbrush I've designated for this task, and this task only.

Fingernails. Reasonable.

Toenails. Same.

Eyebrows no longer have random, freestanding tree branches growing out of them.

The vanity lamps that line the edges of my bathroom mirror are viciously unforgiving. Where did all of these tiny lines around my eyes and mouth come from? Do I smile that much? If I do, then it's from the act I put on for my clients, making these laugh lines superficial and phony. Botox could fix that, blocking nerve function and inducing musculoskeletal paralysis, but who wants to inject botulism into their face? Botulism is a deadly bioweapon and should be illegal to cultivate for cosmetic means. Inhaling a billionth of an ounce causes death in twenty-four hours. I refuse to partake in the superficial use of it, making my hands clean when terrorists get a hold of it and scream "Jihad" once again. The cowards.

My only hope is to find true happiness in the future and wear the laugh lines a little deeper with honesty.

The space between hair follicles on my head is increasing by the day. Each remaining hair is losing a neighbour far too frequently due to the tenacious guerilla force that is androgenic alopecia. Each remaining hair wondering when its time is up. Wondering when its associate sebaceous gland will have pumped too much dihydrotestosterone, inspiring the process of follicular miniaturization. When comes the time where I just buzz it all off? I'm sure that people notice it, despite my best effort to style my hair in a current fashion that isn't a comb-over. But buzzing it to the length that I just trimmed myself is evidence to the world that I've come to grips with my male-pattern issue and have done something about it. Evidence that I'm not afraid of it any longer. Could it be that buzzing my head is the pride-swallowing equivalent to Linda buying jeans that actually fit her?

Perspective has now punched me in the face.

I understand your issue, Linda. I feel your pain.

Our respective questions are: How much longer can we fake it? How much longer before it becomes embarrassing? Linda, are the two of us so superficial that we can't deal with our issues and maintain confidence in the process?

Isaac, your hair is not who you are.

Look at yourself in the mirror.

I am an intelligent and talented man. My hair is not who I am, nor does it define me. I refuse to inch any closer to a comb-over.

I will take the first step, Linda. I will pave the way.

With this, I attach the one-eighth clipper guard, reintroduce electricity to the buzzing blades and mow an even path down the centre of my head. Hair falls into the sink in clumps.

I feel good about this. This is all part of the new me.

—»—

The defiant act against my ego is over, and I now sport a buzz-cut. Sadly, this has only increased the appearance of thinning hair, but I have taken a step in the right direction. No looking back.

Shampoo is splooged onto my hand, and I apply it to my newly shorn hair. What a wild feeling this is. This is amazing.

My new look is going to shock Mandy Klein. She may hate it. This is not what she signed up for. I wish I was going out with Goth Princess from the smoking section instead.

I wonder what she's doing right now?

She could be in the shower, too. She could be washing her perfect Goth body.

She could be thinking of me and washing her perfect Goth body.

...

I should not have masturbated in the shower before the date.

That was the wrong thing to do. I am less turned on now, and all I want to do is rent a movie and sleep. *Turn around, then. Call her from your cell and tell her that you aren't feeling well.* No, I'm halfway to her house.

I should really buy a second vehicle, because I'm getting pretty sick of picking up dates in the plumbing van. It smells like tools, and Gilby and I hate having to vacuum all of his hair off the passenger seat so as not to turn a sexy black dress into an exotic fur. No second vehicle. I should save my money for college. *Excuse me? Are you taking the plumbing van to college with you?* That is a hell of a good point. I can't. It wouldn't be right. I can get away with it in Paradise, but not in Ann Arbor. I would be the "non-traditional" creep who drives a plumbing van to class. It's settled. I'm buying a new truck next fall for my first semester of freshman year. *You shouldn't talk like that, Isaac. You are setting yourself up for serious letdown if you don't get in.* How could I not get in? I have so much going for me.

My life experience.

My SAT score.

Graham McNamara wrote the most beautiful letter of reference I could've ever imagined. It was perfect. It was well-written, and he printed it off on his law firm's letterhead.

He called me an inspiration.

He said that I was one of the most talented people he had ever met.

He predicted that I would be one of the foremost physicians Michigan has ever seen. Most importantly, his letter was on time, as promised, in the mailbox last Sunday. Let's go over it one more time.

Application checklist:

Application form — done.

Signatures — done.

Check made out to U of M — done.

Letter of reference — done.

High school transcript forwarded — done.

Essay question one — done.

Essay question two — done.

Essay question three — not done.

More than anything, I want to rush home and complete essay question three: "Describe a setback that you have faced. How did you resolve it? How did the outcome affect you? If something similar happened in the future, how would you react?"

This is the question I have chosen. It was between this or: "Tell us about a book you have read and you found especially challenging, inspiring or provocative." But writing an essay on

Gray's Anatomy of the Human Body seemed boring and self-indulgent, considering it's a textbook.

I will write on the setback that changed my life and how it affected me. It will start with the day my father, while helping our family friend build the foundation to his new house, jumped off the back of a pickup truck with a bag of cement in his arms and crushed T12 and L1 together so forcefully that the vertebrae splintered into each other. The disc between them exploded, leaving my father a twitching mess for months. It was a miracle he could ever walk again. One thing was for sure — he would never work again. Without income and without disability insurance, the burden was placed on me, and all of a sudden, I was no longer holding the light and fetching tools on weekends — I was the face of Sullivan Plumbing.

I was the ringer.

I was the designated hitter, and my hard-earned dollars paid the mortgage, paid for us to eat, and paid for his ongoing physical therapy bills. This went on for ten years. Then another five, but he had moved out on his own by then. Then another three, as a complaining alcoholic. Which brings us to now. Those are the eighteen years that I have resented the shit out of him for being so careless. When the disc in his back was crushed, so were my dreams of college. My essay will be the tale of how youthful excitement met reality and turned to resentment, sinking to despondency and capitulation, and what it took for a plumber from Paradise to apply for college in his thirties.

An emotional rollercoaster, eighteen years in the making, and it will blow the socks off Admissions.

The light of the restaurant allows me to get a good look at Mandy as she sits across from me reading the menu. It was dark by the time I finally reached her house, and the van lights are oddly placed and dodgy. Dim and yellowish. Not to be trusted when making superficial judgment calls. They make everyone appear under-lit and jaundiced, and jaundice is the yellowing of the skin, eyes, or other mucous membranes due to increased levels of bilirubin in the blood, and although not a disease (in and of itself), it can provide insight into compromised physiological processes that are involved in the metabolism of bilirubin. Most notably, liver function in babies. *Nice one. Thanks.*

The Precocious Sturgeon isn't very busy tonight. How could it be busy? The prices are atrocious. Mandy, don't clam up and order a salad, but if you order surf n' turf, we're going Dutch on the bill. That's only fair. This is a first date that was set up by a mutual acquaintance, and I shouldn't have to pay for the whole thing if she goes crazy with the ordering. *She doesn't have the kind of money you do. You will pay, regardless of what she orders.*

I hate that.

I've met Mandy Klein before, a few years ago, but this is like meeting her for the first time. The bone structure of her face is incredibly symmetrical. High cheekbones. Plump, luscious lips. Mandy Klein is hot for a softball player. *She's not hot, she's beautiful.* She's "girl-next-door-with-a-gargoyle-on-her-lawn" beautiful.

A cute little brown mole, the size of a pencil eraser, sits atop her left eyebrow, but what amazes me is how meticulously she tweezes the tiny hairs around it. That is key, because if the mole was allowed to meld its own thicker and longer mole hairs into the rest of the eyebrow, it would be an ugly mole. Instead, she has made it a beautiful one. *She could have it removed quite easily. A shot of Novocain, straight down the centre of it, followed by scalpel excision.* That would leave a scar. She wouldn't like that. Pirates have scars. *Yes, but so do softball players.*

Her beautiful neck meets two perfect clavicle bones, which are visible and pressing out against her taut skin. Mandy Klein, you are in shape, but let's hope you aren't shaped like a pear. I haven't had a good look at her southern hemisphere. She's wearing black pants, so that's not a good sign. The pear shape is a physiological phenomenon I cannot understand. Simply, the hips, ass, and thighs store more fat than the upper body, but on a cellular level, what dictates that? *Genetics?* Maybe. But that shape is much less appealing to the eye and should be selected against. How has the pear shape slipped through Darwin's theory? Answer: There are too many people on the planet, and there is someone for everyone. Truth: Some men must love the pear shape. They must think it's beautiful. It is very fertile-looking. I have no question at all that she could easily give birth. Maybe the hammer just hit the nail on the head.

"It all looks good. Doesn't it?" she asks, looking up from the artistic menu. Mandy Klein, your teeth are perfect. They look whitened? Did you whiten your teeth for our date? Professionally or a home kit? My teeth are not that white.

"It does look good. Yes. I have no idea where to start."

"Are you getting an appetizer?"

"Umm. Yeah, I think so."

"Maybe we could split one?"

Frugal, Mandy Klein, and a team player. I like it.

"That sounds great. I'll leave the choice to you," I say.

"Really? Pressure!" she says, flustered, flashing her perfect smile.

A dimple is spotted on her left cheek. That is adorable and rare. The bi-lateral dimple is far more common, but not necessarily cuter. Anatomically, dimples are caused by variations in the structure of the facial muscle known as zygomaticus major. The variation being the presence of a double or bifid zygomaticus major muscle dividing on its anterior path, into a superior bundle, landing at the same attachment on the mandible. Thus, the act of smiling magnifies the divide in the muscle, causing the dimple. Bet you didn't know that, Mandy. *You should explain that to her.* No.

"Let's go with the Lake Superior Seared Pink Salmon on Arugula."

"Sounds perfect."

Twenty-one dollar appetizer. Come on, Mandy. *Look at the menu, all of the apps are that much money, which is why she suggested sharing.* Relax. Initiate conversation. *All you've done is look at the menu and scrutinize her face.*

"So, tell me about … what you … umm … do," I say. That was brutal. *She should walk out on you right now for that pathetic stammering.*

"What I do, when?"

"For work."

"It's funny how that's always the first question," she says, almost laughing and almost disappointed. Of course it is, Mandy. What you do says a lot about who you are. "It's like what I do somehow defines who I am," she says.

"Doesn't it?"

"No. It doesn't!"

Looks like someone is ashamed of what she does. Typically, I would let this go, but with the buzzed head and application almost ready for submission, I am in the sporting mood.

"How's that?" I say, hitting the ball back into her court.

"What you do for a living reflects how you make money."

"True."

"That's it. It's how you pay your bills. How you survive. It's what you do outside of work that counts."

Not a bad point, Mandy. Duly noted. However, today, I am playing advocate for the devil.

"Right, but we spend eight or nine hours a day at work. So to me, someone's profession tells me a lot. It's how you spend the majority of your day, and how you contribute to the world. And passionately, one would assume."

"Take our mutual friend, Linda," she begins. "Linda has no education to speak of, and she works at CoffeeBuddy eight hours a day, providing hot coffee and doughnuts to people like yourself. After work, Linda volunteers for a dozen different charities and is busy within the community every night of the week."

Mandy, don't you think it would have been funnier if Linda volunteered for a baker's dozen worth of charities? *Don't say that out loud.* Agreed.

"Linda is great. Yes. I'm just saying …"

"She has a huge heart, and isn't that all that matters?" she asks.

Mandy, don't interrupt me. Linda has a huge heart. Yes. But working at a coffee shop at forty-five still tells me a lot about her. Her income. Her level of education. How determined she is. Is she a dreamer? Does she want to leave her mark on history or is she content to lend a hand when possible? Is she an alpha or a beta? Is she artistic or mathematical or neither? Does she run her own business or is she happy to receive minimum wage and two weeks' vacation?

Something tells me that if I voice this list of examples, the date will end prematurely.

"She has a huge heart. No question. That wasn't what I was …"

"She sure does have a big heart, and she's a hell of a first baseman."

Again with the interruption, Mandy. Not a good sign. Who cares how good of a first baseman she is? I don't. All that tells me is that she can catch a ball and has competent hand-eye coordination. For such a good start, I really opened up a can of worms here.

"Yes. I see that she wins awards in the paper every year," I say.

"Where's our waiter? We've been here for ten minutes and no sign of a waiter. They haven't even taken our drink order yet," she points out, looking around the restaurant — clearly agitated.

What's the rush, Mandy? This isn't Norma's Diner. They let you take your time here.

"I'm sure they'll come soon."

"I hope so, I'm starving."

That's not a good sign. That lends itself to ordering one of the bigger and more expensive entrées. *Tell her that she can order whatever she likes and that it's on you. That will make her relax.*

"So, whether or not it means anything, what do you do in Paradise? I'm interested," I say.

You couldn't let it go, could you? No. Mandy darts a stare from across the table as if being jabbed with a cattle prod. She looks back down at the menu, and her eyes now land on the expensive side. Serves me right.

"I'm currently unemployed."

Looks like going Dutch on the bill is out of the equation. This admittance of unemployment has changed her body language. She is now slouching. Her eyelids are hanging lower than before. Is she aware of this?

"I get alimony from my first husband," she adds. Interesting. Is there more than one ex-husband, fair maiden? "You might as well get to know all the dirt up front."

The tone of resignation in her voice rings with such contrast to her initial character that two Mandy Kleins are clearly distinguishable. Which one is the real Mandy Klein? The adorable and giddy schoolgirl out on a first date, or this worn and tired stable mare — sick of having to re-tell her life story to potential suitors? This Mandy Klein is loaded with baggage, but I have to make the best of this.

"I'm not here to judge, Mandy. Just looking for good conversation and a great meal," I say. And I mean that.

The frustration lines on her face soften. Her brow relaxes. Her posture changes. The tension in her beautiful neck relaxes and the adorable smile appears once again.

"That's good. Yeah. Me too. That sounds really good," reaching across the table to lay her hand on mine.

That's a signal. She likes you, for sure. The invisible plane of personal space has been broken. No Man's Land has been crossed. She has relaxed enough to make contact. That's almost like a first kiss. *You have defused the bomb in time and saved the date. Well done, Isaac. Thanks.*

"So what's new with you?" she asks, while reviewing the menu once again.

You know the menu by now, sweetheart. Are you trying to memorize it? What's new with me happens to be the two biggest skeletons ever to occupy my closet: the application to the University of Michigan for next fall, and the fact that I got fucked by a giant husky named Tim.

"Same old," I reply. Lying.

"I hear you."

Let's not make this a pity party, please. Ask her something else and something less controversial than what she does for income.

"If you'll excuse me. I have to go to the ladies room to tinkle. If the waiter comes, can you order me a glass of Chardonnay, please?" she asks.

"For sure. Yes. Take your time."

What? "Tinkle?" *It means pee. She has to pee. It has to mean pee.* Of course it does. "Tinkle" is an onomatopoeia, the sound of the word reflecting what it describes. *Are you sure that tinkle is an onomatopoeia?* No.

Here is the moment of truth: to be a pear, or not? Mandy collects her silver sequin purse, slung on the back of the chair and stands up, ready to depart.

"Be right back. I must've had too much water after my jog this afternoon."

Mandy, I hope you didn't overhydrate. I hope you don't have water intoxication, because if you have water intoxication, then you have diluted the electrolyte content in the extra-cellular fluid that surrounds every cell in your body. If you have done that, Mandy, then you are risking brain damage, digestive and kidney failure and, in extreme cases, death. *Tell her that.* No. She seems fine. There are no telltale signs of light-headedness, drowsiness, or disorientation, but I wouldn't rule out confusion. *That's mean.* She's fine, and pretty soon she is going to be showcasing her figure down the catwalk to the bathroom.

I smile back at her.

Here comes the pivot.

And turn.

Ass and legs, now in full view.

The width of her pelvic girdle and iliac crest markers are well-proportioned to her height, and more importantly, the length of her femur. Her walking cadence is nice, and nothing is jiggling or swaying unnecessarily. She is definitely not a pear, but the fact that I can see light between her thighs tells me that there could be a child or two we haven't discussed yet. Perhaps that is the *conversation du jour.* Who cares? She's beautiful. And the thought of a woman with kids — a woman who has more important things to worry about than me — has always been attractive. How do I find out for sure? How to bring up the topic of kids without sending her off the deep end again? I certainly can't say, "From the comprehensive analysis of your cadence, it seems that, during childbirth, your pubic symphysis ligament was severed and, postpartum, your pubic bones never really made it back to square one." No. Can't say that. That's not even fair to say. *Mandy is smarter than you think.* I think this menu is expensive, and how can a Sturgeon be all that Precocious? I should find something moderately priced and recommend it to Mandy.

"What's with the buzz cut?" asks a familiar voice.

The voice of an angel.

The kind of perfect voice that should be doing soap ads on TV.

I look up from the leather-bound menu, and to my right stands the most beautiful creature I have ever seen, dressed in a pressed white dress shirt, black tie, fitted black dress pants, and heels.

You have got to be kidding me.

Goth Princess.

Her transformation would leave even a butterfly jealous of the metamorphosis. She has cleaned up so impeccably. The only remains of her former Gothic self is the tiny hole in her lip that typically houses a ring.

The look on her face tells me that she is enjoying my confusion. My wonderment.

"No answer?" she prompts.

"No. Yeah. I buzzed it this afternoon," I say, rubbing the top of my head. *Why did you just rub your head? She knows where your head is.*

"Good thing. Best to get rid of it before the onset of comb-over."

"My thinking exactly." I wonder how she thinks it looks. "How does it look?"

"Sexy."

"Sexy? It looks sexy?"

"Yeah. It suits you."

"You don't think it makes it look worse?"

"No. Me telling you that I thought it looked sexy and suited you should have put that to bed."

"True. Good point," I say, smiling. A real smile. Goth Princess, your charm is more bountiful than before. So are her breasts. *Stop looking at them.* I'm not prepared for this. *Why?* I'm nervous. *What?*

"Where's your date?" she asks.

"Not really a date," I respond. Lie. Full-on lie.

"I think it is, Isaac. Where's she at?"

"You know my name?"

"Where's she at?"

"Tinkling."

She knows my name. *Your last name is scrawled all over the side of your van, and you are one of two plumbers in Paradise.* She would not have required a research assistant to figure that out.

"Tinkling, huh," she repeats, looking in the direction of the washrooms. "She break the seal already?" she asks, hands on hips, as if to call Mandy an amateur.

Goth Princess, I can assure you that Mandy Klein is no amateur. *Isaac, pay attention. She's asking if you have fed Mandy too much wine or beer, pre-dinner, to cause her to have to urinate frequently. She wants to know if you are trying to score.* I'm not. *I know.* Let her know that.

"Nah, she overdid it on the … post-run … rehydrating. Apparently."

We make true eye contact. We both laugh. *That was not a laugh. That was a giggle.* No, I laughed — she giggled. *Disagree. You both giggled.*

"I'm not the only one who looks a bit different tonight," I say boldly. *That was too bold.* Wrong. Something tells me she will dig it.

"Yeah. Not the same chick bumming a light, huh?" she answers, looking to the floor.

Don't look to the floor, Goth Princess. I think you are beautiful. *Isaac, this is getting weird. How old is she?* No clue. *Stop flirting.* I'm not. *Yes, you are. Flirting. Immeasurably.*

"Senior year?" I ask. Hopeful. Come on, Great Designer. Work with me here.

"Victory lap. Couldn't quite get it all done in four."

That makes her nineteen. She may be turning twenty soon, depending on her birthday. *Stay calm.*

"Plans?"

"What's with the twenty questions?" she asks, poking me in the shoulder.

She touched me. Contact has been made. For the second time tonight, physical barriers have been breached. *No, she was just playing with you.* It was a friendly poke. *I have to disagree again.*

"Nothing. No twenty questions. Just interested."

"I was just teasing."

"Oh," I say, smiling bigger than before.

Her figure is perfect, like those japanimé cartoon chicks on the net. *Don't gawk.*

"College," she continues.

"Next year?"

"Yeah."

"Where?" I ask. Say Michigan. Say Michigan. She can't know, yet. It's too early.

"Eastern, I hope."

"Eastern Michigan?"

"No. Eastern Washington."

That's really far.

"Nice. The Eagles, right?"

"I'm kidding," she smirks, poking me again. "Eastern Michigan."

A second poke. Find a way to poke her back. I'd love to. *You're on a date. You can't go around poking other chicks.* I didn't mean it like that. *Yes, you did.* She's too young and riddled with issues. *Why? Because she's a Goth?* Maybe. That's not fair. She seems more grounded than anyone I've ever met. More at ease than Tom Brady with a football, and I could care less if every day for her is Halloween.

I love Halloween.

Dad refused to take me out, but before Mom left us, she dressed up with me and took me trick or treating. Only to the neighbours, though. I didn't care if it was one house only. I loved it.

Eastern Michigan is in Ypsilanti, which is a twenty-minute drive from Ann Arbor. I could give her rides back and forth from Paradise. We could get to know each other.

"You seemed disappointed when I said Eastern Washington."

I was, Goth Princess. I was. *She is definitely flirting.* She's being a brat. She knows she's being a brat, and the look on her face when she knows she's being a brat is disarming. How do I respond to her? Was it even a question? *It was a statement. An accurate observation, from her perspective.* Fine. What do I say now? I can feel fresh blood cascade the cutaneous capillary loops and vessels in my cheeks. How embarrassing. *Say something*!

"What's good on the menu?" I ask.

Deal with that double-entendre of a forehand, Goth Princess. *Isaac, that was brilliant.* Thanks.

She bites her lip trying to thwart an instinctive smile, but the corners of her mouth round upward, giving her away.

She scratches the side of her head with her finger. Her arms are now crossed.

I can see the wheels turning, Goth Princess. You loved that return. You never expected it from me. Don't let my day job deceive you, Goth Princess. I'm more than just a plumber. I'm Clark fucking Kent.

"Depends how risky you are."

"Try me."

"The veal. It's younger, so it's more tender," she says, skewering me.

I am beaten. I want a re-match.

"Two house Chardonnays in the meantime, please," I say.

"Sounds good. And what would your date like to drink?"

"No. One is for Mandy."

Isaac, she was kidding, you moron. She was making light of the awkward situation you are in. She's suggesting that YOU need two drinks. And I do.

"I was just kidding. You gotta keep up with me, mister."

"I'll work on that."

"You'll work on that?"

"Yeah."

"So, that means I'm gonna see you again?" she asks.

Goth Princess, I fantasized about you in the shower not three hours ago, and now you stand in front of me and want to see me again. I believe in you now, Universe. I believe in you now, *Secret*. I believe in you now, metaphysicians, you bunch of crazy bastards. *Respond.*

"I'd like that," I say. That was honest. And concise. *That will work.*

"Good. I'll be back with your drinks when your ... date ... returns from her tinkle."

She smiles.

She winks.

She touches my shoulder.

This was not a poke. This was a touch. Gentle. There was electricity in that touch. Unlike the previous pokes, that touch told me a story about her. My stomach performs a summersault as epinephrine is released in my body, pulling blood away from the gut and sending it to my musculature. The sensation of "butterflies" is predominantly felt during an episode in which the instinctive reaction is either fight or flight, or in love sickness. Love sickness is real. Some doctors have written on this. Chemical changes are happening all over my body at this moment. Could she really be interested in me? *Why would she be?* Such a little tart, she is. Such a breath of fresh air. Immaculate.

She is the *Mona Lisa*.

She is *The Last Supper*.

She is *American Gothic*.

She is *Venus de Milo*.

She is Winona Ryder in *Beetlejuice*.

She is da Vinci's Madonna.

If she were the Madonna, then she would be a virgin. Could Goth Princess be a virgin? Has Lurch Adams deflowered her? I don't believe he has. *It didn't look like he had it in him. Lurch holds her hand.* I saw that.

Why do I want Goth Princess to be a virgin? I've never cared if girls were virgins or not. *You don't want her to be. If you're her first, she will latch on like a tick to a dog and, in turn, poison the relationship with expectation.* This is different. I would prefer if Goth Princess was a virgin. *She's a Goth, so she's likely a freak in bed.* Not so sure. Based on the two encounters, she is down-to-earth, and it would be sensual and real and there would be no need for whips, leather, chains, or any other supplements because there would be no need for supplements. *Having said that, you want her to come with a high level of skill.* Yes, but she can't have attained that skill if she's a virgin, and the tradeoff isn't worth it, in this case. Universe, hear me again: I want Goth Princess to be a virgin, and I also want her to be a sexual prodigy.

The thin red candles on the table flicker, as if my spirit guide had flown through on call, granting my wish.

Mandy lands back in her seat, looking relieved, refreshed, and invigorated. "Where's the wine?" she asks.

"It's on its way."

"Good. I'm thirsty."

I bet you are, Mandy. You were gone a long time, and guess what? In the meantime, Goth Princess revealed herself as our waitress and may be interested in me, and if she's really interested in me, then you are dead to me, Mandy Klein.

On cue, Goth Princess arrives with both glasses of house white and elegantly places them on the white linen tablecloth. White, like purity.

"Oh! Look at that! Lovely. Thank you!" says Mandy, devouring the glass with her eyes.

"Thank you," I say to Goth Princess. Thank you for resuscitating me.

"Do you have any questions about the menu?" asks Goth Princess.

"I'll have the veal," I order confidently. More confidently than I've said anything in my life. "And I will have it rare."

IX

Withholding myself from Mandy Klein was more work than I thought, so I did what every guy does in that situation: I got way too drunk on purpose and passed out. This has always been, and will always be, the perfect solution because it leaves the girl's ego intact without a formal rejection and gets the guy off the hook. *You should have done it.* Wrong. *It was a lay-up.* I realize that … I was there. I was the one pounding shots from her liquor cabinet while she went to freshen up. I hate the term "freshen up." It means that something was not fresh before. It means something was stale. It means that something has passed its "best-before" date. If that is true, how is a five-minute trip to the bathroom solving any of that?

By the time Mandy returned from wherever she went to freshen up, I had consumed half a bottle of lychee-flavored liqueur and could barely see. She told me that she was wearing something sexy, but the room was spinning and all I saw were colours. As far as I was concerned, she was a giant parrot.

The following morning was a breeze. I woke up in her bed, fully clothed, drooling on a stuffed giraffe, and she lay beside me in sweats reading a cookbook. No awkward post-sex conversation. No wondering if the other is chock-full of STDs. No dog choking on the soiled condom beside the bed. No booking of a second date that I intend to cancel. No awkwardly being shown a photo album to ease her post-sex guilt.

None of that.

We simply laughed about how trashed I got, and she recited the drunken nocturnal conversation I had with her about hidden mutual funds fees and how to find the warp whistles in *Super Mario 3.*

Yes, withholding myself from Mandy Klein was the right thing to do, given how taken I am with Goth Princess. Is Goth Princess really interested in me, or is this a joke? Some kind of sick bet? Has she laid down money that she can get me to the senior prom and still be crowned princess? Like in that movie, but the other way around? I crowned her princess the first time I saw her. *No, this is no bet. This is no game. She likes you. She is too grounded for that.* True. She was bored with Lurch Adams and wanted a man. A man with a head on his shoulders and a man who has graduated from bullshit.

Given her ambiguous age, Goth Princess is an old soul, which is the justification I've used to allow myself to meet her for a coffee at the pub this evening. *Who meets someone for coffee at a pub?* I can't take her to CoffeeBuddy. Linda would be there and would wonder what was going on. She'll also have some questions for me as to how the date went with Mandy, and I didn't want Goth Princess there to witness that. *Fair point.*

I have been here for forty minutes. *You were forty minutes early.* I didn't want to be late. In the meantime, I've consumed a coffee and two bar-rail blended Scotches.

This is one of those typical small-town pubs — the kind that has a real brass door. The kind that has a well-punctured dart board. The kind that has framed Biblical scripture written in poor calligraphy hanging on the walls. The kind where chalkboard specials are misspelled. The kind that has a jukebox that only plays songs from the fifties. The kind that has Christmas lights up all year. The kind that has a vending machine to "serve food" — thus, fulfilling their obligation, as per their liquor license. But no one buys shit from that old vending machine. This is the kind of place where, if you're hungry, they'll order in from the diner across the street. This is one of my favourite places on Earth. *Is it because you feel smarter than everyone here?* No. *Really?* Maybe. I am smarter than anyone in here by far, but that doesn't make me feel superior. We all hate our life on some level in Paradise.

Perhaps I do hang out here to feel better about myself.

Perhaps getting served by a waitress with a lazy eye and a rudimentary skillset does make me feel better about myself. But right now, it just makes me grateful.

"Sir, can I interest you in another drink tonight?" asks the lazy-eyed waitress. The question is a good one, and I should answer it, but instinctively, I'm distracted by the waterfall of sub-cutaneous fat spilling over the top of her jeans, garnished with a little dangling belly-button ring (for good measure). This adorned muffin-top could have been easily hidden, Young Waitress. A long sweater or a jacket, a long T-shirt or muumuu would have solved the problem. Even a tractor tire would have worked. Instead, you've chosen to wear a belly shirt. A baby-tee with puffy lettering on it that says *"Daddy's Little Girl,"* coupled with a bikini-clad image of women with devil horns. What could possibly have inspired you to wear that? Why the belly shirt? Worse, did you look in the mirror this morning before you left the house and say to yourself, "I look presentable. I look hot. Men will like this. This is sure to help me find a mate."

I am convinced that she did, in fact, say those things to herself. Why else would she have exposed this ring of surplus flesh?

"What's your name?" I ask.

"Stephanie."

Stephanie, you do not look like Daddy's Little Girl. You look like Saturn.

"That's a nice name," I say.

"Thanks. My mom picked it out."

"Well, it's very nice."

"So, could I interest you in another drink tonight?" she repeats, reverting back to her memorized inquest.

"Stephanie, what if I told you that I could fix your strabysmic exotropia?"

"My what?"

"Your lazy eye."

Isaac, you should not have used the term "lazy eye." Outward deviation of her eye would have been much better. I disagree. I don't believe she would have understood that. *Are you kidding me? The words "outward" and "eye" are in the same sentence.* True. It's still a toss-up. *Fine.*

"Oh … right," she says, looking to the floor and the jukebox at the same time, deflated. Yes, people notice it, Stephanie. *You brought it up too abruptly, Isaac. You caught her off guard. Backtrack a bit.*

"I don't mean to be abrupt, and it's none of my business, but if you're interested, I can give you some suggestions to correct it."

"Yes. If it's not too much trouble."

"Can you sit for a minute with me?"

"Yes. Long as it's not for too long. The boss gets mad," she says, pulling out one of three remaining wooden chairs, stripped of their varnish, surrounding the circular table. Sitting has only enhanced the muffin-top of flab over her jeans, and the bellybutton ring has disappeared. Even the dangling part.

Focus.

"Will you remember this, or do you need to write it down?" I ask.

Don't treat her like an idiot. You should have never asked that. I know she needs to write it down. That is a fact.

"Here," I interject. "I have a pen right here. Write it on this napkin. I know I would need to write this down."

Horrible save. Horrible.

"Okay. Thanks," she says, grabbing the pen. The way she holds the pen in her fingers isn't even right. Who cares?

"The first one is the easiest way to try to correct your outwardly deviating eye."

"Okay."

"When you're at home, put a patch or a large bandage over your one ... good ... eye," I say. This is going horribly. Abort mission. *No, you got yourself into it, asshole. Stick it out.* "Penalizing your dominant ... good ... eye will force, or bully, the other ... bad ... lazy ... eye... to start to function properly."

I should never have referred to them as "good" or "bad" eyes. That kind of rhetoric is uncalled for in this situation. One eye is not better than the other. Nor is this a case of laziness.

"Okay. That sounds easy enough," she says, smiling — revealing too many teeth for one adult space.

What is that called? *Hyperdontia.* Right. Nice one. *Let's leave that for another day.* Focus.

"If that doesn't work ..."

"That might not work?"

"Well. It should."

You are shitting the bed here, Isaac. A doctor never does that. This is becoming Amateur Hour, and pretty soon a clown is going to enter this bar, broom in hand, and sweep you out the door in disgrace as the patrons cheer. I know better than that. A good doctor asks for a follow-up visit to see if it's working or not, and if not, he brings up another solution.

"Let's try this first. It's the best one, by far," I say. *Lie.* The best solution, Stephanie, is corrective recession surgery where I would disconnect three of the ocular muscles surrounding your eye, and then re-attach the stronger muscles further back on the eye, thus weakening the stronger muscles in order to realign it. I would suggest this, Stephanie, but I don't think you can afford it. Truth: I have now made a financial judgment on her ability to pay based on her profession and attire. That is wrong. She is going to tell someone what a horrible experience this has been and that I referred to one of her eyes as "the bad, lazy eye," and I will be stripped of my licence to practice medicine.

Forever.

Enough.

I'm out.

Stephanie is still standing with her pad out waiting for an answer. How long was I out of it? How long have you been standing there, Stephanie? I need to get control of these daydreams. *Are they daydreams, or are they episodes?* They are distracting. I don't need them any longer. I want them to stop.

"I'm fine, thanks. I'll just nurse this water for now," I say.

"Okay. That's fine. I'll be back to check on you."

"That would be perfect. Thank you."

"I'll take a beer," orders an angelic voice. The kind of voice that should do low-calorie yoghurt commercials.

Goth Princess is decked out in full regalia. So beautiful. My stomach flips. That is a cool sensation — like free-falling from the top of the train bridge into the river. Like screaming down a steep descent on a roller coaster. Like turbulence on an airplane, they say. I wouldn't know. Never been on one.

"Can I please see your identification?" asks Stephanie.

"I'm just kidding. Only fifteen months away, though," says Goth Princess, grinning with both thumbs up. That was adorable. And nerdy. And I loved it. "I'll just have a glass of water."

"Okay. I will be right back with that."

Stephanie leaves to fulfill her promise.

Goth Princess gets out of her long black coat and throws it on the back of the chair to my right. I'm glad she's on my right — it's my better side. My nose looks much better from that angle. Maybe I need a nose job. Rhinoplasty. It is horrible to have "rhino" situated inside the proper term for a nose job. *"Rhino" is a proper biological reference to the nose, just like "rhinorrhea" is the proper term for a runny nose.* True, but the general public doesn't know that. There shouldn't be a reference made to a rhinoceros for those already sensitive about the issue. They could have easily called it something else. *Agreed.*

"You meant it when you ordered the beer," I claim. I'm never that bold. Ever.

"Guilty as charged."

"I used to pull the same stunt when I was your age."

You brought up the age thing right away, Isaac. Stupid choice. You are making too big a deal of it. Don't mention it.

"Like … a hundred years ago?" I deserved that.

"Yeah. I was celebrating Henry Ford's first Model T."

"Funny. How was your day?"

That is nice. How nice to ask how my day was. No one has ever asked how my day was.

"It was okay. Thanks. Boring. Same old stuff. You?"

"Oh, mine was fine. I wanna hear what you did."

Really? "Really?"

"Yes, really."

"I had to clean out a P-trap from under a sink, which was

disgusting, and then I replaced a few elements in some hot water heaters."

The sound of my mundane existence makes me hope my application is safe and sound in the hands of the U.S. Postal Service.

"That's not boring. Boring is high school."

"I won't argue with that."

Stephanie arrives with the water and sets it down on a napkin in front of Goth Princess. The glass doesn't land square on the napkin, but that's no surprise. No, it's still a surprise. The glass isn't even halfway on the napkin. Goth Princess waits until Stephanie turns around to properly rearrange the glass. That was kind of her. She has a kind heart. Goth Princess takes a sip of her water, leaving a print of purple lipstick on the rim of the glass. I'm jealous of the glass.

"I like you," she says. *She meant that.* I think so, too.

"Come again?" I say. Maybe if only to hear her utter the words a second time.

"I like you. I think you're super cute, and I just think you should know that."

All said with a half-smile. A half-smile armed with just the right amount of confidence and vulnerability. I admire the shit out of you, Goth Princess. She is too young for me. *She is way too young for you.* This can't happen. This will never work. *You should tell her that this was a big mistake and offer to pay for her... water.* Water is free. I do like her. More than that, I'm intrigued. I want to learn more about you, Goth Princess.

"I'm embarrassed ... I don't even know your name," I admit.

"Really?"

"Well, I was hoping that it was going to be on the piece of paper you slipped me that night at the restaurant, but it wasn't. Your email address didn't have your name in it. And when we set up the meeting here, you didn't sign your email."

"Bronwyn."

"Bronwyn?" I repeat, for clarity's sake.

"Yes. Bronwyn is my name."

That is the most beautiful name I have ever heard. "That's the most beautiful name I have ever heard," I say.

"That's very honest of you."

"I suppose it is."

She blushes. Underneath all that foundation, blushing is visible.

"Last name?"

"Gallagher."

"Bronwyn."

"Yes."

This inspires an awkward laugh between us. I would have never laughed at that if it was anyone else. Gallagher. *That's the last name of the local butcher.*

"Gallagher, as in, Ben Gallagher?" I ask. Please say no. *No has to be the answer.*

"Correct."

She smirks and takes another sip of water.

She's the butcher's daughter. *Isaac, you are infatuated with a teenager whose father owns a widespread collection of sharp instruments meant for disassembling. Run while you still have legs.* No.

"I have to admit …" I say. *Don't do it. Don't admit anything. There is no turning back if you admit the thing that I think you are going to admit to.* "I thought that we had a really strong connection when …"

"You lit my cancer-stick?"

"Yes. Then. But I didn't want to. It was just to buy some time with you."

"I know."

"You should stop smoking," I recommend, unsolicited. "I mean that."

"I'm trying."

"Good."

That is good. Cancer of the lung, gum, or throat is simply deadly, Bronwyn, and I only have so many organs that I can donate to you.

"It's better now since I broke up with Andy. He smoked a lot."

Andy must be Lurch Adams.

"Is Andy the guy I saw you with in the ..."

"Yeah, that was him. He has a really bad jealous streak. I hate that more than anything. Jealousy. It's poison. It's possession. Not love."

"Agreed."

Good riddance, Lurch. You blew your chance, you jealous skid mark.

"I was just so happy at the restaurant, when you seemed to be ... into me."

"Of course I was."

"You don't think I'm a freak?"

"No. Not at all. I think you are probably the most beautiful ever."

I mean that. Great Designer on high, I mean every syllable of it.

She melts me with another smile.

From another set of eyes in the pub, another perspective, this scenario would look quite strange: a mid-thirties local plumber sharing a beverage with a teenage girl dressed like Dracula's bride. Maybe that makes me the freak? I don't care. I'll be out of this town soon. *Hopefully.* What if I don't get in to Michigan? Can I maintain this newfound confidence? Will I continue taking risks? Or will I slide back into the miserable existence of plumbing by day and surfing Internet porn by night? Would I still even look at Internet porn if Bronwyn and I were together? Maybe never.

"You're a bit of a gamble, though. So I'm betting against you breaking your hip in the next few years," she says, poking me in the arm.

She really likes me. I want to kiss you so badly, Bronwyn, that it hurts me physically. I am in pain. Is this how it's supposed to feel?

"The dentures, bunions, and Viagra all start next year," I toss back.

She smiles. "That should be right around the time I can legally have a beer — so that works out great!"

We laugh again. We laugh and mean it.

"Your dad would filet me if he found out about this."

"Your dad's likely already dead," she punches back.

We both laugh. Genuinely. The few people in the bar look in our direction. I don't care. This is a date, you alcoholic fossils. Gawk all you want.

I'm on a date with a teenage Goth named Bronwyn, and I think she's my girlfriend.

Bronwyn laughs so hard she snorts, sending us deeper into the fit of howling. Do Goths howl at the moon? *No. Werewolves do.* Right.

Covering her mouth with her right hand, Bronwyn continues to laugh, shocked by her snort. Don't cover up those perfect lips, Goth Princess. *Do those perfect lips get cold sores?* Pause. I hope not. Cold sores have always been a deal-breaker for me. Cold sores do not move the chains forward ten yards. Cold sores do not move women to pass "GO" and collect two hundred dollars. Cold sores are not like rolling doubles in backgammon. Cold sores are herpes simplex virus strains

I and II, which cause infectious blisters on and around the mouth area, typically lasting two- to twenty-one days before returning to state of remission. Herpes, you are a terrorist. You alter social behaviour, you strike fear when you surface, you hide like a coward when not on assignment, you spread, and you attack highly visible and popular landmarks, causing unsightly damage.

Cold sores are the IRA.

Cold sores are al Qaeda.

My laughing has lessened given the weight of the topic, but not Bronwyn — she is still in gales, unaware of how all of this magic teeters on the answer of a single question. No. I disagree. This is different. I accept her for who she is and her faults along with that. She is not perfect. I am not perfect. This time, the terrorists will not win. I will find out if Goth Princess gets cold sores, and if she does, then I'll just have to pump her full of Valtrex to suppress the nasty bastards.

No. No, I won't even ask. If she gets cold sores, then I trust her judgment to tell me when she feels one coming on. This is a new page of trust and confidence and vulnerability, and I am not going to poison that with my habitual thirst for fault-finding. This time, there are no faults. There are only low-level hurdles.

Bronwyn grabs my right hand with her left, gently. With her right hand, she wipes laugh tears from her eyes, smearing her midnight-coloured eyeliner across her pale cheek. I reach across with my available left thumb and wipe away the smeared eyeliner. This is the first time I have groomed you, Goth Princess. *She knows that. Look at how she is looking at you.* She looks convinced that I will take care of her. She is convinced that the set of eyes looking back at her will never judge her. Will never want to change her. Accepts her for who she is.

"I think we made a scene," she says.

"I hope it's not the last."

I mean that. The laughter has demanded the production of endorphins by stimulating the ventromedial prefrontal cortex of my brain and has left me feeling charged. Research could prove that this bout of laughter has added years to my life, but it has definitely made me alive today.

"I wasn't going to … but there's something I should tell you," she says.

"There's something I should tell you too."

What is she going to tell me? Given the tone of the preamble, it sounds serious. *What's the worst thing she could tell you?* I knew it. Things were going too well. There has to be something seriously wrong with her. Maybe Lurch Adams wasn't dumped at all, but ran for the hills, scratching out his eyes and lighting his hands on fire based on this same news. *Relax.*

"You go first," says Goth Princess.

"No, I already know mine. I want to hear yours."

"You're the first one who is going to know."

"Hit me."

"I got accepted."

"To what?"

"To school!" she bursts.

Early acceptance. She had her application in the mail and postmarked before November 1, I bet. She is smart. Smarter than I am. I should've applied for early acceptance. *You weren't ready for that news.*

"Wow! Congrats," I say. Stunned. Acting. *She can tell you were acting. Your surprise wasn't convincing at all. How about showing a bit more enthusiasm.* No. *Why?* I'm jealous. *She hates jealously, that's why she dumped Lurch, you stupid son-of-a-bitch. Fuck off.*

"Thanks!" she says, touching my hand.

"That's the most perfect early Christmas gift you could ask for."

Now I have to tell her my secret. How is my secret going to compare to hers? *It can't. She got accepted, and you merely applied.* Her information was much more impressive. What am I going to tell her? *Tell her that you got fucked by a husky.*

"But I plan on coming home on weekends a lot … to see my dad and stuff and … other things."

Other things? Is that me? Is that so that I can have something to look forward to while I plumb the shit-highways of Paradise?

"That'll be great. Yeah."

"I think so. Anything to get out of Paradise, right?"

"True. And you start …"

"Next fall."

"Awesome."

I haven't said awesome in years. I look down in my empty glass begging to chug something alcoholic, but no such luck. What is wrong with me? This isn't a contest. This is about sharing information.

"You okay?"

"Yeah, I'm fine."

I'm obviously not fine. *She knows that.*

"You sure?"

"Yeah. I'm really happy for you, Bronwyn."

Drawing back the long band of hair that frames her face, I tuck it behind her left ear. Her left ear that is lined with so many circular piercings from top to bottom that they look like vertebrae. She closes her eyes as my finger runs down her ear, strumming all of the tiny silver piercings on its course down to the bottom of her perfect lobe.

It's vertebrae that changed my life.

Dad's splintered vertebrae are the reason I am here with you now, Goth Princess. Could it be that all my suffering and resentment for the past eighteen years was all worth it to be sitting here with you, Bronwyn? Life is cruel for that to be true. How could the Designer have allowed me to suffer like that, knowing full well that it was all part of a plan?

My inclination is to think that it has been worth it.

It must be times like this when people regain faith. Are born again. I suppose, when the Great Designer introduces something like Bronwyn amidst a chronic track record of suffering and confusion, He is to be praised. The plan becomes a divine plan, and then people thank God for the suffering, because without the suffering, the miracle could not have taken place.

I am not thankful for the suffering. I am thankful for the miracle.

Bronwyn grabs my finger from her earlobe and brings it toward her lips. I can feel her ninety-eight degree breath on my finger. This has caused a chain reaction of goose bumps as the tiny arrectores pilorum muscles, lining each follicle on the back of my neck, contract and pull each hair erect.

Then, a gentle kiss.

The gentlest kiss on the tip of a finger that a fingertip has ever experienced.

The greatest kiss of all time.

Better than *Gone with the Wind*.

Better than *Casablanca*.

Better than *Titanic*.

Better than Mary Jane Watson kissing Spiderman as he dangled upside-down in the rain with half his true identity exposed. Is that the point? Is a ground-shifting kiss designed to expose your true identity? By the reaction caused from a kiss to the tip of my finger, I cannot, in any way, fathom the rest to come. And my true identity as an aspiring doctor will be revealed in due course.

Just not today.

"Now," she says, "what was your news?"

"My family … well … my dad and my aunt and her family … and my uncle and his family are all having a Christmas party this Saturday at my house."

"That was the news?"

"Yes."

"Okay."

"There's more."

"I hope so," she says, ribbing me.

The fingertip kiss has now become something different. She runs the tip of my finger along the ridge of her upper lip — the same ridge that distinguishes the tactile sensory organ from the orbicularis oris muscle surrounding it. My fingertip collects some of her Goth war paint.

I love this. She is a master.

"I was wondering if you would like to come to the Christmas party as my date?"

X

It may have been too soon to invite Bronwyn to dinner with my family. All was normal and boring, until she arrived. Conversations were dry, until she arrived. Town gossip babbled, incessantly, until she arrived. Complaining was at an all-time high, until she arrived.

And then she arrived.

Tight, stretch-denim jeans tucked into sixteen-eyelet black platform boots. Chrome studded belt worn over the jeans. Silver chains running from front belt-loop to back belt-loop. Black, skin-tight, long-sleeve T-shirt with a hole cut out in the cuff of the sleeve for her thumb to poke through. Black, wide-hole, fishnet shirt over the black long-sleeve T. Purple lipstick, black eyeliner, lip ring, earrings, and the two bands of hair framing her perfectly symmetrical face.

I was so thrilled that she had come naturally.

My greatest fear was that she would dress like she does at the Precocious Sturgeon, wearing her day-job mask and sporting her conservative façade. I wanted the band-aid ripped off and for my family to see her as she exists in the wild.

For thirty-six years and nine months, I have lived and never did I think I'd see the day my father was silenced.

He was.

Five minutes before she arrived, I made the announcement that I had invited my new girlfriend to the party and that she would be arriving any minute. The frenzy this created was similar to dropping a pint of blood in a shark tank.

I answered no questions. I pleaded the Fifth.

I simply asked them to wait until Bronwyn arrived.

Not so shockingly, there were no questions from the gallery when the enigmatic Goth Princess made her inaugural appearance. Despite the ringing silence in the room, all seemed fine — until my cousin Alice's daughter, Sarah, scared to death by the sight of Bronwyn, began to cry.

"Don't cry, sweetheart," said Bronwyn and came over to Sarah, who remained half hidden behind her Grandma Maria's leg. Bronwyn shot down to her level and beamed her beautiful smile at Sarah. "You sure are a cutie, aren't you, Sarah. And what a pretty dress." Even a three-year-old is defenceless. Even a three-year-old is unarmed against the charm of Goth Princess. Sarah was easily won over, and the two played hide-and-go-seek for the next fifteen minutes. Bronwyn became Sarah's new best toy: a giant Goth Barbie. Mattel really dropped the ball there. All the self-loathing children from broken marriages would have loved a Goth Barbie — complete with pierced holes, water-transfer tattoos, and plastic-handled copper wire to heat up and melt scars into her wrists.

Historically, there have been nine at my table for the family Christmas party: Dad, Uncle Jim, and Aunt Maria, and their daughter Alice and granddaughter Sarah, and Aunt Grace and Uncle Earl and their son, Mike. Mike is two years younger than me and is the regional sales rep for DeWalt power tools. To my family, his career is the most praised by far. Every year, Dad asks Mike if he's met the DeWalt calendar girl yet. Mike always says, "She keeps leaving her stuff at my place," and the entire table laughs. I never laugh. I refuse to laugh at that. He's obviously never met her, and if he did he would mumble something idiotic.

This is my family. They have always sat in the same seats every year.

This year, there is one more seat.

This year, there is an even number of seats, and the count has graduated to double digits.

Dad and I square off against each other at both heads of the table. My Goth Princess sits to my right. Life is the best it has ever been at this moment. *Can you imagine what they are thinking?* I don't want to.

"What the fuck are we eating again, son?" belts Dad, mouth full of masticated venison.

"Venison," I reply. Is it the fresh, minced rosemary or the spicy olive oil rub that is throwing you off, Dad? No? Maybe it's the hint of dry mustard or the teaspoon of fennel seeds, you ungrateful son-of-a-bitch.

"I usually love venison, but this is too goddamn gamey," he says, spitting a mouthful out into his napkin.

"Y'know, I hear that when you kill an animal, the fear gets released into the meat and it can affect the taste. That you can actually taste the fear. You kill this thing proper, Isaac?" asks Aunt Grace.

"I think it tastes wonderful. You done a hell of a job here," Aunt Maria chimes in.

"You shot this one, huh, Isaac?" asks Mike.

"Yup."

It was a much more heroic effort to simply respond with a "Yup." This is Mr. Buck. Mr. Buck, who I lured into the field using pheromone-rich doe urine as bait. Urine that I collected myself after tranquillizing an unsuspecting doe from a hundred feet and then draining her bladder via catheterization by inserting a lubricated silicone tube up her urethra. Catheterization, in this case, was quite difficult and is reportedly more difficult in females, given their varying vaginal layouts. However, I trusted the anatomical landmarks and was able to skillfully extract the bodily waste without harming the doe. Bodily waste I used later as bait. Sorry, Mr. Buck.

What if someone had caught me? What if someone happened upon me, alongside the unconscious doe, rubber gloves on, and a tube up her doe vagina? *Farmers would have chased you out of town with pitchforks.* True. Bestiality and zoophilia are weird and wrong, but it wasn't bestiality. It was simply a medical procedure. *All that people would have remembered is that you tranquillized an animal and touched its parts. That's all that would matter.* I would become "Isaac, the Deer Toucher." I had to touch it to get the catheter in. *I don't care. No one who is considered normal catheterizes deer. They just don't.* True. But I had to collect a large enough sample of pheromone, and that is legit. A pheromone is a natural chemical that triggers a behavioural response in members of the same species. Will the human species evolve out of pheromone release and response? Maybe. Women shave and laser their pubic hair off now. Pubic hair has many functions: a visual indicator of sexual maturity, protection, and a buffer against sexual friction. However, it's most important function (I would argue) is the collection of secreted pheromone. As much as Calvin Klein and Hugo Boss and Ann Taylor attempt to create exquisite odours, they fail miserably against Nature's default attractant — the almighty pheromone, masked only by the pungent and disgusting scent of raw onions. My prediction, then, is that the more we use crafted scents and the more women insist on shaving, the more likely we are to naturally select against the pheromone as an animal stimulant. *Does Goth Princess shave?* I hope not, but I picture her both ways instantaneously.

I'm hard.

I'm hard, and the tip of my penis has poked out the top of my underwear like a periscope, hunting for the Goth October.

"Is that tough to do, Isaac?" asks Bronwyn.

"What's that?"

"Kill a deer?"

"I think it depends on why you're killing the deer."

"This is a deer, Mommy?" asks Sarah, ceasing her open-mouth chewing and looking up to her mother in horror.

Don't talk with your mouth full, Sarah. *That's how her dad eats*. Wherever he is right now. Drunk in the back of some strip club likely, spending little Sarah's college fund.

"Yes, baby … and don't talk with your mouth full, please," says Alice.

"Like Bambi?" she asks before spitting out the remaining meat onto her plate. That was rude, Sarah. Mr. Buck deserves better than that.

"No, this is a boy deer. They are the ones we eat," Cousin Alice replies calmly.

That was a lie. Alice, you can't still be breastfeeding that child, but your breasts look incredible. *Stop that, Isaac. You can't look at your cousin's breasts.* Why not? I've been looking at them since they first sprouted in the late eighties. Like a time-lapsed video, I watched them transform from bee stings to C-cups. Alice is hot. There is no question about that. For the longest time, she was the only girl I knew very well. All of my other friends were guys, and I didn't have the guts to talk to any other girls, and Alice was the only girl that talked to me, which was confusing for a little while, especially when my cock grew and her breasts grew and her curves formed and she was still the only girl I hung out with. There was a strange chemistry between Alice and me at that point. I would lie in bed at night and beat myself up about the fact that I wanted to feel her up, or see her naked, or worse. Looking back, it doesn't seem so strange now. Simply a young desire to participate in some sexual mapping. Exploratory, perhaps.

Even into our twenties, she seemed resentful of the fact we were cousins and had no legal or moral opportunity to explore each other. I, on the other hand, got over our sexual unease by the time I turned sixteen and began talking to other girls. I pretty much cut her out of my life completely when I started dating Sarah Cliffton.

That hurt Alice.

We were like best buddies before Sarah Cliffton came into the picture.

Incest is illegal and wrong and I can break down, biologically, why it is wrong. But Alice can't. I believe, to this day, that she was in love with me. *Can't be.* It's possible. At the age of twenty-eight, she got knocked up by some idiot from Mackinaw City who owned a towing company and had tattoos and muscles. She lost her virginity on the cracked pleather seats of his towing truck, and that same night, his redneck sperm breached the membrane of her ovum, and little Sarah was the byproduct. I could have gone my entire life without knowing that story. *Why did she tell you?* Likely to see my reaction. *To see if her horrific story made you the slightest bit jealous? That can't be why she asked.* It's just a hypothesis. Truth: I am very sure that, in our mid to late teens, had I made a move, she would have gone with it. *Don't picture it.* Agreed. I won't picture it because she is my cousin. *What if she wasn't your cousin?* Let's move on, please.

I drop back into the conversation. Aunt Maria finishes up her rant on the current mayor. She likely didn't even vote.

"So, how'd you two kids meet again?" Dad asks.

Easy, Dad. Go easy. Bronwyn looks to me for the answer. I should lie. I should say that we met in the library.

"Smoking section of the high school."

172

My response causes Cousin Grace to blanch.

Mike smirks.

Alice looks like she is going to cry.

Dad is deadpan.

Dad is always deadpan. When he jumped off the back of the truck with the bag of concrete, all of the muscles that allow a man to laugh must have suffered some sort of palsy. That, or he gave up on life and laughter, hand in hand.

"I'm trying to quit," says the brave and mighty Bronwyn, breaking the silence. *You didn't have to say that, Bronwyn. I love your effort, though.*

"We really hit it off," I say. *That was brutal and so cliché.*

"There was a definite spark." Goth Princess laughs at her own joke. *My darling, I don't think anyone got the joke. You are playing to a crowd of hillbillies.*

"That's 'cause I was lighting her cigarette. Spark," I add, doing the motion.

This inspires laughter at the table. People are actually laughing. Goth Princess is laughing.

"So what do you do, Bronwyn?" asks Aunt Maria.

Aunt Maria is loving Mr. Buck. She's on her second helping of him. Mr. Buck appreciates that. *He can't appreciate that because he's dead, and to "appreciate" you must have a brain with enough folds to allow for abstract thought, which deer don't have.* I disagree. I think that animals can be appreciative. *True. But not dead ones.* Fair point. Fact: The higher folds of the brain are called *gyri*, and the valleys between them are called *sulci*. *Nicely done.*

"I'm just finishing up my fifth year of high school, and I'm going to college next year," Goth Princess says proudly.

"That's marvellous. I just love hearing good stuff like that. Hey, Jim?"

"Fantastic," Jim replies, refusing to look up from his plate. He could give a shit.

Obviously, Bronwyn makes you a bit uncomfortable, Uncle Jim. Do you think she's a freak? Would you come to our wedding if we got married? Would you come to the baptism of our child, or would you be afraid that the holy water would just sizzle and evaporate off its evil little Goth head?

Aunt Grace is onto her second helping of the heavily buttered and bacon-bit-laden mashed yams. She should not have a second helping of anything. She barely deserves a first helping. Aunt Grace weighs over two hundred and fifty pounds and is cruising in the express lane toward diabetes, congestive heart failure, and cirrhosis of the liver. No woman or man should ever consume that much food or Scotch. Ever. Sadly, when Aunt Grace asks me for seconds, or thirds, or asks me to bring the bottle of Scotch in order to bypass the use of a glass, I will carry out her order with a smile. I'll make a cute comment on how impressed I am with her appetite and how it makes the chef feel good. I will comment on how she can drink all of the men under the table. And she will cackle. But her tears of self-disgust will flow, internally, like the river Styx, transporting her soul to the afterworld, piece by piece.

Uncle Earl sees this. What anger he must feel.

Aunt Grace takes every opportunity to tell Earl that she loves him, but she doesn't love him. She does not. You can't cut your life short and cheat someone you love out of sunrises and sunsets because of a selfish need to overeat and drink. If you loved that person, you would stop. You would stop catering to your compulsion out of a basic, deep-seated desire to spend as much time as possible with your spouse. If you loved them, that is.

Possibly, Uncle Earl has a hand in this, as well.

Silence is a killer.

Given the obesity and diabetes rates in this country, tens of thousands of families allow their loved ones to deviate on a path to self-destruction without ringing a single alarm bell. At Aunt Grace's near and forthcoming funeral, will everyone cry and say that it wasn't fair?

It was fair. She killed herself.

This is called suicide.

She is a Christian, and this is the only way a Christian can do it in good conscience.

And everyone will joke and reminisce about how much she loved life, loved food, loved her Scotch, and loved her family. Perhaps I will be the one in attendance to stand and point out that she was disgusted by herself and hated her life, and that we all have an equal amount of blood on our hands, having facilitated her slow-drip version of euthanasia. Certainly, no one will shine any light on her obvious self-inflicted metabolic syndrome, and metabolic syndrome is a combination of medical disorders due to obesity and laziness which, when combined, increase the risk of cardiovascular disease. *Nicely done.* Thanks, but I still have to download parts two and three of the podcast surrounding that issue. *Then become fully versed in something before you go spouting knowledge. That could get you into trouble at Michigan.* Relax, please.

Everyone sits in silence, chewing.

They say that silence at a table means a good meal, but this silence is painful. This silence has lasted for several minutes. My heart rate is increasing, and my hands and feet are tingling with the crescendo of anxiety at the table.

"So will the two of you stay together when Bronwyn leaves for school, Isaac?" asks Alice.

"Why would they?" announces Dad.

"Why wouldn't we?" suggests Bronwyn, directly at Dad.

Bronwyn, please do not poke the animal in the cage. That animal is rabid with terminal remorse and is unpredictable.

Dad wipes his mouth, swallows, and places the napkin back in his lap. "I think this whole thing is a huge fucking mistake. Isaac, you've made a mistake, and when you go shopping and buy the wrong fucking tool — you return it."

"I wonder how my father would take you calling me a tool, Mr. Sullivan? He has several of his own. Being a butcher and all."

Bronwyn has become Goth Princess. I have used the names interchangeably, but there is a difference. I love that.

"Your father can go fuck himself. You're a defective tool, and you're dressed like a whore, and my son will have nothing to do with you!"

With that outburst, I remove a ninja star from the left pocket of my plaid shirt, and with a single flick of the wrist, it's propelled through the air, across the length of the table, and buries itself deep in Dad's neck.

Everyone shouldn't look so shocked. His comments were uncalled for. No one calls Goth Princess defective. She is the Great Designer's best work. Ever.

The ninja star, resting deep in his carotid artery, is creating quite a mess and looks to be causing more pain than I would have suspected. For that, I am sorry.

I grab Goth Princess, tear off her shirt, and lay her down on the table.

Over her bra, she rubs her breasts for me and bites her bottom lip. I lower my face to hers. We kiss passionately, as streams of blood snake their way toward us from the other end of the table, reaching her jet-black hair and mixing with the dye, creating a beautiful rich cherry. Cousin Alice wails with tears and pounds the table with closed fists.

Enough.

—»—

I'm out.

"Isaac."

"Yes."

"Will the two of you stay together when Bronwyn leaves for school?"

"Of course. Yes," I say, flustered by the daydream. Beading sweat.

Did Bronwyn notice that I gapped out? What would she think if she could witness my mind at work? *She would leave you.*

"I'll likely be at school, too … so no big deal."

Silence at the table. Why? Shit. *That was out loud.*

"Excuse me?" says Aunt Maria.

Hypothesis turns to fact. The register on eight of the faces at my table tells how shocking this really is. I've tried to picture what these faces would look like upon this news for weeks.

All different. All unique. Like snowflakes.

Bronwyn's face is the only one smiling. I love her for that.

"Just kidding," I say.

This causes laughter. Eight faces at the table are now laughing hysterically. The ninth face, the face of Goth Princess, is processing the information differently. Amidst the hyena-like laughter at the table, I connect with Bronwyn as we lock eyes. Her face is unchanged. She believed me. She believes that a plumber from Paradise can go back to school and live out his dream. I hope the University of Michigan feels the same way.

"That was hilarious, man. Nice one."

I am sure that was hilarious for you, Michael. Did he, for a second, think I was telling the truth? Was he terrified that his reign of championing the highest salary this family has ever seen could be coming to an end? How does "Dr. Sullivan" sound,

Mike? I won't be a prick about my MD, but I will insist that you, Michael Sullivan, refer to me as "Dr. Sullivan" the nanosecond my license to practice becomes effective.

"What would you study?" asks Goth Princess.

"Huh?"

"In school. If you weren't kidding … like you say you are … if you were actually going to college, what would you study?"

"Is there Toilets 101?" asks Mike.

The table, again, finds this hilarious. I thought it was weak, and the joke needs serious workshopping, so if you're going to slam me, Mike, get a bit more creative next time.

"I'm serious," says Bronwyn.

"He ain't going to college, sweetheart. Don't get yer hopes up," says Dad, now adding a spoon of sugar to his glass of port.

"That's why I said 'if,' Mr. Sullivan."

"Medicine," I say.

A few hushed snorts and chuckles are heard. Bronwyn heard me. She knew I meant it. I did mean it. She smiles and holds my hand under the table.

"One of my clients told me a while back that, because of my ability to understand plumbing and electrical work so well within the structure of a house, and my ability to look at a situation from an unbiased, holistic perspective in order to solve a problem, without creating others, he thought that would make me a great doctor."

Silence.

"And then he told you to fix his shitter!" bursts Mike.

Pabst Blue Ribbon shoots from the nostrils of Uncle Jim in a misdirected attempt not to spray it from his mouth. The table is a mess of laugher. Hands pound the table in fits of hysterics. Snorts. High-pitched squawks.

Uncle Earl is laughing. My father is even laughing. The first laughter I've seen from him in eighteen years. Laughing so hard he is crying. A miracle. Like when biblical statues cry tears of blood. Yes, this is miracle at my expense, but it's a miracle nonetheless. You should thank Jesus, Dad, for curing your laughter-palsy, because that is who you believe puppets your life like the divine marionette master you testify him to be.

Goth Princess is also crying, but not from the laughter.

She knows.

The pink of her bottom lip is now showing through the worn sections of the deep purple lipstick, and that bottom lip is quivering. How adorable is that. She really believes in me. I want to protect you forever, Bronwyn.

We look at each other.

We look into each other.

My stomach flips.

She squeezes my hand under the table, hard, and her black nails dig into my skin — but lovingly.

There is no question about it. I am in love.

XI

New Year's Eve and, on my shitty old TV, the ball is dropping in Times Square. Millions of marinated party-goers positioning for their kiss.

Some with their lovers.

Recently acquainted singles about to be lovers.

Some of those lovers thinking about other lovers.

Blood-stained surgical gloves pull down my mask, and I get back to work on Mr. Stripes, who looks even more ridiculous with a shaved head. Six-inch wood screws pinning his head down to two-by-fours. *Not a bad set-up.* Thanks. The remaining thirty seconds of the year's official countdown in the background. All I can think of is Bronwyn. Not being here. Out with her dad at a family party somewhere having fun without me. *Or not having fun.*

I bet she looks beautiful tonight.

I bet she wore that little chain that connects her nose ring to one of her earrings. She wore that last week on our walk in Tahquamenon Falls State Park, and I loved it. Just Goth Princess, me, and Nature, and we talked when we wanted to and walked when we wanted to.

Hand in hand.

Peaceful. Simple. Romantic.

The best day of my life.

I wanted to go native and live in the woods with her and hunt food for her and raise children. No need to leave the woods ever. I could be the family doctor as well as her gynecologist and obstetrician. *I miss her.* Me too.

Maybe the butcher granted her permission to take off and party with her friends elsewhere? *If she's with friends, then she's drinking underage and likely around horny teenage boys who are eyeing her up and will be trying to kiss her seconds from now, and kissing leads to touching.* Stop. She won't kiss them. She's thinking about me, and I'm thinking about her, but I shouldn't be thinking about her during surgery. A mistake could be made, and that means a lawsuit and my license revoked. *The dead raccoon on your kitchen table won't sue you. I promise.*

Correct.

Mr. Stripes can't sue me.

Mr. Stripes, who complained of chronic headaches and seizures, which led me to the diagnosis that he had a cavernoma of the brain. Cavernoma being the malformation of a vein in the brain or spinal cord, thus allowing blood to seep out and into surrounding tissue. Let this be a lesson to your remaining family, Mr. Stripes. The cavernoma gene is located on the seventh chromosome. It could be a familial issue and could possibly wipe out your entire family. *Not correct. This malformation would not affect breeding.* True. The real familial threat is continuing to fuck around with my garbage bins.

The ball has dropped in Times Square.

It's a new year. My year.

"Happy new year, pal."

Gilby sniffs at me from his mat in front of the TV.

Happy new year, Goth Princess.

The mask is back over my mouth now. Goggles on.

I pick up the Skil saw and its circular blade becomes hungry once again. As the bone fragments fly, I create more visible brain area in search of Mr. Stripes' defective vein.

The Brain.

Centre of the nervous system and regulator of actions and reactions. So important that, clinically, death is not measured by the lack of a beating heart or functioning lungs or liver, but by the lack of brain waves. Designer, how did you come up with such a complex structure, capable of so much in such a compact space? Like an iPod. What did your trial models for the brain look like? Did they take up an entire lab, like mankind's early computers? And did you eventually pare it down and perfect it to what it is today? Possibly, that's what aliens are. Early trial species. They always have huge brains in pictures. *You have it backwards, Isaac. The bigger the better when it comes to brain size.* That's very true. That's why aliens have the means to reach us from galaxies we can't even see. *Pointless conversation. Aliens don't exist.* Wrong. Aliens have to exist. *You have no proof. Purely speculation.* Logic. Earth is located in the Milky Way galaxy and supports life based on a number of lottery-winning factors: the precise distance to the sun, planet temperature, our planet's size and gravity — integral to supporting an atmospheric blanket trapping the proper gases and moisture and heat energy and water, etc. *You say "etc." because you ran out of examples.* Don't piss me off. Regardless, even if Earth were the only planet in the Milky Way galaxy to support life, would it not be logical to assume that at least one planet in each galaxy does the same? *Speculation.* Fact: There are billions of planets in the Milky Way. Thus, if we increased the odds of "planets with life" to one in every hundred galaxies, the Hubble Telescope Team believes there to be one hundred and twenty-five billion galaxies. With billions of planets in each. Do the math.

Logic.

Odds.

Probabilities.

We are not alone, and the Great Designer is a philharmonic conductor of balance and precision and incomprehension. Higher life-forms on other planets must have doctors as well. Making me part of some inter-galactic club. Sometime in the future, will Earth send me as its representative to the Inter-Galactic Conference of Physicians and Surgeons? Will we all share what we know and cure diseases and genetic disorders? *Listen to yourself. You are not a doctor. You are a plumber playing doctor. That's what you are.*

Hundreds of billions of planets inside hundreds of billions of galaxies, all in motion, and I stand with a Skil saw in my hand on New Year's Eve covered in blood having fully exposed the brain of a dead raccoon.

Sad.

Insignificant.

I am less than a speck.

Unless I'm with Goth Princess. Inside her atmosphere, the gravitational pull and energy between us makes me feel like the Great Designer himself. Capable of anything and all. Maybe that's the point of it all.

Regardless, I'm currently incapable of answering the phone, which is ringing at 12:04 a.m. *It's Bronwyn, and she's calling to tell you she's on her way.* What? No. She wouldn't do that. *She is young and spontaneous and she would do that. Especially if she's had some alcohol.* If Goth Princess is on her way, then I am in serious trouble. Which issue to address first?

The toolbox and power tools?

The carcass with the missing lid?

The surgical mask?

The old table cloth that I've fashioned into scrubs?

Or the fact that I'm in nothing but briefs underneath it all?

The phone is still ringing, Freak. Better to have five minutes than none, and a ringing phone is better than a knock on the door. True. The saw is down, and bloodied latex gloves are removed. *You can't use those again on Mr. Stripes. They are soiled now.* Understood. If this is just a telemarketer offering me a better long distance rate, Designer have mercy on his soul. I grab my home phone, having tracked blood outside my garbage bag perimeter.

"Isaac speaking."

"Isaac. It's your dad here."

He's never called me on New Year's. He's been drinking. My guess is just under half a case. *I wish it had been Goth Princess.* Me too. My hopes, squashed again by my old man.

"Happy new year, Dad."

"Yeah, I'm obviously fucking thrilled about it," he says, spilling over with sarcasm. *Tell him you're busy. There is work to be done.* Can't say that on New Year's.

"What's up, Dad?"

"Well, it's a new year and all, and we didn't get around to fishing much, so I think we should drill a hole tomorrow and sit around the fucker and see what we can catch."

That was him asking. That was his way.

Of all the life forms in all the galaxies, this is who I was granted as a father. And when I meet you, Designer, I will ask what, exactly, I was to learn by that? Perhaps when we meet, I will already know.

It's a new year.

My year.

"Sounds good, Dad. I'll pick you up in the morning."

XII

"Your Cousin Alice told me she's a Goth. What the fuck is that?" he says. Inside our ice shack, the comment lands after bouncing off all four walls and becoming colder in the process.

The first comment in twenty minutes. New ice fishing world record.

"Yeah, Dad. She's a Goth. It's a just a means of expression through style."

"That's not our style, son."

Breathe.

"It has to do with music and literature and art and stuff."

"Evil stuff?"

"No, not evil stuff. Don't let the costume and make-up fool you. Goths are wonderful, peaceful, talented, romantic people. It's not a big deal."

Dressed in his full winter get-up, including the rabbit fur hat with the ear flaps, Dad dips his rod up and down. Up and down in the ice hole I drilled by hand with the most archaic device in the northern United States. *There has to be a machine that does that now.* I don't care. I won't buy it.

"Alice tells me that the Columbine killers were Goths."

I should have known better. I should have known he had an ace up his sleeve. He had it there since we arrived. Since I picked him up. Since he called me last night, mid-surgery. If this were the Wild West, I would shoot him because an ace up your sleeve is cheating, and I've been lured here unfairly. *How to respond now? This is crucial.* I know it's crucial, thank you. *Cousin Alice is obviously jealous. She's trying to wreck this for you.* You think? *Why else would she have likened Goth Princess to the Columbine killers?* Were they even Goths? I bet Goths would reject them, even if they were. *Missing the point. She's making them all seem evil and capable of murder.* That is not a fact. I was not there for the conversation, and give her the benefit of the doubt. Pisses me off if that's the case, though. Perhaps Cousin Alice really is still in love with me. I'm embarrassed at how redneck that is.

"Well, we all know how a few can spoil it for everyone, right?" I say.

"Like the Indians, you mean?"

"Yeah, Dad. Like the Natives."

You shouldn't have agreed. True. I'm just trying to give him a proxy that his back-country brain can understand. I think he gets it now. I think it clicked for him.

"Exactly. That's my point. It's like my son's runnin' around with a goddamn Indian."

Sadly, it has not clicked. My hands and feet go numb.

"No, Dad. It's like your son is runnin' around with someone he loves."

Breakthrough.

Candour like I've never experienced before. This is a new year. This is my year, and Bronwyn and the application have given me newfound strength.

"Oh, Christ. You knocked her up, didn't you?"

"No, I haven't knocked her up."

Dad grabs another beer from the cooler and cracks it open. Is there really a need for a cooler in an ice shack, Dad? Two feet of water has frozen beneath our feet, but the beer still requires cooling.

"Figured you had," he says. "Knocked her up, I mean. I remember a conversation just like this one with your Grampa Sullivan. He'd sniffed out that I'd knocked up your mom, and he damn near held a gun to my head to marry her after I came clean. 'Cause there was no way he was gonna have a grandkid outta wedlock. No fucking way."

Dad chugs.

Now, the only fish biting is me.

"You didn't love Mom? Is that what you're telling me? Never did?"

"Never did. And I told your Grampa that, and he socked me one in the eye hard as he could and he said to me, 'You were man enough to stick your pecker in her. She's yours for life now, buddy boy.' Bruise the size of a hockey puck for weeks."

"Did Mom know you never loved her?"

"I waited till your Grampa Sullivan died, and then I kicked her out."

Jesus Christ. The day after my sixth birthday.

"The day after your sixth birthday, I believe," he says, grabbing for a fresh can of beer.

Mom didn't leave us at all. All the bullshit stories he told me. All the crying myself to sleep at night. Thinking I had been the reason she left. Thinking I wasn't enough to make her stay.

Thirty years of feeling abandoned and hurt to the core and never wanting to see her again, and now all I want to do is weep in her arms while she rocks me.

I bet she begged.

I bet she begged and pleaded to stay long enough for my sixth birthday. Which explains why that particular birthday gift was so generous. Why the cake was the biggest ever. Why she cried through the entire birthday party and why she read to me in bed that night and sang to me, when she hadn't read or sang to me in years. My own mother — bullied out of her house. Bullied from her own house. Bullied from her own child. And I sit, thirty years later, beside the bully himself. Still at it.

Mom, I have no idea where you are, but I will do something great. My name will be in the paper. I will make national news someday, and I will apologize for wrongfully hating you for thirty years. My head is spinning.

Fact: Mom has had to live twenty years knowing that Dad would have twisted the truth. Made her out to be the demon. Made me hate her. Suffering silently.

A life sentence is twenty-five years, and you've almost served it, but your name has been cleared, Mom.

Don't cry.

Do not fucking cry. Not now. Not in front of him.

Another twelve rounds with tears and the enamel on my teeth is ready to splinter. I win by decision. *Nicely done.* I need to cry soon. Now, I can feel it killing me.

Breathe.

Dad does a lateral shoulder rotation with his left arm. Either his rotator cuff is acting up again or he's about to have a heart attack. If the answer is heart attack, I will sit here and let the Great Designer call you in, Dad. No one will be surprised that the local plumber didn't know how to resuscitate you. But I know how. I could resuscitate you and do the bypass myself, if necessary. But I wouldn't. *You couldn't let him die. Doctors take an oath. You would be in violation of it.* True. I would be. But you keep saying it yourself — I'm not a doctor. I'm just a plumber. *Ask him if his rotator cuff is bothering him or if his left arm is buzzing or numb.* No. The rotations continue.

"Goddamn shoulder's acting up again. It's the cold that does it."

Not a heart attack. He's let me down again.

The term "shoulder" is too general, Dad. The injury is to your rotator cuff, comprised of four muscles that are involved in the stabilization and control of the glenohumeral joint during rotation. This could be anything from inflammation to an acute tear of one or more of the tendons that attach to the bone, also known as impingement syndrome. *Nicely done. Thanks.* From the apparent mobility in this shoulder, surgery is not required at this point. A religiously followed physical therapy routine and a few refills of anti-inflammatories would likely do the trick, but I suggest another route and want to administer the shot of cortisone myself. *That is wrong. Doctors can't give needles with the intention of hurting someone, nor can they make an injection more painful.* True. I would never do that to a patient. Besides, there is more than one way to skin a cat, and this conversation about Goth Princess is obviously hurting him more.

"Why did you want to come here today, Dad?"

"No reason. Catch some fish, I guess."

"Was it to try and sabotage my relationship with Bronwyn?"

"I'm done talking about it for now."

"I'm not."

"Don't go ruining the day, son. Let's just catch some fish."

"My plan is to marry her, Dad. You should know that."

He didn't like that one. He's thrown his beer. I bought that beer.

"She's an embarrassment."

"To who?"

"To the whole family, for fuck sakes! To all of us! You've been seen with her in town and seen being friendly with her, and I'm the one who has to field all the questions! I'm the one who has to answer for all this bullshit and make excuses for you! Listen to me! It's going to affect your career. People won't hire a plumber who dates kids dressed like whores. Understand? She's a goddamn circus freak. I'd rather you date a nigger."

In my mind, this was the New Year's Day ice fishing expedition where he put his arm around me and told me how happy he was for me. Happy that I am in love. Happy that I am happy for once in fifteen years. Thankful that I stuck around to take care of him and passed on a normal life and a career of my choice. But even at his age, with a back injury, a bad rotator cuff, and a giant prostate, he still has to have control. He has become his father because cycles are just inherently that way: they can't help but repeat themselves.

The anger is gone from my body. I'm back to feeling sorry for him.

"I'll be leaving in the fall for university."

"Bullshit you are."

"So you should hire a nurse or get Alice to come and check on you in my absence."

"Where? Who took you in? What school?"

"None yet. But one will," I say, pissed that I don't have an acceptance in hand. *You should have said you were accepted to Michigan. Just to see his reaction.* No, that would be a lie. I think I'm done with lying, because if he's a liar — I don't want to be part of that club.

"At your age? The fucking professors are your age. Don't get your hopes up."

"My hopes are up, Dad."

"You have a family and career here. There are responsibilities," he says.

That won't work this time around. The needle has worn through that old vinyl. There is nothing for me here.

"I have a family who thinks I'm dating a circus freak and a career that I'm ready to move on from."

Dad goes back to the cooler but the beers are gone. Nothing left to anesthetize the conversation. "Leave, then. Have your goddamn midlife crisis or whatever the fuck this is. But know that your fucked-up girlfriend isn't welcome at our family dinner table again and neither are you if you keep on with her."

The line has been drawn. The Bronwyn Ultimatum.

I stare deep into the ice hole that I bore out by hand, looking for answers.

Nothing left to say.

My Cabela's Fish Eagle rod with matching Salt Striker spinning reel has served me well but has been poisoned by today's experience. As if the sum of my animosity toward him somehow channelled into it. Radioactive with energy. An emotional time capsule, waiting to be buried.

With precision, I lower my fishing rod through the ice hole, careful not to touch the sides, like a game of Operation, and watch it disappear.

Gone.

Forever.

To be cleansed of its contents and to rust and decay and break down into something valuable again for nature.

I look him dead in the eyes, but his are fixated on the ice hole. The coward. "I'll be in the truck when you're ready," I say.

Across the windy frozen lake, I march toward land. If everything happens for a reason, Designer, then you have left me stumped once again. *Unless the interaction was to encourage you to apply to more than one school.* True. I did make it sound like I had applied to more than one during the conversation from hell. *Not a bad idea. Hedge yourself.* But the schools will have to be in the state of Michigan so I can be close to Bronwyn. My next five including: U of M — Flint, U of M — Dearborn, Central Michigan, Wayne State, and Eastern Michigan. There is no way I'm applying to Michigan State. No way. I'm too much of a Wolverines fan. *Grow up.* It has nothing to do with maturity. More to do with principle. Just like there is no way a Carolina fan would grace the admissions department at Duke. Or a Bears fan would wear a foam cheesehead during a Green Bay game.

Principle.

Would it creep out Bronwyn if you went to Eastern? That's her school. She may want her space. True. The best thing about Bronwyn is how grounded she is. I would just ask her. I would say, "I got into Eastern, and I want to be near to you. What do you think about that?" And she would jump into my arms and kiss and kiss and kiss my face all over in excitement. *Speculation.* She would. *What if you get into Michigan and Eastern? What then?*

...

I have no idea. That's a problem. *That's a nice problem to have.*

True. We would talk it out, and it would be another excuse to spend a day together. I want to see her right now. Debrief on the kind of morning I've had. Vent. *If you re-tell the story, you may cry.* I don't care. I would cry with Goth Princess. I'm safe with her. *You can't tell her how your family feels about her. Ever. It might force her to run away from all of this, martyring herself for having caused a major disturbance.* That is true and a good point. I will tell Bronwyn that I had a falling-out but that it was over my leaving for school. *You are going to lie to her?* No. Shit. I will tell her that my family is not the kind of people I thought they were. *And she is smart and will figure it out.* And if she does, then we will talk about it and I will not budge in my commitment to her. *This is a major relationship issue. If her family forbade her to see you, would you want to know that?* Yes. But, my family only gets together twice a year — Easter and Christmas — so I have a few months to deliver the news. *Fine, take your time preparing for the conversation, but don't wait too long. Withholding the truth is just as criminal.*

In less than sixty days, I will tell her everything. About my father, the bully. About my family, the rednecks. And about my mother, the innocent.

I will tell her about Mom, and I will ask for her support in helping me find her.

And she will help me.

Her family will accept me into theirs, and if they don't, then we will persevere.

And a new family will be created, free of cycles and bullshit.

XIII

It is late January and I haven't heard anything back from the U of M. *It's still too early*. I know, but not really. Michigan has a rolling acceptance policy, and the letter could be in the mail any day. *Any day, up until the university's "decision guarantee" of mid-April.* I need to draw a line in the sand. I need to select a date, late March, when I stop looking in the mail with anticipation. *How about St. Patrick's Day?* Yes. This St. Patrick's Day, I am going to get shit-faced with Bronwyn and wash down the pride-sized pill of reality with green beer. *That's stupid and defeatist. That is giving up too soon.* True.

There is always a chance.

There is always the last play.

There is always Jordan.

There is always Roger Staubach.

There is always Doug Flutie.

The "Hail Mary."

The "Immaculate Reception."

There is always David Tyree's "Helmet Catch," which robbed Michigan alum Tom Brady of his perfect season, which pissed me off. Tom Brady is a superstar and has always been a superstar, even when he was the backup quarterback to Brian Griese for his first two years at Michigan. When Griese would dig himself into a trench by the fourth quarter, I would yell at the coaching staff from my sofa to let Brady play. I knew he was a star. *Griese led the Wolverines to a share of the National Championship in 1997 — so don't talk shit about him.* I'm not talking shit. *Griese was outstanding.* I'm just saying, if Coach Carr had removed his head from his ass and played Brady as a sophomore, they wouldn't have been forced to share the title. They would have owned it outright. *Debatable.*

For Brady's junior and senior year, Coach Carr did, in fact, see beyond the pinkish lining of his own colon, and Brady became the starting quarterback. I watched every game. *You think he's handsome.* He is handsome. *True.* I kind of wish I was Tom Brady.

Here's the new deal: If the acceptance letter hasn't come in the mail by May 1, then the buzzer has rung and the fans have gone home, the tailgate crowd has packed up the barbeques and the game is over. *Agreed. Then what?* The question places an imaginary weight on my chest. My hands and feet tingle. *You haven't applied to the other schools yet.* True. There's a reason for that. I can't imagine going anywhere else.

The dream is Michigan. It's been the dream for too long. I will wait for the acceptance or rejection and go from there.

Enough said. Stay positive.

And I have been positive. In an attempt to prepare myself for the massive change in my life, I have begun to incorporate small changes into my few obsessive-compulsive behaviours.

The milk in my fridge had not gone sour, and I hadn't run out of cereal, but this morning I made a sandwich for breakfast. I sat there, chewing, at my kitchen table, running my fingernails in the cracks while listening to a medical podcast from the Henry Ford Hospital in Detroit about immediate post-concussion cognitive testing for athletes in contact sports. Do I want to be the team doctor for the Red Wings or the Pistons or the Tigers? No.

You might get some second-string groupie action if you were a team doctor. I don't care for two reasons: I would never step out on Bronwyn and betray her trust, and I want to operate.

I want the knife in hand.

I want to feel the hot lights.

I want the weight of a life on my shoulders.

I want the audience of nurses and residents wishing they could be me. So I guess I'm more like the professional athlete than the support staff. I want the ball at all times. Especially when the game is on the line. *What if you choke? What if the ball is in your hands and you can't tie off an artery quickly enough? What if the patient dies on the table due to your malpractice?* Won't happen. I will be a Hall of Fame surgeon. There is no Hall of Fame for surgeons, but if there were, I would want to operate in a sweat-wicking, polyester cross-weave jersey with my last name in block letters across my back and have that jersey hung from the ER ceiling upon my retirement.

For now, I install a Moen Chateau-style faucet with matching side spray on the salmon-coloured marble countertop belonging to Craig and Bev Walton. Surrounding me has to be the most modern kitchen in Paradise: matching stainless steel appliances, an eleven-inch LCD TV in the door of the fridge and professional gas range with matching hood fan. And all this was purchased with online poker winnings. I admire anyone who can work from home and build their dream house. Well done, Craig. But, sadly, no amount of chrome, stainless steel, plasma, or marble can cure Craig of his battle with hyperhidrosis. Every time I see him, he has sweat through the pits of his shirt. Every time I shake his hand, it feels like he's just run a marathon … in a parka … on a treadmill … in a sauna.

Perspiration is a bodily reaction required for body temperature regulation, but hyperhidrosis is a condition characterized by an unnatural and constant increase in perspiration, with no cooling initiative. *Nicely said.* I wonder if Bev thinks his condition is gross? *What does she care? He plays online poker all day.* Maybe that's why he plays online poker all day. Correct. His online poker career is his pre-meditated excuse to stay on his property, away from people, awkward handshakes, and a dry-cleaning bill that would resemble a mortgage payment. I understand your fear, Craig. People are mean. I wouldn't care if Goth Princess had hyperhidrosis. In fact, I'm still looking for something imperfect about her. No one is perfect, and I know that no one is perfect, so the anticipation of finding Bronwyn's imperfection is worse than if it were superficially visible.

Goth Princess has been the perfect lady, and I haven't made it past second base since I dropped her off after the Christmas party with my family.

Our inaugural make-out session.

I caulk a circular line of DAP sealant on the marble countertop.

The past month has been spent seeing her on weekends only. Despite the heroics shown, introducing her to my family, she has not returned the favour. Possibly, this could be for the best. I trust her judgment. *What is she hiding?* She can't be hiding anything. Maybe she is. Is her father, the butcher, a monster? Does Bronwyn's mom sport an invariable black eye due to regular beatings? A black eye is called a *periorbital hematoma*, whereby trauma to the area allows the fatty tissue surrounding the eye to absorb the blood, resulting in the release of various iron-rich pigments, thus turning the area black. The advice to put a raw steak on a black eye, in my mind, is ludicrous. Why someone would expose bacteria-populated animal muscle to a mucous membrane is beyond me. Bronwyn, if your dad beats up on your mom, I will help you through it, and we will get your mom some help.

I lower the chrome faucet into the pre-cut opening in the marble and press down hard. The bead of white caulking and the grey plumber's putty lining the inside of the faucet squeeze out from between the marble and the overpriced water dispenser.

Maybe Bronwyn is more sensitive to the age difference than I thought? *Her dad will be more sensitive than the two of you combined.* True. I'm not afraid of that. *Is she afraid?*

I run my pinky finger along the crease where the marble meets chrome and gather the excess caulking to form a clean-looking, professional seal.

Dating someone from a younger generation has taught me a lot already. For starters, I had no idea how functional my BlackBerry was for varying methods of interaction. The day-long threads of messages back and forth have provided me much-needed entertainment to take my mind off the job and have shifted time spent daydreaming to brainstorming a clever response. The messages are not just conversation — they are a competition in composition, and I love it. The world is changing. The English language is changing. At first, I could barely inter-pret the messages I would receive from Bronwyn. It seems that efficiency, through the medium of mobile messaging, has caused an equally efficient side effect of communicating in condensed prose. Euphemisms are reduced to a series of capital letters. Words are hacked down to single letters — or worse, numbers representing words. My eyes will never forget the first time my phone buzzed and I received my first text message from her. It read, "Wat r u up 2...call me 2nite. Don't 4get. PS. I'm in class now...LOL."

I am rolling with the times and have adopted this digital ver-nacular like the bastard child it is.

From under the sink, I use an adjustable wrench to tighten the mounting nuts.

I don't get to see Bronwyn every day, but I do get to look at her every day. After ten p.m. every night, I talk to her via video chat online. Finding a webcam around Paradise was next to impossible, so I ordered one online, and it arrived six days later. The thought of going into a computer shop for a webcam, at my age, screams pervert. Apparently, Bronwyn's computer has a webcam built into it. I will have to get that when I upgrade for school. I love the webcam, and I am grateful for the technology, but I am old-fashioned and would rather hold her hand. I would rather take her for a drive, listening to music and shooting the shit while she sits with her socked feet up on the dashboard. That's when I'm happiest.

The faucet is now tightly fastened to the countertop, and I thread the water feed lines into the ends of the closed water valves coming up from the floor.

Last Saturday night, we went to see a movie at the Tahqua-Land Theatre in Newberry. Goth Princess and I won't be like the characters in the film. Ever. Goth Princess and I won't take each other for granted and slip into boredom and relationship oblivion. We sat, hand in hand, for half of the movie. The first half of the movie, I sat, heart-pounding, trying to get the courage to reach across and inter-weave her delicate pale fingers with mine. By the time the relationship on screen was crumbling, ours had experienced a growth spurt.

Yes, I was aware of the looks we got in the lobby, coming and going. And yes, I was prepared for them. They didn't hurt. Even the snickering teenagers didn't hurt. Even the woman clutching her child as Goth Princess and I walked past didn't hurt. She has made me stronger.

Dad was right, however. People are talking. The rumour is spreading. Yesterday at CoffeeBuddy, Linda barely said two words to me. I imagine she can't believe that I chose Goth Princess over her talented softball playing compadre, Mandy Klein. I imagine she said to her friends, "I know the girl is legal, but it still isn't right in my books. There should be different kinds of laws for that." And I bet people nodded. I wonder if anyone has informed her father, the butcher, about Isaac Sullivan, the thirty-something town pervert, chasing his helpless daughter.

Believe the rumours, Paradise. Believe them all.

Talk about it until you are blue in the face and then die from oxygen deprivation.

Bronwyn and I are in love like elbow joints and PVC pipe, but not really, because those fit into each other and we haven't got that far yet, which is fine with me because she is a perfect lady. The kind people wait lifetimes for.

The water feed lines are secure, and I move each of the plastic valve handles to face north/south, arming the faucet for battle. So far, no leaks.

After returning from the movie, Goth Princess and I sat in the van at the end of her lane for an hour, talking. I can't remember what we talked about. We kissed. We kissed for ten minutes before I got my hand up her shirt, massaging her breasts and rubbing her nipple ring between my thumb and index finger. She seems to respond well to that. *Will the nipple rings affect breast-feeding?* I have no idea. *I hope not.* True. There were sections of the make-out where we simply looked at each other, panting passion-charged breath into each other at close range like we were figuring out some sort of emotional math equation. I didn't care what it was. I loved it. I had never been so turned on in my life. By the time I reached for the button on her tight black jeans, she just as quickly moved my curious hand away and whispered in my ear, "Not yet."

I am getting what I asked for: a woman who respects herself and is making me wait. And I love it. "Not yet," means that the day will someday come, and so will I, hopefully not too quickly.

The aerator has been taken off the faucet, and I am letting it run for the first time. I will do this for one more minute, flushing out anything that may have been left over from the manufacturing process. *You have done a great job here, Isaac.*

"Looks like you've done a great job here, Isaac."

I whip around to make eye contact, only to stare directly into the dark circles in the armpits of Craig's grey T-shirt. Even the neck of the shirt is dark. I refuse to venture a vision at what his underwear looks like.

"Thanks. Yeah, things look to be working fine," I answer.

But I'm not so sure your thyroid is, Craig.

"Well, I really appreciate it."

Would he appreciate some medical advice? *Don't get into it.* Why? There are ways to combat hyperhidrosis. *It's none of your business, and you're not a doctor.* Since when does health advice have to come from a doctor? *It doesn't. It can also come from friends and family but not the fucking plumber. Get paid and leave.*

"Nice choice with the Moen taps. Best value for the money, in my mind," I add.

"Yeah, the wife picked them out. They're good for somethin' right?"

"What are? The taps?"

"Wives."

You knew he meant wives. True. I was just hoping the reiteration of the sentiment might sound a giant gong in his head that he's lucky to have one. *Change the subject.*

"Any big plans for the day?" I ask, wiping the excess caulking from the marble post-fastening. *Is that the best you had for subject changing? The sweaty bastard is basically a prisoner in his own house. What big plans could he possibly have?* Think. Got it. "You gonna watch the State of the Union tonight on that big fancy TV of yours?"

"Yeah, I suppose I will. No use, though. The country's going to hell in a handbag if you ask me."

But I didn't ask you, Craig. I didn't. You were just begging for the opportunity to spout your bullshit from that clammy red neck of yours, that's all. *You can't use his disorder against him like that. That's why he makes a living from home.* Truth: Now is not the time get into a political debate with a man who is about to pay me. My witty comebacks burn up on re-entry.

"Well, I guess only time will tell."

Nice out. *Beautiful out.* That was a Jack Nicklaus bunker shot. Gorgeous.

Craig lifts the bottom of his T-shirt to wipe his forehead, exposing his chubby belly. The ball of lint buried inside his belly button is the size of a small grape. That is just gross. *How is that even possible?* It's perfectly round, as if rolled by a dung beetle. Perhaps a lint beetle rolled it, a beetle who lives inside it and feeds off dead skin cells and hydrates from the pool of sweat that accumulates at the base of that cavernous belly button when he lies on his back.

"I sure as shit didn't vote for him," he states. Yeah, I got that, Craig. Move on before I get pissed off. "Never thought I'd live to see a goddamn coloured runnin' the country for Christ sakes. That's for goddamn sure."

Rage.

"What do you do about your hyperhidrosis, Craig?"

Bad idea. Too late. The question dings him in the centre of the forehead like a stone from David's slingshot, and a stunned gaze washes over his face, already beading with perspiration.

"Excuse me, Plumb?"

"Your hyperhidrosis. What are you taking for it?"

"I'm not sure that's any of your goddamn business," he says, crossing his arms. You should never cross your arms, given your condition, Craig. Your body language is giving you away. Capillaries dilate in his face and redness flushes. Look at yourself, Craig. One simple question from me and your tough, racist demeanour is crushed, based on something superficial — perhaps as superficial as the colour of one's skin. Can you imagine if someone with hyperhidrosis was president, Craig? Is it wrong to NOT vote for someone based on the colour of their skin or how much they perspire? He won't learn from my lesson today, and he is right — it is none of my business.

"Look, I know it's none of my business, but I happen to know a lot about it and think I could help."

That is true, and I mean that.

"What do you know about it?"

"Did it start when you were a teen?"

"No."

"Okay. So that means it's secondary hyperhidrosis and it's being caused by something."

"Like what?"

"Have you been to a doctor about this yet?"

"Yeah."

"And?"

"They gave me oxybutynin, but the shit made me dizzy."

This is going well. He's relaxing into this conversation. "Any other suggestions from the doc?"

"You never answered me."

"When?"

"When I asked what could be causing it."

"Didn't your doctor explain?"

"Would I be asking if he did?"

Good point. *Pay attention, Isaac.*

"Could be thyroid. Pituitary. Anxiety. Onset of diabetes. Could be mercury poisoning. Could be a side effect of a number of things ... emotional, glandular, or ingested."

Nicely done. Thanks.

He's worrying. I should let him squirm. *No, alleviate his worry.* I want to alleviate his racism. *That's not the role of a doctor.* True.

"I wouldn't worry about it, unless it is hinting at a larger issue," I suggest.

"Doc said it wasn't ... based on the first round of tests."

"Okay. Good. In that case, there are some advanced procedures that can really help. Everything from disabling sweat glands with botulinum toxin — which I don't recommend — to severing the sympathetic chain and nerve ganglia that run parallel to your spine, which is called an endoscopic thoracic sympathectomy."

Stop showing off, Isaac.

"Sounds like hell."

"It works, ninety-plus percent of the time."

"You're kidding."

"Isn't it your career to tell if someone's bluffing?" I ask with a warm smile. He smiles back.

"And how the fuck does a plumber know all this?"

"Podcasts and journals."

"Come again?"

"Ask your doctor about ETS surgery. Outpatient. Easy as pie. Will you remember all that?"

"I will. Yeah. ETS."

"Good. And that will be two hundred and twenty-five for the taps and installation."

"Is cash better for you?"

"Cash is fine."

"And thanks ... you know ... for the advice. I really appreciate it," he says, peeling twenties from a silver money clip. He
meant that. *He seems happier already.*

"No sweat, Craig."

The joke flies over his head. *Not a horrible thing.*

I've done it. I helped my first patient.

XIV

February 14. Valentine's Day. Still no results in the mail from Michigan. The only interesting mail, to date, has been a flowery letter of apology from Mrs. Bennett on West Portage Lane with the tardy cheque stapled to a McDonald's coupon. I wanted to press the plastic red button that would open the hidden door to my nuclear silo and launch a laser-guided MIRV Peacekeeper Missile into her living room. Sadly, with the destructive power of twenty-five Hiroshima-vintage nukes, I would incinerate myself in the process and maim several hundred more around the Paradise town limits. That would be gruesome.

As much as I want to be a doctor, there is one scenario (and one only) in which I would beg to be back in Paradise, in a crawl space with my torch and solder and by my side. That is a wartime scenario. Long gone are the comforts of a clean and organized O.R. Long gone are endless supplies. Long gone is the luxury of taking one's time. More specifically, there is a process within the selfless wartime scenario that scares me the most. And that process is called triage — the quick-time decision-making process by which the wounded are filtered by priority, based on the severity of their situation. In most cases, this involves doctors being forced to select wounded soldiers with unlikely odds of survival and cast them aside to die so efforts and supplies are reserved for those with a probable chance. The thought of this brings tears to my eyes every time, and even now, while driving to a job with Gilby by my side, I have difficulty seeing the road. *You are too sensitive to be a doctor.* No, I'm not. It's not the melted, hanging flesh due to radiation or napalm burns that disgusts me. It's not the missing limbs thanks to Claymore mines and Bouncing Bettys that turn my stomach, and I will have had enough practice with dismemberment due to the high volume of "donor-cycle" accidents. It's not even the torn faces from molten shrapnel or the horrifying screams of dying soldiers begging for their mothers. No. As gruesome as all of that is, I am fine with it, because I have a specific job to do with each and every one of them. I have a focus. Any classification of wound or injury is nothing more than an obstacle standing between the patient and recovery — an obstacle I will have been selected and trained to overcome. *You haven't been selected yet.* I know.

What devastates me is the concept of introducing the principles of Las Vegas to the arena of war and gambling on who is granted medical attention. That, to me, is sickening. That, to me, is a violation of human rights, and I would rather fix toilets in Paradise than have to make those kinds of decisions.

A doctor is not a machine, and a machine will never be a doctor. A machine can be programmed, but it can't play jazz. Understanding the weight of a human life and that each human life has a mother and a family drives and inspires me to give my all and roll with whatever complications arise using skill and holistic intellect. And, mostly, a doctor must have the cerebral capacity to value life, in order to save one. Therefore, being emotionally numb as a surgeon cannot serve a better purpose because it negates working harder than the programmed status quo.

So, again, I disagree. I am not too sensitive to be a doctor.

Gilby sniffs in my direction. Hi, pal.

A message chimes from Bronwyn. It reads, "cant wait 4 2nite…big s'prise 4 you…yuv bin a good boy ;)…"

I have been a good boy. I have been a patient boy.

At my age, any waiting time over three weeks seems unreasonable, but this is Bronwyn's show. I just have to show up and play ball. What's the surprise? It's quite possible that I could get laid tonight. I must trim up and buzz my hair, making myself properly groomed for the occasion. One thing is for sure: It's weird when you use the same length guard for your pubes that you use for your head. Still not used to that.

"Cant wait myself. First time alone with u that isn't my plumbing van. LOL," I reply. Proud of myself for integrating as best I can into her world of tech lingo.

Why add the LOL? In no way did you laugh out loud. You didn't even snicker. I grinned. *Yes, you grinned but that does not deserve an LOL.* Larger issue: Texting and driving is not safe, especially when texting provocative material. I have almost lost control on the gravel shoulder many times, and I'm sure the MacDermotts are still wondering why their mailbox was vandalized so badly. *You should have come clean and told them that you hit it with your van.* No, I didn't want that kind of attention. I already seem to have enough these days. *Tampering with someone's mail or mailbox is a federal offence. You could go to jail, and then your medical dreams would be dashed, for sure.* Good point.

New text arrives.

"tracy odonohue just called me a freak," reads the text.

"obviously tracy hasnt met me ;)" I type back, intermittently looking up to the road where mothers and school buses whiz by, carting children off to school. *Pay attention to the road!* True. *But nice text to Bronwyn. Deflecting the comment onto yourself was charming.* Thanks.

—»—

Mr. and Mrs. Trelford's lawn needs cutting. *That's an understatement because it looks like Jurassic fucking Park in there.* I'm expecting the neck of a brontosaurus to emerge and for the thing to look at me while grinding its teeth on plant matter hanging from the sides of its jaws. What would I do if that happened? I would wave a friendly hello at the brontosaurus. That's all. Nothing would surprise me in Paradise, especially a dinosaur. Gilby has noticed the forgotten yard as well.

"I should cut that for them, hey, pal?"

Gilby looks at me with knowing eyes.

"Yeah, you're right," I reply.

Gilby always knows what's best. Next week, I will offer to cut that grass for the Trelfords, and Mrs. Trelford will prepare me a homemade soup and tea biscuits, I bet. Why are there so many old people in this area? *The young ones have left Paradise.*

I am next in line for departure. I have taxied down the runway. I have put in my time.

New text from Bronwyn. "LOL. U r 2 cute. Xoxoxo. more reason to look ahed to 2nite. Cya soon ;)"

Something serious is going down tonight. I hope I can perform to what she's envisioned. *I've never heard you say that before. Seriously.* I've never cared before, that's why. *Don't put this sexual situation on a pedestal.* Why not? *It will mess with your head.* How? *Anxiety.* This is true. I am kind of nervous about tonight, if we are going to be having sex. Maybe I should take some Viagra, just to make sure that I perform like a champ and that I'm bigger and harder than ever. Viagra is really sildenafil citrate, which was originally developed to treat hypertension and angina but wound up giving all of the clinical test subjects erections, because sildenafil citrate releases nitric oxide into the corpus cavernosum of the penis, which binds with an enzyme that I can't remember the name of, which causes a chain reaction I completely forget that makes a penis stand at attention. *Points off for the lapse in memory.* Understood. I will do some research before I buy some Viagra for tonight. *Horrible idea. You don't need them, and how are you going to find Viagra in Paradise?* Good point. It's a prescription drug. Is there an underground, black market sex-enhancement industry? *Do you really want to find out?* No. Getting caught buying Viagra from an undercover cop in a town like this would be as socially devastating as getting caught with the catheter and your fingers in the unconscious doe.

On my way home, I will buy a package of Durex numbing condoms. *Do you really want to be numbed?* No. But I really love Bronwyn, and would like to *make* love to her for longer than seven seconds. It's been a while. *Does Bronwyn know that you love her?* I haven't told her. Actions speak louder than words. *You should tell her anyway.* I don't want to tell her too soon and scare her off. There is nothing worse than being on the receiving end of a profession of love when it is not reciprocated.

It is awkward.

It is horrible.

It's likely worse for the other person. I'm not sure it's worse — it's just different. The professor of love has to deal with rejection and humiliation, and the professee is forced to think quickly and get out of the encounter, while trying to be as empathetic and tactful as possible. I would never want to put Goth Princess in that position if she doesn't love me yet. *Question: When do you stop being a pussy and take a risk and tell her that you love her?* Good question. Answer: When it hurts more not to tell her than it would to tell her and not have that love reciprocated.

And my gut is telling me that time is imminent.

— » —

I was right to think that dinosaurs could exist in Paradise. I'm back at Mrs. Dunfield's house to install a water softening system, and I am certain that she qualifies as something from the late Mesozoic. What does a ninety-year-old woman care about hard water after fifty-five years in the same house? My only thought is that she is sick of the soap lathering poorly due to the amount of dissolved minerals in the water. *That makes sense.* At ninety, I would want a nice lather to wash my deteriorating human form as well. *Maybe she is sick of having to replace the elements in the hot water heater due to calcium buildup?* Also a good reason, but she doesn't do that. *Correct.* I do. I am the replacer of all things plumbing. Whatever her reason, the course of my life leads me back to her house and to the scene of the yard-cleaning crime.

Gilby and I sit in the van, parked in her driveway.

No sign of Albert. I'm still not sure Albert exists.

Maybe Albert is the brontosaurus that has strayed from the MacDermotts' front yard. That would have made sense based on the girth of the feces. *Isaac, leave the van and get to work.* I really don't want to. All I can do is think about Bronwyn and this evening's romantic events. Truth: Time won't tick any faster whether I install the softener or sit home and watch the second hand on the clock travel, second by second, until it's time for me to pick her up.

Dinner tonight is sautéed rabbit loin with braised fennel and balsamic vinegar, topped with a freshly chopped and warmed salsa verde, served on polenta. I shot the fat wild rabbit last weekend and followed up the kill by performing gastric bypass surgery on him. On a micro-scale, this surgery was much more difficult to perform than on a human, I would assume. Also, there was no laparoscopic technology at hand. No big deal. There is always an old-fashioned way to do it. Decreasing the size of the stomach — thereby decreasing the volume of food that can be eaten — was quite simple, and creating the partitions with wood staples worked better than expected. The re-routing of the GI tract, affecting food absorption, took longer than the time allotted, and another pint of blood would have been required in real life. It's a shame that he was such a fantastic candidate for the Valentine's Day recipe, because I am convinced that, post-surgery, the altered physiological and psychological response to food would have resulted in significant weight loss, increased liver function, heightened social acceptance, and increased breeding opportunity. For a rabbit, I imagine that is important.

Regardless, he will be delicious.

"And this is where I want it, Isaac," says Mrs. Dunfield, pointing with her ancient finger, loosely covered by a layer of rice paper skin, exposing all of the blue vasculature in her hand. "I want it there so it's accessible."

"Beside the hot water heater?"

"Yes. I want to keep it all in one area so people don't get confused."

"What people? Me?"

"No dear, the people who buy this house when I pass on," she replies, articulated with a grounded sense of destiny, delivering a thunderous left hook to my previous playful remark. My remark is unconscious.

Mrs. Dunfield couldn't give a shit about hard water — or softened water. She has begun the process of renovating her house to inflate the sale price when her kids are forced to transfer its deed to the highest bidder and portion off the inheritance money.

This original red brick house was built by Mr. Dunfield, one year before he was drafted to fight in World War II. A war that saw four hundred thousand American deaths and four percent of the world's population perish in an effort to defeat an all-star cast of misguided tyrants.

A war from which Robert Archibald Dunfield did not return home.

I would argue that a house built by a war hero should be granted indefinite historic protection, as this particular house continues to stand in a country that is not German-speaking — thanks to the sacrifice of the man who built it. It is an historic site of hard work, patriotism, love, the American Dream, and hats.

Hundreds of hats.

This is the Paradise Hat Museum.

This museum should be the default Saturday meeting place where elderly women of Whitefish Township congregate to play a game of bridge over hot tea and homemade cookies, dressed in their finest outfits, their best hats, and matching silk gloves.

The town should buy it from the family and hire full-time help to keep it clean and dust the hats on a regular basis. The help should tend to the property and maintain the gardens and clean up Albert's lawn sausages so I don't have to.

I am going to see that this happens.

"Marvin, up the road there, told me no one would buy my house with hard water."

What does Marvin know? He breeds cats. "What does Marvin know? He breeds cats," I say. Mrs. Dunfield snorts with laughter and pats my arm in appreciation. "What about hooking up to town water, instead?"

"Is that more expensive?"

"It is. Yeah. I'm not trying to make you spend more money, but I just think that a town water connection would raise the value of the house more than a water softener."

"Why's that?"

"Because whoever buys the house … or looks after it … will want town water and won't factor in the money you spent on the softener," I say.

That was an honest answer.

Here is some more honesty: I have no interest in hooking her up to town water. It is a messy and time-consuming job that would take forever to complete.

"They would have to dig up my yard with those big machines. Isn't that right?"

"That's true. We'd have to bring a back-hoe in to do the job properly," I say.

Mrs. Dunfield crosses her arms and looks deep into the corner that houses the hot water heater. This is a big decision, obviously. Why should a woman of her age have to make such big decisions? *Don't get involved in her business.*

"Look. This is none of my business, but why don't you enjoy the money you would spend on the softener, or the town hook up, and let whoever buys or takes care of the house … let them deal with it," I recommend.

That was out of line. *You are just the fucking plumber, and you take orders from clients.* No. Not anymore. Not for the last few months I call myself a plumber, anyway. I am a prescriber of ideas now.

The risoris and zygomaticus muscles in her little face retract, resulting in a smile. The smile, explaining in detail how all of the thousands of wrinkles were formed. This is followed by a high-pitched hearty laugh and an extension of her frail hand to shake it. I reciprocate.

We shake.

"You sure tell it like it is, Isaac."

I did.

"I couldn't agree more. Let the young ones figure it out," she says.

"I would say we have a plan, then."

"Yes. Good. Now, come upstairs to the laundry room while I have you here. The damn washing machine is leaking."

Of course it is. Getting out of this place in under two hours is more impossible than shooting the laughing dog in *Duck Hunt*.

The washing machine is leaking. There is no question about that. Ironically, the hard water (which the softener would have treated) has calcified the inlet connection, and the whole thing is beginning to disintegrate. *I'm not sure that classifies as irony*. It's not. But it's something, given the previous conversation.

"So what's going on back there?" she asks, hovering.

Don't tell her this is because of hard water damage. Professionally, I should.

"Just a case of wear n' tear," I report back.

"Meaning what?"

"I just have to clean things up back there. No big deal."

"Okay. That sounds fine. Cost?"

"I won't charge you for the parts. It's just a couple hoses and some new clamps."

"I don't need a discount, Isaac. You charge me what is fair, please," she insists. Interesting, coming from the woman who thought fifteen dollars for dog shit removal was fair. Bless you, Mrs. Dunfield, but your perception of fair is warped by your experience with the Depression, and it's not your fault. Having said that, you asked for it — so I'm charging you full pop.

Should I pick up some soda for tonight, or is it safe to serve Bronwyn wine or beer, given her age? *Treat her like an adult*. I do. But the law says that she can't drink alcohol, and I don't want the police or her butcher of a father upset with me for illegally serving her. *Then don't*. How is Valentine's Day the same without red

215

wine and champagne? *Are you trying to get her drunk?* No. *Then pass on the pre-dinner drinks, serve her a glass of champagne with the meal and look past the legal implications. They can't send you to jail for a glass of champagne, and the risk is worth the reward of treating her like an adult.* Good call. Although my thinking is that the bottle of champagne will get finished.

"I can get this done in no time. I just have to get a few things from the van."

"Take your time, dear. I have homemade lemon cake on the kitchen table if you get hungry."

As I open the back doors of the plumbing van, I have to wonder if there are less than a hundred jobs remaining in my plumbing career. Is the countdown on? Or is my life *The Truman Show,* and are there higher powers at work, conspiring to cage me in Paradise for the rest of my life? If this were a TV show, that would make Goth Princess an actress.

That would explain her interest in me.

Paid interest.

Goth Princess, if you are an actress, then I hope you are nominated for many Golden Globes and Emmys, because you are playing your role to perfection. You have come along at the perfect time, and your improv skills are genius. Audience members must have loved tuning in to see the family Christmas party, and I'm sure that, second to the current election, your darling face would have occupied the lion's share of viewership in America. *Isaac, your life is not televised, and thinking that people care that much about what happens to you borders on delusions of grandeur.*

True. My life is not a TV show. That is, unless the bubble extends to Ann Arbor. *Stop it!* Fine.

I gather the replacement hoses from the bin. The hacksaw needs a new blade, and its original blue paint has worn completely away, reminding me to change it.

It will see one more job.

Four stainless steel screw-band hose clamps. I'm getting low on those.

Slot screwdriver.

Gilby sniffs at me from the passenger seat. Are you anxious for the date tonight, too, pal? I bet you are. Bronwyn loves you. She spoils you with kisses and petting.

It's important that Bronwyn loves you, pal. If she hated you, I would have to end it with her. *Honestly?* Yes. If she hated Gilby and I love Gilby, then how could I possibly love her? *That is potentially broken logic.*

"Back in a second, buddy. Hang tight up there."

Finishing the job took longer than I thought, so in addition to payment, lemon cake seemed like a good idea. Mrs. Dunfield and I sit in silence, breaking off bite-size pieces of the bitter loaf and washing it down with sips of piping-hot orange pekoe. Is this what the elderly do when they visit with each other? Do they simply eat and sip and stare and ponder? Perhaps at ninety, all has been said, and the physical presence of another human being is all that's required to maintain sanity. *Say something.* I have nothing to say. *Two options: Talk about the cake or discuss the potentially cancerous sunspot forming just north of her clavicle.*

"The cake is wonderful, Mrs. Dunfield."

The comment breaks her from her daydream. I have daydreams, too, Mrs. Dunfield. Not as many, these days. Not since Goth Princess. But they still sneak in.

"I'm so glad. Have as much as you like."

"I love the poppy seeds."

"You know, I always put extra poppy seeds on my lemon cake. That's so funny you would mention that."

There are a large number of poppy seeds. Much more than the recipe calls for, I'd bet. It's almost like a poppy seed crust. How many bags of poppy seeds do you own, Mrs. Dunfield? Are there hydroponically grown poppy plants in a secret chamber of this old house where you harvest the seeds and make morphine to soothe your aching arthritis? Regardless, the lemon cake is delicious.

Gilby is still in the truck. I should go soon.

I press my index finger against the plate, collecting the crumbs from the flowered china. As I look up to say my final thank-you, I spot a familiar face on a picture tucked away in the corner, on top of an antique four-foot mahogany radio. The kind of radio that would have broadcast updates during the war. The kind of radio families used to huddle around.

I focus on the picture. It's Bronwyn. No, it can't be Bronwyn.

It is Bronwyn, but she's dressed in old-fashioned clothing and no traces of Goth. None at all. *Is Bronwyn a recent Goth convert?* Not based on what she told me. This must have been for a fashion shoot of some kind? Bronwyn wouldn't do a fashion shoot. *Why not?* She's beautiful enough. *Agreed.* Why is there a picture of Bronwyn in Mrs. Dunfield's house? All of a sudden, this quaint little tea party has gone balls-deep into weird.

My hands and feet tingle, numb.

"You look like you know that young woman, Isaac."

"Oh, I apologize. I was staring, wasn't I?"

"Don't apologize."

"That picture …"

"Was taken a long time ago," she says, dabbing the sides of her mouth with a floral napkin. That can't be possible. That photo couldn't have been taken more than a year or two ago.

"I know that young woman, Mrs. Dunfield."

"I am well aware of that, dear. I think we all are, around Paradise," she grins back.

Larger issue: Why has Bronwyn not mentioned Mrs. Dunfield and their apparent relationship? *You didn't ask.* True.

Based on her reaction, she must support my relationship with Bronwyn. This is good news. I wonder what Goth Princess has told her about me?

"Was this a gift?" I ask.

"It was. Yes."

"Last year?"

I did not expect the laughter resulting from my question. It seems that this was the least intelligent question I could have posed. Possibly, the least intelligent question ever posed. Tears of laughter well up and run down her cheeks, wiped away by the same napkin that cleaned her mouth moments ago.

"Dear, this was taken in 1933."

"Excuse me?"

"I was all dressed up to meet Robbie for the junior prom, and my father hired a man … I can't recall his name now … but he was the man in the area who had the technology to take nice photos, and he would come over to people's houses to do family portraits, and he was also the wedding photographer in the area. He took our wedding photos, too, but that's another story. Anyway, he came over to the house, on account of my father calling him, and he took this photo. The next year, that photo was wrapped up under the tree for me, framed, just like you see it right now. That was a big deal back then. That would have cost my father a lot of money in those days," she says proudly, nodding repeatedly and ever so slightly.

This is not a picture of Bronwyn.

This is a picture of a young Margaret Dunfield, and I can also put another mystery to rest: Mrs. Dunfield was, in fact, breathtakingly beautiful in her youth.

"That's incredible," I admit.

"What's so incredible?"

"The story … but also … I thought it was someone else, actually. You two could be twins. It's scary, the resemblance."

"Who, dear?"

"A young woman I know in town."

"A woman you're interested in?"

"Actually … yeah."

"And what's the lucky young lady's name?"

"Bronwyn," I say.

"I just wanted to hear you say it," she says, raising her cup of tea in preparation for sipping. "That would be the free spirit I call my great granddaughter."

No amount of poppy seeds could have prepared me for that. Guilt multiplies like cancer cells.

I want to return all the money she's ever underpaid me and then offer to shovel the dog shit off her lawn every week for nothing.

"She seems very excited about you," she says.

"I feel the same way."

"Never mind what they say in town. I'm sure they're all talking. They've had something to talk about in Paradise since the beginning of time."

"I don't care what they say, Mrs. Dunfield."

"Call me May, Isaac. I get the feeling we'll be seeing each other more often."

Smiling, I dab my thumb on the plate, capturing every last crumb of the lemon cake. Prepared by hands that share nucleotides and a similar genetic blueprint as Bronwyn.

"Treat her well, Isaac."

"Like a princess," I say.

—»—

I close the door to the van and stare ahead blankly, reliving the stranger-than-fiction moment that has just occurred.

"Pal, if my life wasn't already strange enough … I'm now dating the heir to the Paradise Hat Museum," I say to Gilby.

Gilby sniffs at me and begins to pant. I agree, buddy.

My cell phone beeps to signify that I have voicemail.

I scroll through the missed calls. One call from Norm Calder, who I know wants me to adjust his ozone water purification system, and one call from my home phone number. *That's weird.* Two possible scenarios: I've been burglarized and the cops have called me from my own phone, or Dad has taken food from my freezer and has called to admit to it.

If a burglar has trashed my place and taken my stuff and ruined my venue for entertaining Goth Princess tonight, I will hunt down the bastard and beat him to death with all of my stolen items. On the other hand, if Dad has stolen the fixings for the meal tonight from the fridge, thinking they are left-overs, I may transfer that beating to him. *Perhaps he's trying to sabotage Valentine's Day with Goth Princess.* Possible. However, that would take effort, of which he has none.

I skip the first message and go to the second.

"Son, it's me. I took a porterhouse out of the freezer. Just thought I'd let you know. I got a date tonight, believe it or not. Needed something to cook. I'm gonna split it with her. I'll take the strip and give her the good part. The filet. I'll pay you for it next time I see you. You need to shovel the goddamn lane. The roads are all clear, and then I could barely get down your fuckin' drive. Get that done, for Christ sake. Anyways, I took the mail in for you, and you got something here from Michigan. Looks like the admissions department. Just wanted to let you know that there's mail here for you. I'm lookin' at it right now, and I'm gonna leave it for you on the kitchen table.

I didn't open it. Talk soon. And shovel the goddamn lane."

I hang up without deleting the message. Gently, I set it back in the passenger-side cup holder, where it always sits.

The answer is a ten-minute drive away, and oddly enough, I feel unprepared for it.

This is too much at once. I'm still processing the Dunfield/ Goth Princess connection, and when it rains, it pours, and it is torrential right now. This is the kind of torrential that sounds more like hail and strips the paint off cheap siding.

The answer sits on the kitchen table.

XV

The plumbing van has a V6 engine with two-hundred and seventy-nine horses — all of which are currently being recruited. Despite the amount of snow that has fallen over the past two weeks, the roads are bare, making it reasonable to push the needle past a hundred. *How is driving one hundred miles per hour reasonable? Fuck off.*

I have never driven this fast. Never. Gilby is uncomfortable with the speed and begins to force whines from the back of his throat. Don't worry, pal. The roads are good. I wouldn't put you in danger. *What's the hurry, Isaac? The mail isn't going anywhere.* True. But the last eighteen years did go somewhere. Somewhere I can never again access, and the mail on my kitchen table will dictate the next eighteen, and the eighteen after that. So that's what the hurry is about. *Relax.*

Fact: Dad stole a steak from my freezer to share with a date after threatening to disown me. If I had the technology, I would cut open his head and investigate what happens between the synapses in his brain that's different compared with the rest of humanity. To see where the connection to reality gets lost. To see how he can manipulate and destroy a bond between a mother and a son and still sleep at night and then manipulate and destroy the relationship with that son and then steal one of his son's steaks. *Let the steak go.* No. I'm pissed about it. I'd rather

the steak in my freezer than him in my life. *You don't mean that.*
No, I actually do. That was a really good piece of meat.

My rearview lights up with red and blue lights, and my hands
and feet go numb. The only times I've been pulled over in my life
have been police officers asking me to fix something at their house.

This time is different. This time I am travelling at a law-
breaking speed. No, this is beyond law-breaking speed. This is a
cognitive dismissal of the law, entirely.

Could I outrun the cop? No. Not a chance. They have
souped-up cop engines and cop tires and cop transmission. They
have the *Blues Brothers* car on steroids. *A car chase would ruin
your chances of getting into Michigan, regardless of what the letter
says on the kitchen table.* True, but so could the speed at which
I'm travelling. The speedometer now reads one-ten, and at this
speed, the state trooper will cut my licence in half, impound the
van, and force a court date. Fact: If found guilty, I will have a
record. *Fact: You will not out-run the cop, so pull over immediately.* How was I so careless to let a reckless driving infraction
sabotage my acceptance to Michigan? *Pull over and talk to the
cop. He will understand. You likely know him and have installed
something for him, and he could be sympathetic. The alternative is
a car chase, and that will lead to prison, and you will be talking to
Goth Princess through two-inch bulletproof glass.* More than that,
I wouldn't be able to see Goth Princess tonight, and she will think
I stood her up. No. She would be my one phone call. *Pull over!*

I slowly apply pressure to the brake pedal and signal to the
officer that I will be pulling over.

The tires crunch into the snow covering the gravel shoulder
of the highway, and I come to a stop.

Right turn signal, still ticking.

I can get out of this mess. I did the right thing by pulling
over. *You waited too long.*

From my rearview, I see both doors of the police cruiser open. Passenger Side Officer gets out, standing behind his doors as a shield. Not looking too concerned. Resting his forearms on the doorframe and looking up at the sun through his aviator sunglasses. Driver's Side Officer is next to emerge, walking toward the plumbing van, right hand casually resting atop his gun holster. They must be trained to do that. He can't want to shoot me. *You were going too fast. He may think you are unstable.* I'm not. *Or Drunk.* Fair point.

"This not what we wanted, pal," I say to Gilby. He is silent, as if embarrassed for both of us.

Driver's Side Officer is only feet away now, and from my mirror I can tell that Driver's Side Officer is really Officer Bob Patterson. Bob Patterson, who hired me last year to install an ultraviolet purification system, which I connected to a reverse osmosis filter after his artesian well tested high for E. coli. I may have saved his kidney and liver function, so he owes me.

Knuckles tap on the glass of my window. I roll it down.

"Officer Bob."

"I need you to get out of the van, Plumb."

"Why?"

"You know why."

"Was I going a little fast?"

"I would call it a complete disregard for the law."

That sounds worse that it really is. *He is pissed. You need to get out of this and quickly.*

"How's the water system these days?" I say. *That was pathetic. Fuck off.*

"Plumb, based on your speed, I have to impound the car and take you to the station. I need you to get out, please. Don't make this any more difficult."

In the rearview, Passenger Side Officer is picking his ear. He's found something and is inspecting it closely. Flicked it. Now he's going back for more. Likely some dry skin, which is really called xeroderma and could be safely treated with emollients or a non-scented moisturizer. Passenger Side Officer has nothing to race home to. He has no date tonight. This is so unfair. *It's your fault. You were the one who chose to speed.* Speeding home to my golden ticket. Yes. And Goth Princess and I were going to celebrate the news and then she could proudly tell her father that she is dating someone who is going to Michigan and then he would approve. *You're speculating.* Fuck off. *Doctors don't say "fuck off." They don't talk like that.* True. *They also don't get hauled into police stations, and this will only damage your opportunity if you are charged criminally for driving so recklessly.*

"Plumb, I'm not asking again," says Officer Bob, taking three cautious steps back. Resting his hand atop his holster once again. Passenger Side Officer seems to have taken note of this action. His gun is now drawn.

"Bob, not today. I just can't."

"Plumb, last chance," he says, flicking the protective snap open, giving him access to his firearm should he choose. My heart is pounding. I feel nothing but trouble swallowing. My right gastrocnemius contracts, pinning the pedal to the floor. Gravel flies. My brain did not give this direction. This was not my decision, but I am forced to go along with it. Accomplice to my calf muscle.

Change in plan. The mission now is to simply get home and read the contents of the envelope before they haul me off to prison. The van peels off the shoulder, fishtailing as I attempt to regain control. Bullets ping as they puncture steel. Puncture me.

Enough.

I'm out.

Sweat beading down from my winter hat, I slow the van down to eighty-five. Still fast enough, but not offensive. Gilby is happy with this decision. I need to focus, and this is no time for daydreaming.

"Sorry, buddy," I say, scratching his head with my right hand. *Get both hands on the wheel immediately.* True.

I round the long highway bend I titled "Murphy's Corner." In my thirty-six years in Paradise, I have rarely rounded this bend without passing a car or truck, tractor or tractor-trailer that has broken down. I've dodged the bullet all these years. It's never been my vehicle in distress on this corner.

I'm begging that today is not the day.

Today can't be the day. However, a long line of cars has formed around the bend, and I am forced to a stop completely. I don't have time for this bullshit, and Murphy's Corner has delivered on its promise once again. *Maybe there's an accident up ahead?* Could be. *Should you get out and see if someone needs help?* The line of cars extends too far to see what the issue is. Fact: The line of cars is not moving. *Pass them all on the shoulder.* No. That is illegal. *Is it?* Not sure. Not worth the risk. *Fine. Turn around and find another route home.* Horrible idea, because the only other route home from here will take forty-five minutes, and I don't have forty-five minutes.

I can't wait thirty minutes.

I can barely wait ten.

Or one.

I pound on the dashboard three times with my open palm, producing a hairline fracture in the plastic. That's not good. *That will cost money to replace.* Not if the acceptance letter grants me permission out of Paradise. *True.*

Three-point-two miles to my letter.

Five kilometres.

Five thousand metres.

Half a million centimetres.

I would convert the distance to inches, but no one uses inches. Inches are dying. Not even me, the plumber. I refuse. I measure in metric ... like doctors. Regardless, I am a certain number of thousand inches from home.

Sitting in park has increased my blood pressure. How long will it take to run five kilometres? *Not longer than forty-five minutes.* I can run five kilometers faster than that. *Not in the snow and not in winter boots.* Time will have to tell.

I turn the van off and race to the passenger side to let Gilby out, and the two of us tear down the shoulder en route to the envelope.

I have martyred my van on Murphy's Corner. Someone will eventually tow it, after it causes more traffic backup. It will be impounded. My hope is to never see it ever again, and I hope it rots in that pound until nature nags at it for centuries and it is reduced to nothing but a footprint.

One hundred metres down the shoulder and I am already significantly winded. This was a horrible idea. *Push harder. Run faster.* The taste of Mrs. Dunfield's lemon loaf is back in my mouth. Tart as it was the first time around. Now stomach acid. Mouth fills with saliva. Too much to swallow, so I spit it out, but it's too thick, and the saliva whips onto the side of my cheek. Covering it. Freezing onto it. Lungs wheezing, and now I taste blood, which is a likely result of the alveoli in my lungs being overtaxed in their hurry to transfer carbon dioxide back out of the blood stream. Thus, some of the blood cells are pushed through the alveolar walls and forced out in my breath as an aerosol, which is why I'm tasting blood. The other possibility is that the air temperature is so cold that it's freezing cells in my bronchioles, causing microbleeding. Regardless, I can taste blood, and am blacking out.

Enough.

— » —

I'm out.

The van slingshots out of Murphy's Corner like Apollo 13 barrelling out from the dark side of the moon. Stay focused, please.

Suddenly, an explosion. Based on the weight transfer, I can tell that the rear left tire has blown. I knew it was balding. *You did nothing about it.* Chaos theory.

The sound of the alloy wheel grinding against the pavement triggers my right foot to pile on the brake, causing the van to shift sideways down the highway.

"Hang on, pal!" I scream. Gilby should be wearing a seatbelt.

The right wheels bite into the pavement, and the van trips over itself quickly. I understand momentum and inertia, and in a matter of seconds, the van will roll down the highway into oncoming traffic.

Enough.

I'm out.

Just over a mile away from home.

Isaac, you need to pay attention! Agreed. Focus. Are the daydreams creeping in to sabotage my efforts to get home? Possibly. Perhaps they are occupying my mind to make the nail-biting journey fly by more quickly. Like movies on airplanes. In which case, I should be thankful. No, you can't thank a daydream. A daydream is not to be thanked. It is not real. It is not even art or a movie or a play. It's not entertainment. It's a compulsion of the mind. A departure from reality. How can that be beneficial or thanked? What I am thankful for is that they've taken a back seat since the application to Michigan and the introduction of Goth Princess into my life. For the past few months, I've had something more to focus on than myself, and that has been refreshing. No more time to focus on depression or feed it regular meals of negativity.

Not when there are goals to be met. When odds are being challenged.

Less time to plan an exit strategy when passion has taken over, inspiring the much needed resurgence of endorphin floods and increased levels of serotonin activity. *What will you do when you reach your goals? How will you combat depression once the checklist is complete?* Answer: The list can't ever be complete. If goals have been met, then the bar was obviously not high enough, and new challenges must be introduced. Therefore, if we are not fighting for something, we must be in the process of dying.

Less than a mile.

The speed of the van is increasing, and my heart is pounding through my chest. Both hands and feet are fully numb, but I am in control. What will Goth Princess say when I tell her the news? I suppose that depends on what the news is and how I deliver it. *Stay positive.* She is likely starting to get ready for the evening. Picking out her Goth best. Lorne Fenton's hill approaches — the last glacier-carved knoll before the descent to my laneway.

Gilby is looking at me. I know, pal. I should slow down. How fast am I going?

The speedometer reads eighty miles an hour, but it looks closer to eighty-one or two. That is beyond the legal limit according to the State of Michigan, and that is too fast in my books as well. My eyes shift over to the odometer, which boasts 298,036 miles and counting.

May what lies on the kitchen table not allow this van to hit three hundred thousand miles. May Gilby and I retire this van with a respectable level of mileage and move on to Ann Arbor.

Hear that, Great Designer.

Hear it.

My prayer.

My first real prayer, and I mean it with every cell, and for the entire duration of that prayer, I feel like someone or something is listening to me. Or whispering back while I speak. Like one of those religious experiences people talk about.

Goosebumps.

I will pray more often, and I will tell Bronwyn about this. We could pray together. *She might not be into that. Don't turn into a religious freak.* I'm not. No one knows about the Great Designer but me, and soon only Goth Princess and I will know.

No one else.

Goth Princess talks about the universe a lot. She talks about energy and the universe and putting intentions out into the universe. Perhaps we are speaking the same language. Perhaps she is already in contact with the Great Designer. I wouldn't put it past her.

From the odometer, my eyes mark back to the township road in front of me to see Mr. Buck, standing sideways like an Egyptian hieroglyph, head raised and one eye burning a hole through the windshield.

Not surprising.

Not surprising, at all, to see you, Mr. Buck. Have you come to get in my way? Resentful of your contribution to medicine? Have you come back from the dead to play tricks on me? To spoil my progress?

As tenths of seconds fly by, I storm toward the ghost of Mr. Buck.

Enough.

Nothing has changed. The giant animal remains.

XVI

Even in slow motion, accidents happen too quickly. Before the impact, I closed my eyes and have yet to open them, but I know something bad has happened.

I can taste something bad has happened.

Can feel it.

There is a pressure on my chest. A pressure greater than proving a parent wrong or asking out a girl or being piled on in football. The only thing harder than breathing in is breathing out.

My eyes open slowly to find my windshield missing and a large wooden pole where the engine should be. That is a telephone pole, and I have hit the telephone pole, and I have hit it hard.

Gilby?

I can barely move my head but force it far enough over to find the passenger seat. Empty. Where are you, pal? Are you okay? Passenger window, blown out. *He was thrown.* I hope he landed on something soft. *Blood on the window.* Likely mine. I'm sure he's fine. He's Gilby. He's a soldier. But what have I done to myself?

I look down and see my familiar steering wheel and its column pressed deep into my chest.

The status of my injury is critical.

Your genius design has been badly damaged on account of me, Great Designer. I apologize for that.

From what I can assume, the steering wheel has crushed my ribcage, forcing fractured ribs into my lungs and causing bilateral pneumothoraces.

The now-audible sound of a flopping punctured lung has only confirmed my diagnosis.

I have two minutes. Tops.

Why did I swerve? *He was huge. You had no choice.* To hit him square would have sent all of his ten points through the windshield, impaling both of us. *You made the right choice.* Obviously not. My choice was impulsive. Let me replay it one more time, Great Designer. Like a video game. Press the reset button and give me one more try. I will get it right. I promise. Please. I would brake hard as soon as I spotted him over the crest, and I would throw Gilby down into the passenger side foot space, and I would hide under the dash, and I would hit the bastard so his antlers wouldn't get me, and I would eat him for Easter dinner with Bronwyn in two months.

Bronwyn.

She is at home getting ready.

I'm so sorry, Goth Princess. I have ruined this for us. I have ruined Valentine's Day and the next fifty after that. I will never know the look in your eyes when you are proposed to. How you like your eggs cooked on Sunday. If you prefer to be the big spoon or the little spoon. All the places you are ticklish. How beautiful you would have looked pregnant and what cravings you would have had, though I bet it would have been peanut butter and pickle sandwiches on rye with gummy worms on the side.

Trapped in a cage of bent steel, I want to roar with anger. I want to explode with frustration. Breaths are getting harder to push out.

Based on the last exhalation, I am six or seven more cycles from the last.

Bronwyn will wonder why I'm late to pick her up. She will stand at the end of her lane for hours, dressed beautifully for our big night, cursing me and texting me and trying to call me and texting me and then cursing me some more.

She will think I stood her up.

The thought of this breaks me further.

No, you are wrong, Isaac. She will know that something has happened, and she will have the butcher drive her over to your house, and on the way over, she will tell him that we are dating and in love, and he will be supportive. Proud and liberated, she will arrive at the house, alive with neighbours and family and the preacher from Dad's church and police asking questions and offering supportive hugs.

When you see this, Bronwyn, your sympathetic nervous system will trigger a mass release of epinephrine and norepinephrine in response to the shock and trauma you will experience. This will cause your pupils to dilate, and you will sweat. Your heart rate will increase, you will salivate less, and your digestion and pancreatic function will decrease. Your bronchioles will dilate, and bladder contraction will be inhibited. All of this will happen as a result of the news, but you have to cry.

You have to cry, Bronwyn.

When your body realizes that it's not in danger, adrenocorticotropic hormone will be released by your parasympathetic nervous system to restore stability and homeostasis, and you have to cry the ACTH out. If you don't, Goth Princess, it will linger in your system, chronically releasing corticosteroids, causing damage, so please don't hold it in.

Cry, Goth Princess.

It will keep you healthy.

Telephone poles are approximately a hundred yards apart, so my odds were approximately one in a hundred. This can't be an accident. Was this part of the design, Great Designer? Do not attempt to take me now. Not now. I will not come when you call me, and I will haunt the Paradise Hat Museum for eternity.

Perhaps my wishes for death set a ball in motion a long time ago. Where daily doses of negative momentum encouraged and rolled it for over a decade as it grew in size.

The ball gathered speed.

Couldn't be stopped.

Crashed into a pole.

The answer sits on the kitchen table.

Will it get thrown out amidst the rush of company to the house? I hope someone opens it, and I hope it's Bronwyn, and if it's not Bronwyn, I hope it's Dad, and I hope the results listed on the handsome Michigan letterhead cause a torrential release of ACTH. I hope he weeps over the times he said I couldn't make it. And the times he said I was born to be a plumber. And the times he called me stupid like my mother. *What if you didn't make it?* Then, I hope he weeps harder.

He knows the letter exists. *It will get opened.*

Three more cycles until the last, but I am still fighting.

A millipede emerges from a crack in the telephone pole. Racing, as his kind do, as fast as possible to wherever he is going. Unable to comprehend what has just happened, he moves to a safer place. He moves and winds, hundreds of legs in synch, with purpose to live another day. Mr. Millipede has no aspirations of wealth, fame, or graduate degrees. He is racing, simply to live. To experience. To create. I should have been more like you, Mr. Millipede. I should have been racing to live — not to get a better job. Not to get an application in on time. Not thinking that a diploma with the dean's signature and navy blue seal would solve my problems. Even when I thought I had figured things out, my cushy seat atop the food chain had continued to cloud my perspective.

Run fast, wherever you are going, Mr. Millipede.

I dig deep, with the help from every last mitochondria in every last functioning cell, to take in one more breath. Very likely the last.

I don't know exactly what to call you, Great Designer, and I trust you won't be offended by that when we meet. If we meet at all.

Pressure lifting from my chest.

Awaiting What's Next.

Acknowledgements

Special thanks to:

Sylvia McConnell and the entire team of wonderful professionals at Dundurn Press; Chris Bucci at Anne McDermid & Associates; Dr. Jonathan Streit, my "medical facts editor" who was a medical student at the University of Michigan and living Isaac's dream; Rob Snider, who owns and operates Rob's Plumbing in Port Elgin, Ontario; Professor Daphne Athas and Marianne Gingher in the Creative Writing Department at the University of North Carolina–Chapel Hill for your encouragement and support; Professor Derek Goldman for fostering my creative strengths at the University of North Carolina–Chapel Hill (Dr. Goldman is now a professor at Georgetown University); Kelda Card, my loving and supportive wife, and Elodie Card, my daughter, whose sheer existence influenced this novel; Craig McConnell; Joe Monaco; Uncle Jim Buttrey, the consummate sportsman, for your special interest in Isaac and advice on all things hunting; my loyal and wonderful friends, especially Marc Rigaux, Mike Laba, Matt Hehn, Adam Kunkel, and Rowan Cainer for your candour and input on this project.

My entire family and especially my parents, Clive and Mary Card, and sister, Breanne, for encouraging me, day after day, in all of my interests over the decades; and Earl Farrell, who taught me many years ago how to set a goal and see it through.

More Fiction from Dundurn

Blind Luck
by Scott Carter
978-1926607009
$18.95

Dave Bolden's life feels like it's on repeat. He works his eight hours at an accounting firm, goes home, gets drunk, and wakes up the next day to go back to work with a hangover. But his life changes when an eighteen-wheeler crashes through the windows of his workplace, killing everyone except him. Shortly after the accident, he is approached by an eccentric businessman, Mr. Thorrin, who interprets Dave's survival as luck and sets out to exploit what he perceives as a gift. Thorrin wants Dave to participate in gambling, stock manipulation, and extreme betting, all based on this belief. What transpires is a series of extreme tests of luck, orchestrated by Thorrin. The more Dave denies that he is lucky, the more he finds himself in situations that make it appear that he is. As the stakes rise both financially and personally, he is left to decide whether his run of good fortune is a gift or a curse.

Waiting for Ricky Tantrum
by Jules Lewis
978-1554887408
$17.99

Jim Myers is a painfully shy kid living in Toronto's west end Bloorcourt Village. Rarely is he able to muster enough courage to say anything beyond "ya" or "dunno." After school he hangs around with his neighbour and only friend, Oleg Khernofsky, playing basketball against a NO PARKING sign in a laneway. In the evenings, he haunts Nicky's Diner, a restaurant owned by Oleg's uncle.

On the first day of junior high, Jim crosses paths with Charlie Crouse, a brash, mouthy kid full of wild stories about his past. Charlie takes Jim under his wing and introduces him to the electronic strip poker machine at the Fun Village Arcade in Koreatown, a Queen Street hooker who calls herself Steffi Graf, and the diverse sounds and utterances of his landlord's three lovers. As Jim and Charlie's friendship grows, however, the realities of looming adulthood seep into their lives with surprising consequences.

DUNDURN
www.dundurn.com

Visit us at
Dundurn.com
Definingcanada.ca
@dundurnpress
Facebook.com/dundurnpress

www.ingramcontent.com/pod-product-compliance
Lightning Source LLC
Chambersburg PA
CBHW022015010726
47494CB00003B/1044